# Praise for books by
# ASHLEY THORPE

"Phenomenal! Magic, myth and history woven
into a heart-pounding adventure."
**Sophie Anderson, author of**
*The House With Chicken Legs*

"I enjoyed it immensely. It's a deep dive into Jamaican
folklore, belief systems and vivid storytelling."
**Alex Wheatle, author of *Crongton Knights***

"A gripping, vivid magical action adventure that taps
into deeper themes of grief, identity and power...
Also, an excellent talking cat in a hat."
**Louie Stowell, author of *Loki***

"Tremendous, nail-biting action filled with brilliant characters
you can't help but root for; this is children's fiction at its finest.
Thorpe is a talent to watch!"
**Lizzie Huxley-Jones, author of**
*Vivi Conway and the Sword of Legend*

"An electrifying adventure that will leave you breathless."
**Tọlá Okogwu, author of**
*Onyeka and the Academy of the Sun*

"An amazing, fast-paced adventure filled
with action...had me at the edge of my seat."
**Alex Falase-Koya, co-writer of**
*The Breakfast Club Adventures*

*For Noel, Cislyn, Ivy and Justin with love and gratitude.*

First published in the UK in 2025 by Usborne Publishing Limited, Usborne House,

83-85 Saffron Hill, London EC1N 8RT, England. usborne.com

Usborne Verlag, Usborne Publishing Limited, Prüfeninger Str. 20,
93049 Regensburg, Deutschland, VK Nr. 17560

Text copyright © Ashley Thorpe, 2025

The right of Ashley Thorpe to be identified as the author of this work has been asserted
by him in accordance with the Copyright, Designs and Patents Act, 1988.

Cover illustration by Gashwayne Hudson © Usborne Publishing, 2025

The name Usborne and the Balloon logo are trade marks of Usborne Publishing Limited.

A CIP catalogue record for this book is available from the British Library.

ISBN 9781805075653  9585/2  JFMAMJJASON /25

Printed and bound using 100% renewable energy at CPI Group (UK) Ltd, Croydon, CR0 4YY.

MIX
Paper | Supporting
responsible forestry
FSC
www.fsc.org
FSC® C013604

# ASHLEY THORPE

USBORNE

# CONTENTS

Map of Xaymaca ............................................ 6

Prologue ...................................................... 9

1. The Magical Mangrove Hotel ...................... 15

2. The Enchanted Larimar ............................. 20

3. Midnight Magic ........................................ 26

4. Spirit Waker ............................................ 33

5. A Deluge of Duppies ................................ 39

6. The Space Between Worlds ........................ 48

7. Cat in a Porkpie Hat ................................ 55

8. A Long Day Ahead .................................... 61

9. Picking Up the Pieces ............................... 67

10. Three Questions ..................................... 71

11. Jancrow .................................................. 80

12. The Summoning ...................................... 85

13. The Soulless Sailor .................................. 91

14. The Xaymaca Express ............................. 101

15. Cerasee Tea .......................................... 113

16. Those Who Live For Death ...................... 121

17. Spirit Sight ........................................... 127

18. Night Watch .......................................... 136

19. The Safehouse Siege ............................. 144

20. Fractures ............................................. 153

21. Sekesu's Town 159

22. Sankofa 165

23. Spirit State 175

24. Undone 182

25. The Library 186

26. Betrayal 193

27. The Blue Mountains 200

28. Ambush 206

29. Blackheart's Shroud 215

30. Nanny Town 223

31. Cai's Lament 229

32. Deeper Than Blood 234

33. Visions of the Past 240

34. Ghosts of Xaymaca 247

35. Proposition 258

36. Brothers 267

37. Battle for the Blue Mountains 277

38. Spirit Waker Vs Spirit Waker 282

39. Darkest Light 286

40. A Reckoning 290

41. Return of the Heroes 295

42. Memento 303

Epilogue 308

Author's Note 315

Acknowledgements 317

# Map of Xaymaca (/ zah-my-kuh /)

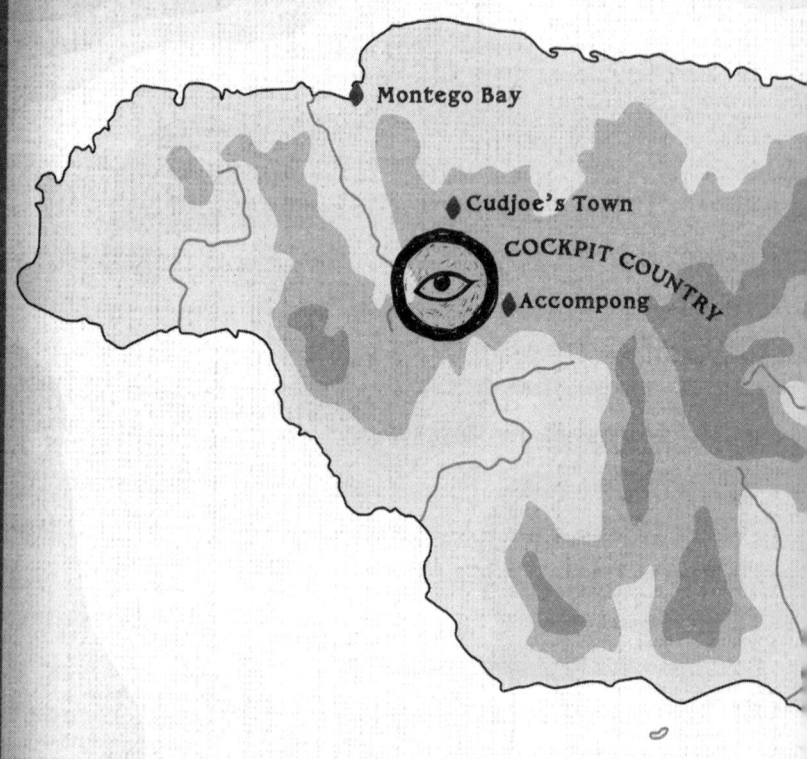

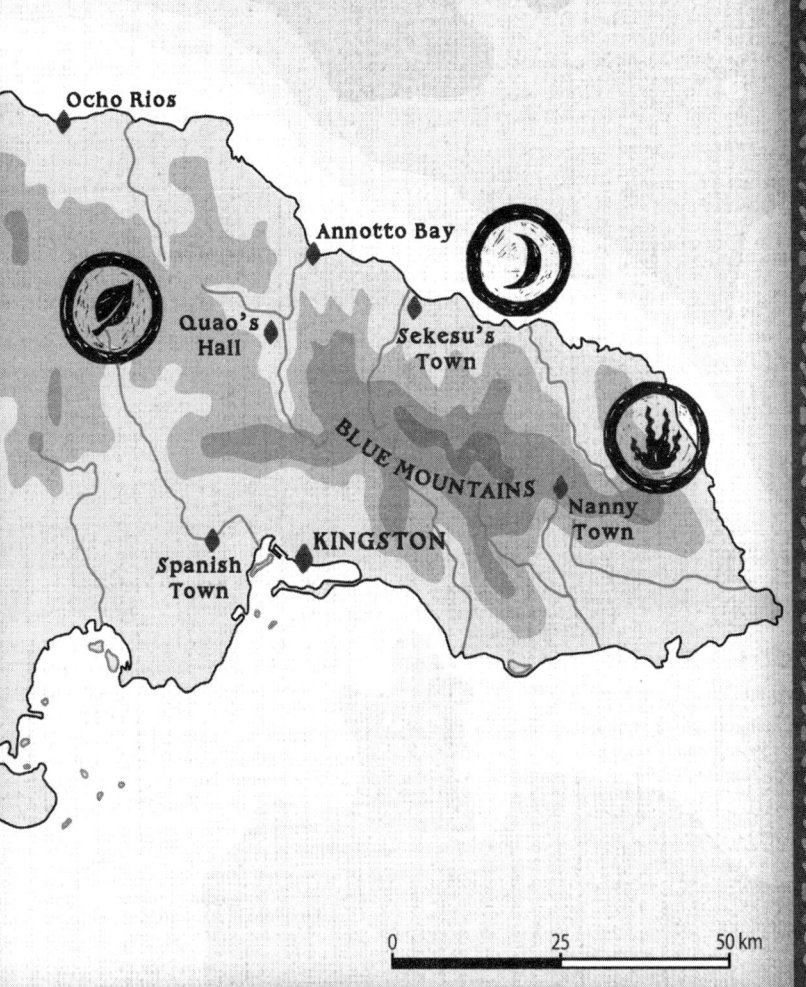

Ocho Rios

Annotto Bay

Quao's
Hall

Sekesu's
Town

BLUE MOUNTAINS

Nanny
Town

KINGSTON

Spanish
Town

0          25          50 km

# PROLOGUE

## Accompong Town, Xaymaca 1953

In Accompong, Obeah magic ran deeper than the roots of its Kindah Tree, the leafy giant that stood sentry at the heart of the town. On an evening of ritual celebrations, the townsfolk gathered under its branches. Dressed in rich kente cloth, and with feet bare to feel the earth between their toes, they danced in the fading light of the sun. Giving thanks to their African ancestors for the gift of magic, they waited excitedly for the youngest generation's powers to awaken.

Would their child become a diviner and receive visions of the future? Would they become a healer, able to cure people by absorbing the qualities of plants and herbs? Perhaps a gifted enchanter, able to control objects or an element? Or perhaps that rarest of all abilities…they might become a spirit waker, a living link to the spirit world, able to communicate with the ancestors themselves and awaken latent magic in others.

A young woman in a blue headwrap sat apart and watched the celebrations from a distance. Unlike the revellers she was an outsider, born in Xaymaca's capital city, Kingston. She'd arrived in this remote Maroon township only a year ago, during a time of great personal loss and heartache. The wound, unhealed, opened up again at the sight of the village children, dancing without a care. Because she knew that her daughter would have been old enough to awaken her magic here too.

No more than six years old, the children moved instinctively, losing themselves to the melody and rhythm. The drums called to a voice deep within them, urging them to wake up. Their first sparks of magic appeared – born from the great energy called Obeah.

As they leaned into these flashes of magic, the sparks became colourful auras, encompassing them, as though the spirits of the children manifested outside of their bodies. They realized with glee what kind of mage they would become. There was the rich blue of the enchanters, the deep red of the diviners, and the placid green of the healers. However, there was no majestic purple of the spirit wakers among them.

The hand drums and singing crowds grew louder, more jubilant. The young woman, though, felt more distant. She blinked away tears for the daughter she'd lost. A shadow fell at her feet, along with two long black feathers. A large turkey vulture – or jancrow as Xaymacans called them – loomed by her side. The white tip of its curved beak looked deadly, and a beady eye glared amidst the grisly pink skin of its head.

"Are you going to follow me everywhere I go?" asked the woman, turning away from the bird.

"You never told me to go away," answered the jancrow. "Because you know mi can help you. We can help each other."

In the humid, breezeless air, somehow the young woman felt a chill. Her fists clutched her dress at the knees. The jancrow wasn't a bird, not truly. Just the vessel for a spirit waker, who secretly controlled it to do their bidding.

"Your daughter and your husband, you can have them back, my dear. In this life. In a new world of our creation. But to do that you know what we ha'fi do. We ha'fi harness the great magic of the Four Heroes of Xaymaca."

The woman's knuckles grew paler from gripping her dress so tightly. "Why don't you show yourself to me? Your real self."

The jancrow cawed. "Mi will reveal everything to you as we build a new world."

The young woman hesitated. "Can I trust you?"

"I awakened your magic, nuh? You sought a spirit waker to commune with your lost family, and you found one. *I* am the only one who truly understands your pain." With the instincts of a predator, the jancrow shuffled even closer in the woman's silence. "I will help you turn that pain into power, the likes of which you've never seen. Now is our chance to steal the magic of the Four Heroes and reunite you with your family. Your heart and spirit, entrust them to me – your spirit waker!"

Tears dropped from the woman's face to the backs of her hands. She watched mothers and fathers embrace their daughters and sons, welcoming them to a new life of magic, a world of boundless possibilities. She would never know that joy. Not unless she acted now. "A-all right," she assented, barely a whisper.

"Say it!"

"I entrust my heart and spirit to you!"

The blue of the young woman's enchanter aura, now peppered with black, fizzled at her skin. What was this feeling deep in her chest? It felt too bleak to be hope. The jancrow hopped away and spread its long dark wings. "Use your magic as soon as the coral stone is revealed. Do that and I'll take care of the rest. This is just the beginning."

To her ears, the young woman's heart pounded as loudly as the hand drums being played.

The elderly chief of the Accompong Maroons arrived at the Kindah Tree and signalled her blessings to the revellers. Then, as was tradition, she removed the bright red coral stone from underneath her headwrap to welcome the new mages to the fold. The gemstone contained the powerful magic of one of the historic Four Heroes of Xaymaca, and it gleamed in the waning light. Now was the young woman's chance.

She rose to her feet and unleashed her magic, sparking sapphire. Her shadow stretched and spread over the ground like spilled ink. It reached the shade of the Kindah Tree, and the deed was done. Each person's shadow had merged with the tree's under the setting sun, which meant that now the shadow enchantress was connected to them – had power over them.

They froze in time, no longer able to control their bodies. The fear in their eyes was the only tell that something was earth-shatteringly wrong.

The jancrow swooped down towards the stricken chief who held the magic gemstone. The chief could only watch in horror as the bird swiped the red stone from her open palm and escaped to the sky once again.

From beyond the edges of the young woman's shadow, two air enchanters hovered above the ground where she had no chance of reaching them. She panicked as they unsheathed their swords and charged at her. But before they could act, they themselves were cut down by a figure cloaked in black.

The two air enchanters crumpled in a lifeless heap. The tall man who had attacked them wore brilliant white robes under his black cloak, and a startling ram's-skull mask covered his face. Long silvery locs of hair suggested an old age that belied his youthful movements. The jancrow glided back over, dropping the coral gemstone into the masked man's hand. This was the real spirit waker. The spirits of the air enchanters seeped into him like steam reversing into a boiling pot.

"It appears mi ha'fi reveal myself sooner than mi wished," he said, the whites of his eyes just visible under the dark hollows of the mask. "Do you know who I am?"

She knew, all right. The one who had sold his soul to the devil. The one who summoned duppies – evil spirits of the dead. The one who sought to control the hearts and minds of those who had lost their way.

"Blackheart Man."

"Yes," he said, lifting a hood to cover his exposed locs. "Which means that *they* all know who I am as well." He gestured to the revellers still frozen under the young woman's shadow enchantment. "Our plan has to remain a secret from the other Maroon towns for it to succeed. Do you understand? There can be no survivors."

The young woman forced herself to look at the townsfolk who she'd lived among for months. Those who'd tried to bring her back from despair and given her a home. A darkness of spirit that wasn't there before crept in to strangle her emotions. But one incessant feeling consumed it all. The memory of her child, and the chance to bring her back.

"Yes," she answered. "I understand."

# Chapter One

# THE MAGICAL MANGROVE HOTEL

## Ocho Rios, Xaymaca 1962

### Evie

It was a wonder that The Mangrove Hotel was standing at all. The charming mustard-yellow building with a terracotta roof was nestled in the gnarled branches of mangrove trees like some overgrown Eden. The cluster of trees burst from the sea, suspending the hotel in the air like a gleeful child in the hands of a parent. And this marvel was only possible because The Mangrove Hotel was brimming with magic.

The mangrove branches even reached inside the hotel, dangling vines and fragrant flowers finding homes along the colourful walls and ceilings. The Mangrove had been Evie Bell's home for nine of her thirteen years. She adored it. But on this particular evening, all that was on her mind was escaping the place.

A walnut grandfather clock in the lobby chimed eight times, reverberating to the hotel's two upper floors. Evie peered from behind her rickety linen cart, over the balcony of the second floor, down to the lobby below. The brilliant white of her maid's uniform was somewhat grubby from wiping off her dusty hands. Beside her, Arthur, one of the porter boys, snuck a peek down too. The hotel owner and Evie's adopted mother, Ms Bell, had just handed over keys to two of the many guests who'd arrived especially for tonight. The couple gasped in astonishment as enchanted vines crept from the balconies, wrapped around the handles of their brown leather suitcases and lifted them up to the first floor.

Evie watched the guests with a frown. So many visitors and hardly any were mages themselves. They had no magic. They just wanted the thrill of being close to it. Okay, so maybe *she* didn't have any magic either, but certainly not for lack of trying.

"All right, make sure you follow the plan to a T, you hear?" Evie commanded Arthur. "If we mess up, Ms Bell's not going to lay back and give us another chance at this."

"Yeah man, relax yourself," Arthur replied. His small brown eyes were barely slits when he flashed a self-assured smile.

"But how you mean 'relax', Arthur, when we're about to pull the heist of our lives?"

Arthur snorted. "The heist of *your* life, sistah. This'll be child's play for me." He held his hands up like a mime and wiggled his thieving fingers playfully.

Evie rolled her eyes. "Cho!" she huffed. At least *someone* was enjoying this. Evie's stomach was in knots.

The Carnival of Magic, or Myal as it was known to locals, took place one night a year, at a different location on the island each time. It only happened when the moon was full and the veil between the living world and the spirit world was at its thinnest. This year, Myal would take place on a golden beach in the town of Ocho Rios. And although Evie was forbidden from rowing across to Ocho Rios after sunset, she'd already made up her mind that she was going to the carnival to see her long-dead parents.

Evie stepped up onto the second-floor balcony railing, feeling the thrill as she glanced down at guests pottering around below her feet. The height didn't bother her. The enchanted hotel was her playground, and although she wasn't a mage herself, she had complete faith in Obeah – the divine energy linking the living world to the spirit world, and the reason magic existed in their world at all. A large plant stem unfurled itself from the railing, dipping to the floor below. Evie walked along it like a tightrope artist before hopping to a giant flower. Her added weight caused the pink flower head to wilt slowly, tilting her down to the ground floor and spitting her out with yellow pollen smudges to add to the dust marks on her uniform.

As she approached the front desk – where Ms Bell was deftly flicking at the rotary wheel of a telephone – Evie made efforts to brush off the worst offending dirt from her uniform and patted her plaits to ensure no hair was out of place (as it often was). She was prepared for whatever the answer to her request to attend Myal would be.

"No," said Ms Bell with only a cursory glance up. She swivelled slightly away from her adopted daughter, signalling that the conversation was over, and pressed the chunky phone receiver closer to her ear to further the point.

"But mi nah even ask you anything yet, Mama!" Evie had expected a chance to at least debate her case.

Ms Bell kissed her teeth. "Mi know when you want something, young lady, it's written all over your face. And the only thing you could possibly want on Myal night is to be over there and to take the larimar with you."

Bingo.

To fully embrace the Carnival of Magic you had to take magic with you, and the shiny blue larimar gemstone was the very source of the hotel's magic. Evie was definitely walking out of there with it.

Ms Bell began her phone conversation, switching seamlessly to her posh, Anglicized voice rather than her natural Xaymacan patois. A shadow fell onto the floor behind Ms Bell, and Evie tried not to glance upwards and draw her mama's attention to the source of it. Arthur appeared just behind the hotel owner, suspended on a long, enchanted vine, which hung precariously from the ceiling. Sweat seeped through his white hotel shirt as he shimmied his way down, tongue sticking out in concentration and small hands passing one beneath the other, halting only when Ms Bell gesticulated in her chair without warning.

The larimar was locked in Ms Bell's office, through the peeling lacquer door behind the front desk. Evie had entrusted Arthur's deft hands to make the gemstone heist, while her job was to do what she did best: talk. But Evie hadn't accounted for this phone call, which crucially took Ms Bell's attention away from her. Heaven forbid her mama needed to check a logbook or file from the office and caught Arthur in the act.

Ms Bell and Evie both jumped as a hotel cat leaped onto the desk. The phone receiver dropped from Ms Bell's plump hand like a slippery fish before clattering on the tiled floor and bungeeing back on its cord.

"Clinton!" Ms Bell screeched at the brown-black cat. "Lawd have mercy. You'll make me catch my death, and mi only forty years young!"

Clinton slow-blinked disinterestedly before narrowing his yellow eyes at Evie. He always had a grumpy-looking face anyway, but given Evie and Arthur were in the middle of their covert operation, she imagined that the Burmese cat was glaring with disapproval. Clinton mewed, switching his attention to Arthur, who was using the commotion to good effect as he picked the lock of the office door. Arthur glanced back and shot a look at Evie, with a furrowed brow and widened eyes. While Ms Bell apologized profusely to the person on the other end of the line, Evie cleared her throat and accosted Ms Bell again.

This next act would hold her attention for sure.

# Chapter Two

# THE ENCHANTED LARIMAR

## Evie

Evie slammed her palm down repeatedly on the service bell on Ms Bell's desk. The high-pitched *tring* rang out across the lobby.

Ms Bell's mouth hung open mid-speech, her sharp eyes shooting daggers. "Rahtid…" she uttered in disbelief, forgetting herself and apparently the person receiving her call too. "What in the world yuh think you're doing, Evelyn Bell?"

"Requesting your service," Evie replied, emboldened by Arthur successfully slipping through the office door and pushing it gently closed.

Ms Bell gave her apologies once more to the recipient of her call, and promised to ring back. Then she placed the receiver in its cradle, pushed back her chair and drew herself to her full height. Granted she wasn't much taller than Evie, but Ms Bell had that headmistress aura about her. Even the burly cooks in the hotel kitchen wilted when she gave them a dressing-down.

"You can wash pots and clean Clinton's dutty litter tray for a week for this! You are *not* going to Myal."

"But why?"

"How you mean 'why'? What mi tell you about dark magic? You want La Diablesse to lead you away to your death, hmm? Or you want to get your spirit snatched outta your body by Blackheart Man?"

Evie sighed, exasperated. All the older folk insisted on telling kids stories about monsters and duppies to stop them misbehaving. About the devilish woman La Diablesse with one human foot and one cow's foot, and of the demonic Blackheart Man who sold his soul for power and had to take the spirits of human victims to pay the devil back.

"Mama, I'm not the child you think I am. Can we stop with all the ghost stories and be real?"

Ms Bell looked amused despite herself. She stood hands on hips, her tight grip creating the only visible creases on her freshly pressed uniform. "Okay, madam. Let's be real." She lifted a hinged portion of the desk and walked out so that she was directly in front of Evie. "I thought that after your thirteenth birthday you would have matured, and that you'd be ready to keep the larimar close to you. But you're not. Magic is powerful and dangerous."

Evie bristled. She embraced magic and wanted to understand it to feel closer to her dead parents, who she suspected had been mages. Yes, she might make trampolines out of giant flower heads and swing from ceiling vines, but she wouldn't apologize for being curious about the larimar's magic just because Ms Bell had no imagination. Once, magic had been at the heart of Xaymacan culture – she'd heard all about it from guest mages. But now, magic was on the fringes, especially in the modern industrial cities. What had once been celebrated now made some people fearful, which birthed the ghost stories of warning.

"It's not magic that's dangerous, it's the people who use it to do bad things," said Evie. Ms Bell looked taken aback at being challenged again. "And my reasons are good. This is my one chance to commune with Mami and Papa! To find out what really happened to them and where I came from."

Without Evie realizing it, this discussion had become more than an act. It was no longer about buying time for Arthur. It didn't matter that he was busting a safe open on the other side of the office door – this conversation, long overdue, was real. It wasn't just that Ms Bell didn't trust her that upset her. It was that she didn't seem to respect Obeah, despite magic being all around them at The Mangrove.

A flash of guilt lit Ms Bell's face, then she deflected it. "Yuh don't listen to me. Have I not done everything to take care of you? To keep you safe from harm?"

"Mi not saying you haven't!" Evie cried.

"This is for your own good, Evie. The larimar is too powerful and you're not a mage. You aren't ready to handle magic and the responsibility that comes with it!" Adopted mother and daughter glared at each other, resentment bubbling like a brook. Lately, Ms Bell was always talking about "responsibility". She seemed disappointed that Evie wasn't another version of herself: serious, regimented and effortlessly polished.

Arthur re-emerged from the office with an oblivious grin, silently patting his pocket to signal his success. His smile slipped under Clinton's unimpressed gaze – the cat letting out a low mew as if to attract Ms Bell's attention. Arthur swiftly grabbed at the dangling vine and was lifted up to safety, as the enchanted plant drew back towards the ceiling.

The larimar heist was over, and all Evie needed to do now was back down. But a line had been crossed between her and Ms Bell. Evie's body shook despite her best efforts to control it. "It's *my* gemstone," she said petulantly. "My parents wouldn't have left it to me if it was so terrible. But I suppose it's okay for *you* to use its magic on this place when it suits you!" Evie regretted the words as soon as they left her mouth, but it was too late to take them back.

Ms Bell looked as though she'd been struck – shock turning to hurt, and hurt to bristling anger. "Plenty o' people would have taken the gemstone from a four-year-old girl and run away with it. But I adopted you as my own – gave us both a life. This place gives us a life, Evie!"

It was Evie's turn to feel guilt, and it doubled as she thought again about how she alone had survived that day. The day Ms Bell found her. "Mi just want to see them, Mama." A sob caught her and refused to let go. "Why did the larimar save me and no one else? Mi ha'fi know."

Ms Bell softened. She wrapped her arms around Evie with a sigh. "Mi know how much it means to you to feel close to your real parents, so mi thought that it would be okay to let you keep the larimar with you once you were old enough. But even I don't truly understand its magic, and it's a powerful enchanted instrument. You aren't ready – and certainly not to expose yourself to the wutless crowd attending Myal."

With that she lifted the desk at its hinge again and sat back down without another glance. Her brows hung like heavy rain clouds over her eyes. Evie lingered, realizing words weren't going to be enough – she was never going to make Ms Bell see her the way she saw herself. So she pushed away the feeling of guilt at what she had to do. Her scuffed leather shoes squeaked on the tiles as she turned and made her way back down the lobby.

As Evie entered the housemaids' quarters, Arthur was sitting on an armchair brandishing the ocean-blue larimar which had been set on a silver pendant. Grinning, he tossed it to Evie, who snatched it from the air.

"Ms Bell's gonna be vexed," said Arthur, already washing his hands of the deed.

"Brudda, you been here long enough to know Ms Bell is *always* vexed."

Arthur chuckled. He'd been at the hotel two years, ever since Ms Bell had brought him home from town to make an honest living as a porter, rather than pickpocketing unsuspecting tourists. She'd watched him pull his tricks while on an errand at Ochi's busy market, but had also noticed his meagre frame and worn clothing. Ms Bell certainly had a habit of picking up strays! But it turned out she was a great judge of character because Arthur had quickly become Evie's best friend.

"I'm coming with you, you know," Arthur said, in a way that dared Evie to say otherwise. But she was grateful that she wouldn't be doing this alone.

"Then dress to impress and meet me at the dock once the clock strikes eleven," she said, placing the pendant round her neck and tucking the chain under her collar. "With the power of the larimar to help me, we'll see who's 'not ready' for Myal."

# Chapter Three

# MIDNIGHT MAGIC

## Evie

Outside the hotel, the national flag of Xaymaca – in its tricolour green and black with a yellow cross – hung limply from a mast. As the grandfather clock chimed eleven, Evie climbed out of her second-floor window and down one of the mangrove branches until her feet touched the veranda below. Keeping low by the front windows, she made her way towards the largest mangrove tree where steps leading to the dock had been carved into the twisting trunk. Hanging lanterns illuminated the steps, and she was greeted by the sound of the sea lapping against the cedarwood planks.

About four hundred metres across the water was Ocho Rios Bay Beach, where the Myal was taking place. There were lit fires, raised voices and a large crowd of revellers. The guttural punch of djembe drums reached her ears and vibrated through her body from across the sea. Finally, Myal had come to *her* town. She drew the pendant, containing the larimar, up from under the white collar of her navy-blue dress. Dangling from its silver chain, the gemstone glistened in the moonlight. This was the night Evie had been waiting for.

Arthur appeared by her side, breaking her from her reverie with a start.

"You look like you've seen a duppy," said Arthur, equally alarmed by her reaction.

"Mi lawd, that's cos you snuck up on me! How you manage to tread so soffy-soft all the time?"

An undersized black porkpie hat rested atop Arthur's short, neat hair – a prop to make himself look older than his thirteen years. He had a suit jacket slung over one shoulder, and a crisp white shirt with the collar buttons undone to let in air on this warm night. Dark red braces held up his smart black trousers.

"You going to carnival or church?" Evie asked.

Arthur cocked his hat and shrugged off her teasing. "Appearance is everything, yuh know. People trust a man in a suit." He winked and began untying a rope holding one of the rowboats. Evie side-eyed Arthur as she stepped into the vessel. She knew exactly what he was getting at.

"Hear me now, no picking pockets," she ordered as she steadied herself. "You promised to leave that behind."

"Come now, sistah. You just had me steal a gem!" Arthur scoffed. "You can't invite me to Myal, with so much magical booty to collect, and not expect me to take a little look!"

"You invited yourself!"

Arthur waved her away, climbing into the boat himself. "With all the excitement we've had tonight, who can remember who said what?"

Evie kissed her teeth in reply.

"If mi can score a magic artefact or two and sell them on the black market, I'll never ha'fi thieve again!" Arthur continued. "I'll get offa this island – set sail to New York, Paris, no, London Town. Maybe I'll become a lord or a duke... That'd show everyone—"

"Stop," said Evie abruptly.

"Stop what?"

"Talking about leaving." Evie couldn't meet his eyes, so stared across the dark water to the distant bay.

"Oh..." Arthur caught himself. "Sorry." He fell silent, continuing to untie the rope.

Evie frowned, annoyed at both Arthur's lack of tact and her own display of vulnerability. The shipwreck that only Evie had survived meant that she lost her parents very young. Arthur's parents, however, left him in the care of a cruel auntie and uncle while they sought work opportunities abroad. When he could stand it no more, Arthur ran away to the nearest big town: Ochi. Without a true family, all either of them had now was found family. Evie thought Arthur of all people would feel the same and want to stay here, stay together. And from the photographs she'd seen, she had no desire to leave home for London, as many Xaymacans were tempted to. The Caribbean was always living colour; England was just pigeon grey.

"Look, you know how much it means to me to find a spirit waker and communicate with my family. You mess up and get caught then you're on your own, you hear?"

Arthur shook his head with an easy smile. "Evie, mi don't get caugh—"

A rapid shuffling over the planks made the pair squeak with fright. But the ambush had only come from a feline friend.

"Clinton!" They exhaled, sweet relief and annoyance rolled into one, as the hotel cat mewed at them.

"Get back up there, Clinton," Evie whispered. "Mi nah have any treats for you. Go catch a mouse or suttin' like you're meant to." Clinton slow-blinked and mewed again louder than before.

"Mi swear this cat is the biggest snitch!" said Arthur, flustered.

"Let's just get outta here. Out of sight, hopefully out of mind!" said Evie, picking up her oars and pushing off from the dock.


Anticipation skyrocketed as their boat drew towards the dock of the bay.

"So, you've got the larimar; we're here. What next?" Arthur asked.

"All kinds o' mages will be here: diviners, enchanters, healers," said Evie excitedly. "But being a carnival to honour spirits, all I care about is finding—"

"A spirit waker."

"Right. I hand a spirit waker the larimar and they'll act as the medium between me, my mami and papa."

Arthur looked uncertain. "Just be careful, you hear?"

Evie raised an eyebrow. "That's *my* line. Anyway, don't believe everything you've heard about 'dark magic' and duppies. We're just going to make contact. We're not here to raise the dead!" Evie leaped out of the boat and onto the boardwalk before it had been properly moored. "Tie her up and let's go!"

Their feet battered the planks as they walked quickly. Evie's eyes fixed on the dancing, chanting people on the beach. Everyone was dressed so beautifully, so colourfully. She only hoped she slotted in, with her patterned red bandana and her pleated blue summer dress that would make moving and shaking to the music easy.

She took off her leather shoes to feel the grains of sand between her toes, and marvelled at fire enchanters breathing flames onto wooden torches like dragons, illuminating the darkness. She watched a queue of restless people gather to have their fortunes told by a diviner, whose aura glowed red.

"Mi laaaawd Jesus, will you look at that!" Arthur pointed.

Four giant papier-mâché busts were worn by performers. At around two metres in height, they became central parts of the celebrations. The busts were of the Four Heroes of Xaymaca – Queen Nanny, Cudjoe, Quao and Sekesu – the figures who'd led enslaved Xaymacans to drive the British out of the island in the early eighteenth century, using ancestral magic. Nanny represented the spirit wakers, clothed in purple with her famous white headscarf; Quao the healers, swathed in green; Cudjoe the diviners, in red, and Sekesu the enchanters, in blue. Many of the revellers were draped in the colours of the magic type they practised. Evie had to find a willing spirit waker, marked out by purple.

She reached up to her collar automatically, feeling the outline of the larimar necklace beneath it. The heaving crowd stepped to the rhythm as musicians pounded their hand drums. Evie was a slight thirteen-year-old, which made manoeuvring through the bodies both easy and intimidating all at once. An elderly healer to her left held out a calabash full of a steaming concoction to a young woman who looked drawn and weak. A flamboyant enchanter in a top hat built a large castle of sand with the touch of his hand, to the rapturous applause of onlookers.

Two figures draped in muted whites and black stood out because they *weren't* dancing or, apparently, enjoying the Myal at all. They were both of Taíno heritage: a broad, imposing man with long dark hair and markings on his face and forearms, and a boy about half his size with a quite distinctive bowl cut and piercing eyes. The boy was about Evie and Arthur's age, but something about his posture, raised chin and soldier-like manner made him seem older. However, it wasn't the pair's physical appearance that caught the eye so much as their hefty scabbards holding curved swords. Who on earth were they? Evie was about to point them out to Arthur, but he spoke first.

"I'll…er…meet you back at the dock after midnight," he announced with a roguish grin.

Evie followed his gaze to the fancy enchanter with the top hat and narrowed her eyes at her friend. All it took was a whiff of magical treasures and Arthur was all over it. She couldn't muster the energy to argue about him abandoning her before she'd even found a spirit waker. "Yeah man. Go, go." She waved him off, but Arthur had skittered away before the last word had even left her mouth.

Feeling suddenly exposed and alone, Evie turned from left to right, searching for any sign of a spirit waker in the crowd.

As the midnight hour approached, the golden moon hanging low in the sky, Evie stopped in her tracks. Peering through the mass of revellers, she spotted a purple sash over white robes, and her heart leaped.

A spirit waker had finally appeared.

# Chapter Four

# SPIRIT WAKER

## Evie

Evie quickly took her place in a queue forming in front of the elderly spirit waker. The man smiled in greeting, his eyes squeezing to slits beneath bushy grey brows, a tall Rasta hat covering his head. Everyone waiting to be seen was there for one of two reasons: to find out whether they had latent ancestral magic in them or, like Evie, to commune with their ancestors or lost loved ones.

The next person in line placed cufflinks in the elderly medium's palm. Evie realized they must have belonged to someone who'd died – the objects allowing the spirit waker to find a thread to their owner in the spirit world. Evie was engrossed as the spirit waker took a seat on the ground with his client. His eyes flashed purple before flickering shut as he channelled a spirit. There was a violet aura surrounding the pair, and they conversed animatedly. After a minute, the client rose to her feet with a start before profusely giving her thanks to the medium for his help, full of relief and wonderment. Evie's hopes blossomed at the sight.

When it was her turn, Evie removed her necklace as she approached the spirit waker. He stared down at her clasped hands, narrowing his eyes as the gemstone caught the light.

"Please help me," Evie began. "My mami and papa – mi need to reach them."

The medium's small eyes studied Evie. "So young… How long have your mami and papa been gone?"

"Nine years," Evie answered.

The medium nodded in understanding, studying her closely. "They were mages?"

It was something Evie wondered often, but the way the spirit waker asked seemed expectant of a "yes". Instead, she replied honestly. "Mi don't know."

Her answer perhaps conveyed how much she wanted to know, because the elderly man continued to appraise her. Then he pointed to the gemstone. "And this larimar. What is its significance to you?"

Evie looked at the blue stone in her hands, and it suddenly began to glow, as though it was manifesting her hopes. It had never done so before. "It was all they left to me," she uttered, entranced. "It saved my life."

The medium reached out. "May I see it?"

Evie held the pendant out on her palm and the spirit waker

took it. He gently placed a hand on Evie's shoulders and, with a reassuring nod, brought her down to kneel on the ground with him. She sat with fretful anticipation as the medium chanted. His body sparked – the magic consuming him, a link to the spirit world forged. His energy created a tingling sensation on Evie's skin, as though a light electrical current had flowed through her. Then the medium's eyes opened, his purple aura dimmed and just as quickly as he had begun, he released her.

"Wha-what happened?" Evie spluttered.

The medium shook his head. "They can't be reached. Sorry, my dear." He thrust the larimar back to her and climbed to his feet. Evie sat stunned for a moment.

"No…no that can't be right," she said. "They gave the stone to me. It *must* have their magic. Mi ha'fi reach them!"

"You can't communicate with spirits who don't want to talk back," the spirit waker said sharply.

It was as though a cold wind had snatched Evie's breath away. Her disappointment was immense. Her parents' spirits refused to come? She bristled, her sadness turning to anger. "No!" she said, rising from the sand. "Mi don't believe it. Are you even a spirit waker? Mi gwarn speak to one of the others who actually knows how to use magic."

The medium looked straight through her and nodded to the next person in the queue. "Next," he called.

A man nudged past Evie as she stood paralysed by disbelief and disappointment. As others in the crowd brushed past her impatiently, more anger built up until it propelled Evie forward, batting her way back through to give the elderly spirit waker a piece of her mind. Then a hand on her shoulder stopped Evie in her tracks. She looked up in surprise, meeting the eyes of a tall woman. Her face was elegantly set under a large, brimmed hat. She was wearing a stylish, scarlet dress and jacket to match it.

"Be calm, unless you want to anger the spirit wakers and everyone here who believes in the power of Obeah," said the woman, her voice like silky honey. "We can't have bad energy here tonight, all right? You must heed the words of a spirit waker, show respect and accept your lot. Go on home, darling."

The woman's warning was delivered gently but her aura was authoritative. Burgundy lipstick popped against her deep ebony skin, her face not unkind but firm. The woman patted Evie's shoulder sympathetically and disappeared into the crowd.

Evie felt like begging any spirit waker to help her – she might not have a chance like this again for a long time. But the thought of being perceived as lacking respect for Obeah held her back. Overwhelmed, she quickly walked away, placing the necklace around her neck once more. She fought away tears, determined not to cry in such an exposed public setting.

As she made her way towards the dock, she found Arthur waiting with a beaming smile, his pockets bulging.

"Look 'pon this haul!" he exclaimed, showing off a ruby

36

necklace, some rings and other fancy ornaments. He lifted his hat to reveal a squat, silver candle holder resting on his head. "Mi nah sure what this does exactly…" he said, popping his hat back on. "But it belonged to one uppity diviner who laughed at my hat. So mi thief it from right under his nose. Classic misdirection: you make them look to the left while you disappear to the right." Arthur noticed Evie was subdued and his expression changed. "Everything okay?"

As Evie opened her mouth to speak the whole beach suddenly shook. Revellers cried out in shock, some falling to the ground. The tremors grew so strong that the musicians stopped entirely and people ran for cover.

"Earthquake!" someone yelled. But almost as soon as they had, Evie recognized it wasn't that. The very sky was shimmering, glowing as if a distant star was emerging from some hidden place right between the atoms of their world.

From the rift, which extended from sky to sand, luminous figures emerged. They howled like deranged jackals, a sound that was not of this world. Goose pimples prickled all over Evie's body.

The ethereal beings wasted no time, moving across the beach at a ferocious pace. They snared revellers who weren't quick enough to escape them. Evie watched open-mouthed, fixed to the sand in fear, as the ghostly creatures took hold of people and seeped into their bodies, until they began to cry like jackals themselves – their bodies jerking and hunching over as though possessed.

As though...*possessed.*

Evie turned to Arthur sharply, uttering words that she could barely believe herself. "They're...they're duppies!"

# Chapter Five

# A DELUGE OF DUPPIES

## Evie

They were evil spirits, the stuff of folk tales that Evie had dismissed, right there in plain sight. Duppies were real! Their long, greying faces were human-like but everything was in grotesque, exaggerated proportions. Their gaping mouths contained broken teeth, there were dark holes where their noses should have been, and their bulbous eyes with pinprick pupils were devoid of life. The duppies swarmed the crowd that had become a terrified stampede.

"Mi lawd Jesus and all twelve o' dem apostles! Let's get outta here!" Arthur yelled.

They sprinted down the boardwalk, or rather Arthur shuffled as fast as he could, every crease and crevice clinking with stolen magical artefacts. He held onto his hat with one hand as the candle holder threatened to drop out. Evie glanced over her shoulder as a shriek pierced through the air. Seeing a hideous duppy flying towards them with its empty eyes and screeching mouth, she reached out for Arthur's hand to drag him along with her.

"Quick, Arthur! It's comin—"

In her haste, she tripped over an uneven board and clattered to the ground. Her bare toes throbbed with pain, but that was nothing compared to the feeling of sheer terror. Fear consumed Evie – and soon the duppy would too...

"Evie!" Arthur cried, trying desperately to pull her up.

She held on to Arthur and screamed as the duppy closed in on them both. But before the evil spirit could possess her body, the pendant snaked itself out from beneath her collar, the larimar inside it glowing brighter than ever before. She felt a static tingle as it released a pulsing energy that made the duppy recoil. A second later, the creature flew away to find another victim.

Utterly perplexed but relieved just to be alive, the pair scrambled to their feet again and dived into their boat. As Arthur picked up the oars and rowed, two figures splashed into the water, wading after them.

"Wait! Please, wait!" a desperate voice called. It was silky smooth despite being laced with fear. Evie turned to see the glamorous woman in the scarlet hat and a chiselled young man alongside her. He must have been in his late teens or early twenties, and he looked like he was of Taíno heritage, with tan skin and wavy black hair that fell the length of his neck. His molasses-brown eyes were sharp to match his angular features.

"Stop, Arthur. Let them aboard," said Evie.

"No way! We're not stopping till we reach the mangrove."

Evie grabbed his arm. "We can't let them get attacked by those things!"

"Cho!" he huffed, but conceded.

The pair waded to the boat and the young man held one side of it, allowing the lady in red to climb aboard. She took great care to keep her dignity, her long dress pressed down to cover the length of her legs so that she emerged from the water like a mermaid. Then the young man clambered aboard himself, his garnet-coloured shirt and white trousers sodden.

"Thank you," said the woman, as Arthur picked up the oars again.

"Yes. We're in your debt," said the young man, looking back at the beach in horror.

Evie wanted to turn away from the nightmare scene but couldn't bring herself to. Many revellers hadn't escaped the duppies; she could tell because they were no longer running away. They'd been possessed and were moving jerkily, sparking red, blue or green, as the evil spirits took control of limbs and ancestral magic that didn't belong to them. There were mages on the beach still fighting for their lives, using enchantments – sand, water, fire, smoke – to attack the swarming duppies. There were flashes of silver through the chaos as the stoic Taíno pair she'd noticed earlier used their great swords to ward off the spirits.

Evie was still shaking from their miraculous escape. Her hand drifted to the larimar under her collar. Had the gem's magic somehow protected them?

"What happened?" she asked in a daze. "They're duppies. But who summoned them?"

"It can only have been a spirit waker," the woman answered. Evie felt her stomach drop. "Only they can commune with the spirit world and summon evil spirits here."

"So someone is making the bad spirits possess the bodies of the carnival-goers?" Arthur asked.

"It seems so," said the young man. "But the duppies aren't attacking just anyone. Only mages seem to be the target."

"But we nah have any magic. How come they came after us?" said Arthur.

The young man cast a glance at the woman in red, but Evie struggled to read his expression.

"Did you bring something to Myal? Something that could have attracted them?" the woman asked.

Arthur glared at Evie, a caution. But this woman had already stopped Evie from making a mistake at Myal. She was knowledgeable in the ways of Obeah. It was, perhaps, a chance for Evie to find out more about magic. Now was not the time to be left in the dark.

"I came to commune with my parents," she confided, fiddling with her dress. "I was left something of theirs. Something enchanted."

The woman appeared to be waiting expectantly for more

before she nodded in understanding. "I see. I'm sorry for your loss, my dear."

To Evie's surprise, she saw true sadness in the woman's expression rather than the look of pity most people gave when they learned about her parents' death. It was as though a distant sorrow had been pulled from the woman's own memory. But she quickly gathered herself.

"I'm Lana, Lana Walters. And this is my aide, Jujo. What's your name?"

"Evelyn. But everyone calls me Evie. And this here is Arthur."

"Pleasure is mine," Arthur muttered, without a hint of pleasure in his tone.

"Where are we headed?" asked Jujo.

Evie pointed to the great cluster of mangroves wrapped around the hotel in the distance. The lamps on the tree path up to the veranda shone through the darkness like fireflies. "The Mangrove Hotel. We'll be safe there. Magic protects us— Ow!"

Arthur pulled back the oar that had slapped Evie on the back. Lana and Jujo blinked at him while Evie glared daggers.

"Sorry, Evie. How careless of me," he said pointedly. "*Very* careless."

The hotel had once stood on a lonely isle until Ms Bell brought Evie and the larimar back home with her. Then the neighbouring mangrove had become enchanted over time, taking on a life of its own. The Mangrove Hotel became a big draw for visitors to Ochi, but at Ms Bell's request, the fact that the larimar was the source of the hotel's magic was never revealed to anyone, so as to keep it safe. Evie shouldn't even have told Arthur about it. So she took the hint, but not without making a mental note to clap him back at some point.

"Why, that's incredible," said Lana, peering through the dark at the building taking shape through the branches. "Magic can affect a building like this? I've never seen anything like it. At a less…traumatic time I should love to study it properly."

"Study?" said Evie.

"We're researchers from the University College of the West Indies," Jujo explained. "And our interests in Obeah are somewhat more academic than the average mage or Myal guest."

"We want to understand this gift we call magic," said Lana, "in the world we know and beyond."

Evie didn't want to look a fool by asking what Lana meant by "beyond", but the question nagged at her.

"You mean the spirit world?" she asked, eyes darting back to the beach which she could barely see through the smoke and flames. The duppies still circled, shimmering in the night sky, but the possessed mages had disappeared.

"That's right," said Lana, following Evie's gaze. "Magic penetrates the realm of the dead as well as the living. Our bodies may fade here, but Obeah connects all spirits across the divide."

Jujo nodded. "We want to understand whether this bridge of spiritual energy can become physical. Without the need for a spirit waker at all."

Evie's excitement grew as the seed of possibilities was planted. Her mind raced, and the image of a smiling woman and man with features like hers took root there. "You really think it's possible? To travel to the spirit world?"

"Even for the most gifted mage, Obeah is a force that cannot be fully understood," said Lana. "Everything seems impossible, until it isn't."

Evie moored the rowboat at the hotel dock and led the way up the carved-out steps to the veranda. Her legs felt like lead, but as fearful as she was of the repercussions of disobeying Ms Bell, with duppies and possessed mages on the loose she simply had to tell her adopted mother what had happened at Myal. So much for slipping back inside unnoticed!

"Who'd have thought such a place as this could exist?" said Jujo, breaking their silence. "Only a very powerful enchanter could mould nature like this... Or a powerful enchantment tool."

A lamp light came on above the front doors, providing a cool glow on the veranda. The doors swung inwards, and Ms Bell appeared in a bronze-coloured bed robe and headscarf – her expression thunderous.

"Get inside," she ordered. Then a surprised look passed over her face as she noticed the unexpected guests.

"Mama, something terrible happened," Evie began. "Mi know, mi disobeyed, and you must be vexed—"

"A-true!" Ms Bell answered, controlling her anger a touch more in the presence of visitors.

"Th-there were duppies. They came from the spirit world. And, and…"

"Duppies?" Ms Bell repeated, horror compounding her anger. "What mi tell you about Myal? Get inside!" she ordered. "And don't think mi can't see you hiding over there, Arthur."

A porkpie hat hovered behind a potted plant, and someone cursed under their breath. Arthur emerged sheepishly, taking off his hat to tip it. The magic candle holder fell to the stone veranda with a *clunk* and a shower of red sparks. Arthur laughed nervously before picking it up and hiding it behind his back.

"May we come in, Ms Bell?" Lana asked. "Please."

"Check-in hours have passed, madam and young sir," said Ms Bell, agitated.

"Please, Mama," said Evie. "We can't leave them outside on a night like this with evil spirits about. And they're soaked through."

Ms Bell exhaled through her nose. "All right, all right, come. Quick!"

Evie followed Ms Bell inside. She heard a strange clunking from behind her on the tiles of the veranda. Heavy footsteps. Jujo was wearing leather shoes but the weight of the sound didn't match his steps. Confused, Evie turned her attention to Lana. Under her long dress it was impossible to see what sort of shoes she wore. But, strangely, only one of her feet was making the sound.

Evie noticed that Ms Bell had stopped in her tracks, with the desk partially lifted at the hinge. She too was staring at Lana, and there was something in her eyes that gave Evie chills. She had never seen her guardian so tense.

"What…what did you say your name was, madam?" Ms Bell asked, her unease drawing out each word.

Now it was Lana's turn to halt where she stood. Her tight-lipped smile became an emotionless cast; her once warm features suddenly icily cold.

"I didn't, but I've no doubt my reputation precedes me." She raised her manicured hands, swooping them both in an arc. Cast in the shadow of her arms, the hotel doors flew off their hinges, splintering as though a cyclone had struck. Distant jackal-like howls grew ever louder in the night air until the echoey lobby was filled with the frightful sound.

"They call me La Diablesse."

# Chapter Six

# THE SPACE BETWEEN WORLDS

## Evie

Fear.

Fear like Evie had never known enveloped her. This had to be a nightmare. There was no way she'd brought the devil-woman into her home. La Diablesse was just a story anyway! Wasn't she? But then she'd thought the same about duppies before tonight.

"M-Ms Lana?" she uttered, not knowing what else to say.

"Evie! Arthur!" Ms Bell screeched, her voice rising in octaves. "Come quick!"

Arthur dashed for the front desk, which shook Evie from her inertia. But as she moved, spectral duppies with ravenous eyes and long flailing limbs swooped in through the open doorway, rounding the high ceilings and balconies like sharks circling prey. The patchwork of vines and flowers that adorned the hotel withered and died when touched by their ghastly aura. The mangrove branches blistered and crackled.

La Diablesse and Jujo stood in the eye of this ghostly storm exuding calm. Evie realized they had to be the ones who'd summoned them here.

Hotel guests had stirred at the commotion, emerging from their rooms on the upper levels. As they fled, their screams joined the deathly chorus of the duppies. One of the evil spirits shot down towards Ms Bell, who turned with a terrified shriek, arms raised. The duppy swooped overhead and back upwards again. It was as Jujo said, the duppies only attacked mages. But Ms Bell collapsed to the floor, fainting from the sheer terror.

"Mama!" Evie ran to her guardian's aid, but Jujo beat her to it. He crouched at Ms Bell's side placing his right palm over her forehead. A scarlet glow emitted – the red of a diviner. "Leave her alone!"

Evie moved on instinct, reaching for the necklace beneath her collar. She had to try something, anything, to save Ms Bell. But as she withdrew the chain of the pendant, her body froze as though someone was holding her still with an iron grip. Yet there was no one near her. Evie was terrified; her body wouldn't obey what her mind was telling it to do. What kind of magic was this?

Evie heard the *clop, clop, clop* of a hoofed foot. She could only watch, unable to do a thing or say a word, as the devil-woman plucked the pendant from her hand and lifted the chain from around her neck. La Diablesse stepped away from her, marvelling at the larimar, eyes wide with delight. Evie collapsed to the polished floor as La Diablesse's shadow receded. That was why she hadn't been able to move – this woman was a shadow enchanter.

"You don't even realize what you held, Evie," she said. "Look around you at the magic that has affected this place. This is no ordinary enchanted object or charm. This larimar contains the very magic of one of Xaymaca's Four Heroes. It belonged to the earth enchanter Sekesu."

Evie stared at the larimar in shock. Sekesu had lived and fought centuries ago. How did her magic end up here? How did it end up with her parents?

"Imagine our surprise, after years of searching, that the gem should be flaunted right in front of us. And at Myal of all places."

"Please," Evie begged. "I need it. I need answers. Without it I...I—"

"What you must understand, Evie, is that this is bigger than you," said La Diablesse, her hand closing to a fist. "Our mission is bigger than all of us."

Jujo rose to his feet again, the red glow he emitted disappearing.

"What did you learn?" La Diablesse asked him.

"This woman found the girl drifting in the bay with the larimar as a child," said Jujo. In his open palm was another gemstone of lava-like reds and oranges: a coral. "She doesn't know about the larimar's origin but kept its power secret to profit from it."

Jujo handed the coral stone over to La Diablesse. The devil-woman opened her jacket to slip both gems into her breast pocket, but she froze when she realized the larimar was glowing.

"I won't let you take it!" Evie cried, dashing at the woman and catching her off guard. Evie reached for the larimar, getting a finger to it as La Diablesse tried to snap her hand out of the way.

The contact with the gem triggered an explosion of energy, just like the blast that warded off the duppies on the beach. The shock wave blew La Diablesse through the front desk. It shattered, scattering papers and knocking down shelves. A terrified Arthur was left exposed, crouching but no longer hidden behind the broken desk.

Jujo had also got caught in the blast, his body sprawled on the lobby floor. But just as Evie was eyeing a way to escape while they could, La Diablesse stirred, pushing herself up with a grunt. The front of her dress was torn from the blast and Evie stared in horror at the sight.

A hoofed cow's leg banged on the floor as La Diablesse climbed to her feet. Where her wide-brimmed hat had been displaced, two small horns protruded from her hairline. Her irises were now icy blue, glaring with ferocity. Arthur scurried away with a yelp upon seeing the true vision of La Diablesse.

"So…you *do* have magic in you, Evie." La Diablesse swiped her hat from the floor and placed it back over her head.

Evie was frozen with fear and confusion as the devil woman

levelled her gaze at her. La Diablesse thought the magic was Evie's rather than the larimar's. She had to be mistaken. Didn't she?

"Evie!" Arthur called. "Run!"

But as La Diablesse advanced, Evie found herself stuck in the clutches of the woman's shadow once again.

La Diablesse placed the glowing larimar and coral in her breast pocket. "Let me show you the true power of the combined magic of Xaymaca's heroes."

In an instant, La Diablesse was in front of Evie. As the devil woman thrust a palm towards her heart, Evie had the sickening sensation of bursting apart like vapour.

When she regained her senses, Evie found herself submerged in water, with La Diablesse's hand gripping her throat. At first she wondered if she'd somehow been transported into the sea. But it felt different somehow. Rather than normal water, it was like being trapped in a forceful current of energy, bright light and immense weight. Evie could hear a moaning sound, like whale song. With a fright, she realized that this sea was full of spirits of the dead.

La Diablesse floated in front of her, her irises glowing blue as her gaze bored into Evie.

"It would be an act of mercy to reunite you with your parents now," she said venomously. "My gift to you."

Somehow Evie knew that she was not dead. Not fully. But it

felt like she was being dragged towards death – like her resolve was being drained. Her heartbeat slowed despite her struggling to break free. The floating spirits of the deceased were heading towards a light – a large break in the water's surface. Evie understood that she shouldn't go towards it, but her spirit seemed to call for it. She desired to follow the other spirits into that light.

"Evie!" a faraway voice called. It echoed faintly as though it were oceans away.

Suddenly, the sea of spirits came crashing down around them, and they were back in the hotel lobby. Evie collapsed to the floor, gagging as though she had water in her lungs. She heard a thrashing sound beside her and Arthur's cry of pain.

"Stop, La Diablesse!" Jujo barked. "You shouldn't go to that place. Remember our orders!"

As she lay weakly coughing on the tiled floor, Evie watched the others from the corner of her eye. Jujo had a hold on La Diablesse's wrist. She glanced at Jujo with a glare that could cut steel. The young man promptly let go, and she swayed wearily on her feet.

"Let's go, then, before the shamans find out where we are," she said. "We have what we came for."

Evie watched them both disappear through the open doorway, La Diablesse seeming to have less energy than before. The swarm of duppies followed them, screeching out into the darkness like a colony of oversized phantom bats. Evie's chest rose and fell, snatching for air, her body too drained to move.

Then she felt a tugging at her dress.

"Ay, Evie! Wake up now." Arthur's voice went from distant to loud. "Ay! Come now!"

She opened her eyes again and tried to focus. But the more she did, the more confused she became. She found herself staring up at the miserable furry face of the hotel cat.

"What? Clinton, get outta here." Evie found the strength to bat the Burmese cat away.

"Lawd have mercy, you're all right!"

Evie blinked once. Twice. The words had come from Clinton's mouth. But that was unmistakably Arthur's voice. She sat up and the cat backed away to give her space.

"My gosh! ...Arthur?"

## Chapter Seven

# CAT IN A PORKPIE HAT

## Evie

"What in the…but how yuh get so big?" Arthur exclaimed. "The devil woman…musta turned you into a giant!"

"Arthur, wh-what happened?" Evie gasped.

"How you mean 'what happened'? You—" Arthur suddenly caught sight of a paw as he pointed, and realized he was on all fours. His eyes grew larger and his head dropped, as if by focusing harder on the paws they might become hands again. Then he let out an almighty yell as he bounded round the lobby.

"Arthur!" Evie tried to raise her voice above the din. But Arthur's cat-cries kept going.

When he finally stopped, he panted. "Okay… Okay… Everything gwarn be all right." Then he caught his reflection in a full-length mirror and proceeded to test out his lungs again.

Evie crawled over to where Ms Bell lay. She shook her

guardian gently and when she wouldn't come round, Evie pressed her ear against her chest.

"Thank heavens," she said as she found Ms Bell's heartbeat.

Evie cradled her head in her hands, fully taking in what she'd lost – the larimar had been her sole link to her parents. The reason their home existed. "I must be dreaming…"

"*You?*" Arthur called. "*I* must be dreaming cos last time mi check, mi couldn't even grow a moustache never mind whiskers!" Arthur sank his face to his paws with a moan. "La Diablesse…"

Evie's heart still hammered, the adrenaline yet to seep away. "What happened?" she asked again. "One minute mi was here and the next…" She shuddered, thinking about that awful place that had felt like it was draining her spirit.

"The devil woman had you," Arthur explained. "She had you by the neck and it was like your spirit left your body. You were physically here but there was nothing in your eyes…in your…body."

Evie shivered. "Mi…felt like mi wasn't here. It was like another world entirely. Somewhere beyond."

"Mi tried to free you from her. It was a stupid thing to do, but my body just moved by itself. Next thing mi know, mi trip over the damn cat. And then, I'm travelling through a wall of ocean and mi see you – mi see the devil woman – and then mi back here on the floor in agony."

"Arthur…you were there too? In that…sea of spirits?" Evie got to her feet shakily, eyes never leaving Arthur. "Somehow, your spirit has ended up in Clinton's body!"

"Mi laaaawd," Arthur moaned. He looked about the room before turning back to Evie. "Then where mi body go?"

A very human yowl sounded from the first floor. They looked up in disbelief to see Arthur's confused face peering through the railings of the balcony.

"Clinton?!" they cried in unison.

"Get that cat! Mi want mi body back!" Arthur commanded, rushing towards the curved staircase with Evie tailing him as quickly as she could.

On the first floor, Clinton – in Arthur's body – cagily stood on all fours, back arched and poised to break into a run himself.

"Here, kitty, kitty."

There was trepidation in Arthur's voice, and Evie's head spun at the absurdity of hearing a boy as a cat coaxing a cat as a boy. Clinton wailed when Arthur darted at him. He tried to run on his human hands and feet, but face-planted instead. Evie dived on top of him, but the cat-boy scratched and hissed, forcing her to let go if she wanted to keep her eyeballs.

Clinton scampered off again, struggling to coordinate a sprint in Arthur's wiry body. He made his way down the stairs head first, backside up in the air, fumbling his way down. Evie chased and leaped off the railings towards him, crashing down on top of Clinton, so that they rolled down the few remaining steps together.

"Ay! Steady or you'll bruk up mi body!" Arthur complained.

Clinton let out a dazed mew as his head hit the floor.

Arthur's porkpie hat popped off and Evie uttered a startled cry. There, inside the black hat, was a gleaming blue gemstone. The larimar encased in the pendant.

"Arthur!" Evie took the larimar in her hands and studied every side to check it was the real thing. "How did you...?"

"Mi switch it with a necklace from my beach haul," he said, picking up the porkpie hat with his paw and placing it on his head. "And put it in La Diablesse's breast pocket while you were both in that spirit ocean place."

"Arthur, yuh wonderful, wonderful boy!" Evie clutched the pendant, giving it a kiss and placing the chain back around her neck. "Mi can still reach my parents, and whatever terrible plans La Diablesse and Jujo had are ruined."

"How 'bout first we use it to get me back inside *my body*," said Arthur, butting his cat head against his real torso. "He's out cold... Quick, try something."

"I..." Evie's hands trembled as she held the gem. She saw La Diablesse's terrifying scowl and the ocean of dead spirits. What could she do without properly understanding Obeah and the magic that caused this? What if she somehow made things even worse? "Mi don't know if mi can, Arthur. Mi can't make sense of this. La Diablesse must be a shadow enchanter – mi found that out first hand. And she said that the larimar belonged to Sekesu, so it should only be able to enchant earth and plant life, not spirits."

Arthur blinked his cat eyes and sighed. "All right, all right. We don't have time to hang around. La Diablesse left in a hurry, so let's get outta here before she realizes the switch happened and comes back."

"But what about Ms Bell and the hotel guests?" Evie asked.

"Mi think most o' them already making an escape," Arthur replied, glancing out of the hole where the front doors had been. And, indeed, they could hear guests scrabbling out of windows, see them racing down to the dock, and hear the splash of bodies in the ocean, not even waiting for a boat to become available.

There was a murmur from the now demolished front desk. Ms Bell stirred.

"Mama!" Evie rushed over and crouched down to help her sit up. "Mama, easy now."

The hotel owner looked around confusedly before sitting up with a lurch, her breathing rapid.

"She in a whole heap o' shock," said Arthur, sitting agitatedly at their feet. And if Ms Bell wasn't alarmed before, she was at the sight of a talking cat in a porkpie hat. She fainted again. "Mi didn't think that one through…"

"We ha'fi…drag her, and Clinton, to the boats," said Evie, grabbing a thick leg but moving it entirely nowhere.

"*We*? I'm a cat!"

"Cho!" Evie couldn't shake off the thought of La Diablesse discovering their ruse and returning with a vengeance. They were out on the mangrove alone and vulnerable. "Let me see if there's anyone left here who can help. Don't say another word! Last thing we need is anyone getting spooked by a duppy cat."

*   *   *

In a matter of minutes, the remaining guests and staff had fled the mangrove. Rodney, the hotel's gentle giant of a night porter, had helped Evie to carry Ms Bell and Arthur's real body down from the veranda to the dock. Arthur himself, in his cat body, was occupied with dragging a sack full of as many stolen magical goods as he could manage. They piled into a boat and the porter took up the oars. Once Ms Bell came round, Evie explained everything that had happened and how Arthur had fallen victim to the devil-woman's magic.

"We'll head west to Mahogany Beach," said Rodney, rowing furiously. "Cos we don't know what a-wait for us down on Bay Beach. You can stay with me at my sister's house for tonight."

Evie was only half-listening. A nauseous feeling came in waves as the boat bobbed across the water, and she stared helplessly at The Mangrove Hotel. It blistered and ruptured – the magic dying at an accelerated rate from the duppies' touch. She was wracked with guilt. Ms Bell silently wept as her residence became a ruin in front of her eyes. The gnarled branches of the mangrove fell away, and the building it once cradled collapsed with it.

When this night began, Evie had been desperate to escape the hotel. But now, she already felt the ache of having no home to come back to. And even if there was, she daren't think about what La Diablesse would have in store for her. She had something the devil woman wanted badly enough to kill for, and it frightened her more than she knew was possible.

## Chapter Eight

# A LONG DAY AHEAD

## Cai

Where there had been a carnival atmosphere at Ocho Rios Bay Beach not an hour earlier, now there was an eerie twilit silence. The sand was littered with ashen fabric, decorative wares, jewellery and spatters of blood. It was the picture of a desperate exodus rather than the aftermath of a celebration.

As the last of the remaining duppies disappeared from the living world, defeated, Cai sheathed his akrafena. The short, curved sword with a decorative golden hilt and squat round pommel slipped into the leather scabbard at his hip. With the sleeve of his off-white robe, he wiped sweat from under his dark fringe. He'd fought off twenty-three of the spirits – he'd kept score – and wondered how that compared to his mentor Mucaro's tally.

Cai peered to his right where Mucaro had also concluded

his fight with the duppies. His long black hair, which had been tied up at the beginning of the night, now fell loose behind his shoulders. Mucaro's gaze landed on Cai with the sharpness of an owl – his namesake in the language spoken by their Taíno ancestors. His weathered face relaxed upon seeing that Cai was unharmed.

"How many yuh get?"

"Twenty-three," Cai answered cagily.

Mucaro gave an unenthusiastic nod. "Thirty-five."

Cai could feel a vein throbbing at his temple. He was still not up to his master's standard, even though he desperately wanted to be. He was a shaman, well, a shaman in training at least. The society of mages he and Mucaro belonged to had a special purpose – to guide spirits of the dead out of the living world and to send them on their way to the spirit world. There were similar authorities known by different names around the world: reapers, shinigami, santa muerte, yama... But Xaymaca's shamans – whether they had enchanter, healer, diviner or spirit waker magic – had another duty as well: to vanquish any evil spirits that were summoned to their world. So Cai and Mucaro had attended Myal as protectors, in the unlikely event that such a misuse of magic occurred. But they could never have imagined a summoning of duppies on such a vast scale would take place.

"And still, so many mages got possessed and escaped," Cai fretted. If only he'd been stronger!

"There were simply too many duppies attacking for us to be

able to save every mage," said Mucaro. "Two of us versus tens of them."

"So what now, master? We'll need our entire squadron out hunting them, nuh? To force the duppies outta dem host bodies before they cause chaos. As if magic don't have enough of a reputation among common folk without this disaster!"

Mucaro nodded calmly. "We'll call home for reinforcements as soon as we can. But even if we're successful in hunting them all, two questions remain: who summoned the duppies in the first place, and for what wicked reason?"

"Mi was about to say that," Cai insisted. "Do you think Blackheart Man was…" He barely dared to voice the thought for fear of the answer.

"Among us?" said Mucaro impassively. "It's more than likely, mm."

Cai's muscles tensed and goose bumps formed. He drew his fingers to the feather necklace around his neck, a necklace that had belonged to his departed brother.

Out in the bay, amidst a tangle of mangrove branches, a large yellow building collapsed into the ocean as though it had been struck by a wrecking ball. It was a peculiar sight to behold on a night of already peculiar events.

"Do you see that, master?" Cai called, pointing to the crumbling building. "That has to be a failing enchantment, nuh?"

"Or a clash of magic," Mucaro replied. "A swarm of duppies left there minutes ago. That place coulda been a good lead for us to learn who's behind all o' this. Pity."

"Maybe we can comb the beach for clues? Or track some footprints?" Cai suggested, eager to impress by taking the initiative.

"Good idea," said Mucaro, and Cai flooded with warmth. "You all right to search the beach yourself while I take those lost spirits to the realm beyond?"

Cai hadn't noticed the meandering spirits of dead revellers that Mucaro pointed out, roaming the shoreline. He swallowed back his disappointment that Mucaro wouldn't be allowing him to take his first spirit to the realm between life and death, as shaman were trained to do. He'd hoped to get his master's blessing by now. "Yes, sir," he answered instead.

As Mucaro approached the spirits, his loose hair and off-white robe flowing around him, he withdrew his gleaming akrafena again. The spirits were alarmed at the sight of the sword, but there would be no pain. They had no physical forms after all. The akrafena would cut through the atoms of this world and their spirits alike, to send them to the realm between life and death.

Mucaro recited Taíno words of ritual, taking a seat on the sand and preparing his own spirit to project from his body. His long sleeves were drawn back, revealing markings that began to glow harlequin green. His spirit would temporarily leave his body and depart their world, taking the spirits of the dead with him. Cai longed to perform that ritual himself. He knew that in that space between worlds, the call to the realm of the dead would be powerful, and he needed to be strong-willed enough to make it back alone to his body. But he wanted his chance to prove himself.

He tore his eyes away and focused on the ruined beach in front of him. There had to be a lead – a trail of blood, a whiff of magic, some footprints among the many that would help them find out who was behind all this.

It was as he was inspecting the wreckage of a diviner's stand that he heard a whoosh of air. He turned sharply, trying to locate the source.

"Who's there?" he demanded when there was silence once more. But he could feel someone. Or something.

The wind whipped at his fringe again, and the drooping sleeves of his robe flapped as he reached for his akrafena. He looked up, in the nick of time, as a blue blur shot down at him. He dodged and the attacker landed in a cloud of sand and dust. Cai backed away, giving himself plenty of space to react to the speed of his opponent.

The sand cloud cleared revealing a man in a sharp blue suit and trilby. His eyes were mostly whites with pinprick pupils.

"A possessed enchanter," Cai uttered.

The duppy let out a shrill laugh and its host body levitated off the ground, readying itself to attack again. Cai smiled. Of all the types of enchanter, this mage appeared to be a master of air. Cai snapped his fingers and a bright flame was born, licking at his palm. He was a fire enchanter, and wind would only feed his flames. The advantage was his.

The possessed enchanter hesitated, sensing that the challenge would be greater than expected. He lifted his cane in both hands, holding it like a staff. Cai, in turn, raised his akrafena with his other hand.

Not far away, Mucaro's body sprang back to life – his spirit returned from the space between worlds. This spooked the possessed enchanter. Realizing that the odds were now firmly against him, he bounded away in a giant leap. Cai shot the flame from his left palm like a missile, but the enchanter landed just out of reach and leaped again beyond the bay.

Cai tried to keep pace with the air enchanter, but running through deep sand was tricky and the distance the possessed man could cover with each jump was impossible to make up.

"Well, that's our only lead gone," Mucaro said as he caught up to Cai, the possessed man now vanished into the night. "You revealed your hand too early. Gave away the advantage."

Cai's jaw clenched. He hated mistakes. He could ill afford them if he wanted to become a true shaman any time soon. "He'll still leave a trail," he said, refusing to give up.

"Yeah man. This time we need to think many steps ahead, you hear?"

"Yes, master."

"All right." Mucaro nodded. "Something tells me we have a long day ahead of us, hm."

Cai sheathed his akrafena once again. He hadn't slept, but adrenaline had quickly replaced fatigue. He was ready for the hunt.

# Chapter Nine

# PICKING UP THE PIECES

## Evie

Rodney the night porter had kindly taken Evie, Arthur, Ms Bell and Clinton (in Arthur's body) into his family home and made space, even when there wasn't much to go around. The narrow house contained a small living-room-cum-kitchen, a front room with a table for eating together, and two upstairs bedrooms for Rodney, his sister and her husband and child.

Arthur had been melancholy silent, and made it clear he needed space. Evie and Ms Bell were left to try and settle in the musty living room and put the pieces of their broken selves back together as best they could. Tiny lizards ran across the walls before disappearing into the cracks. Evie thought herself lucky to even have a roof over her head. She wished she could find some solace in having survived La Diablesse. But she was fearful after their encounter, and feeling the weight of guilt for everything she'd caused. Neither she nor Ms Bell could seem to find words of comfort or consolation. Yes, they were alive, but much like the hotel itself, they were in ruins.

"I'm…I'm so sorry," was all Evie could say.

Ms Bell looked up with her large, tear-stained face. "No, I'm sorry."

Evie was startled. She didn't think she'd ever heard those words come out of her guardian's mouth.

"I've warned you against falling into magic, but all the while mi did so myself without fully understanding it. I'm just so glad that we're safe. If anything had happened to you I…" Ms Bell wiped away tears. "This was bound to catch up with us at some point. The magic of the larimar was never meant for the hotel. But you ha'fi understand, mi just wanted to make a life for the two of us."

Evie placed a hand over Ms Bell's, and Ms Bell responded in turn.

"Mi never tell you about my life before this place. I was engaged. My fiancé came home from the Second World War – he was a pilot. But the island was too small for him after that. He'd always talk about England, Europe."

Evie sat in shock. She'd never imagined that Ms Bell had been engaged.

"Mr Campbell went to work until he'd saved enough to take a ship across to England. That was 1947. He was going to work for a year and then send for me. I waited. I would have waited years more. Eventually the letters stopped and I understood that the call to England was never going to come. Mi heart break."

Evie gripped Ms Bell's hand tighter. She was sorry for every squabble – every single time she'd been stubborn.

"Child, I had nothing and no one. I struggled to get past the heartbreak and find the will to carry on. Then, one day, I was at the water's edge and mi saw the wreckage from a ship. Then mi heard the crying. It was you, Evie, carried over the water like the very ocean was your cradle. The larimar stone was glowing and you drifted. I waded out to reach you. It was a miracle."

Evie had heard that part of her story before. But now tears pricked at her eyes, fully understanding everything that had passed before they entered each other's lives.

"We found each other when we needed someone the most." Ms Bell smiled. "I decided right then that I was going to adopt you as my own. And yes, I kept the larimar to myself, away from the authorities. It saved your life. I knew it held a great magic beyond my understanding, but still I used it to create something for us. Something to make sure we didn't have to rely on anybody else. I can never be sorry for that. But, Evie, I am sorry that I kept it from you, locked it away when you just wanted to understand where you came from. You wanted to use the larimar to find out who your real parents were. To make a future for yourself, you have to make sense of your past. I know that better than anyone."

Evie leaned into Ms Bell's soft body. She didn't tell her

guardian that the larimar was safely back under the collar of her dress or that after learning that the gemstone belonged to the hero Sekesu she now had even more questions about who her parents were. How did they come to have the gemstone? What magic had they wielded, if any? And what did that make Evie?

# Chapter Ten

# THREE QUESTIONS

## Evie

A restless night barely brought any sleep, and when it did Evie's dreams were full of terror. She was back in the sea of spirits being called towards the light – to the realm of the dead. There were two figures haloed in the light, a man and a woman. Their hands were outstretched. As hard as Evie tried to make out their faces, their features were a haze. Their voices too, as loudly as they called to her, were unfamiliar. When one of the faces did become clearer, she recoiled. For it was not her mother but the devil woman. La Diablesse wasn't reaching for Evie's hand but her neck.

Drenched in sweat, Evie became aware of others stirring around her. Her makeshift bed was a light blanket and a spongy mat on a boarded floor. Ms Bell lay beside her, and Clinton – in boy form – awkwardly lay on his side by their feet. Dawn hadn't fully arrived, the autumn sun remaining absent for now. It must have been before six o'clock.

Evie got up to use the outhouse and saw Arthur's yellow eyes gleaming at her from a chair across the small living room.

"Did you sleep?" Evie whispered, kneeling beside him.

"Not a wink. Not in this body and with everything that's happened." He studied Evie's face. "You neither by the looks o' things."

She shook her head, the shadow of her awful dream shrouding her waking thoughts. "Let's step outside so we don't wake Ms Bell and cat-boy."

The pair moved to the front room and took a seat on the floor.

"I keep replaying last night in my head over and over," said Evie. "I brought this all on us. If I hadn't gone to the stupid Myal... This is all my fault."

"You can't be thinking like that," said Arthur. "It won't get us nowhere. Besides, Ms Bell isn't blaming you. She said it herself, the truth was bound to catch up with you."

Evie held her head in her hands. "The Mangrove's gone, just like that. La Diablesse is real. Duppies are real. It feels like a nightmare."

"Cos it is," Arthur agreed. "And now we ha'fi decide what to do to break free from it." He lay on the floor with his paws stretched in front of him, thinking. "Mi did never realize Ms Bell had such a tragic tale," he said, shaking his head absently.

Evie startled. "You heard that?"

"Yeah man. There's not much worse than being abandoned by those who are meant to love you."

Evie placed a hand on his back, stroking his fur. "Sorry, Arthur. Your parents... That story must have been hard for you to hear."

Arthur was a barrel child. His father had gone to England for business opportunities, just like Ms Bell's fiancé. A year later he'd sent for Arthur's mum and his eldest two children to join him. But they didn't have money enough for Arthur yet. Left in the care of his awful aunt and uncle, all he had to remember his parents by were cardboard barrels of gifts sent from England from time to time. He waited longingly for his call to follow his family overseas. When he could wait no longer, he'd run away.

"It's okay," said Arthur. "I don't need them the same way Ms Bell didn't need her fella. I'll thrive without them and show them."

Evie offered a watery smile. He was hurting but he was strong. She'd always liked that about him. He was determined and quick-witted. He did what he had to in order to survive. There was no one she'd rather be with in a dire situation like this...even as a cat. They were strong together. She fondled the larimar pendant around her neck. Tears pricked at her eyes making her blink.

"I'm worried that I'm forgetting, Arthur," she said.

"How you mean?"

"My mami and papa – I'm scared that I'll forget them.

I dreamed that they were reaching out to me. It felt like they were right there. But I couldn't remember their faces. I couldn't place a single detail..." She choked on a sob and had to stop.

"Hey." Arthur drew closer. "You'll see them again – with the larimar and the right spirit waker to reach them in the spirit world, mi sure of it."

Evie wiped her face with her hand and took a steadying breath. "So where do we go from here?"

"Well..." Arthur began, taking hold of his swag bag with his teeth and dragging it from behind one of the chairs. "What if we tried consulting this?" The candle holder he'd pinched from the haughty diviner poked out of the bag.

"You think it can tell the future?"

"It belonged to a diviner so it must do, nuh?" Arthur insisted. "Have a look for some matchsticks in the cabinets."

Evie guiltily rummaged through Rodney's lacquer cabinets and drawers until she found what they needed: a single candle and box of matchsticks. Placing the candle inside the holder she then struck a match and lit it. The flame sparked and glowed diviner's red.

"Something's happening!" said Arthur.

"Seems that way," Evie replied. "What should we ask it first?"

"How do I get back into my real body?" Arthur asked without hesitation.

The candle flame flickered, wax melted down and smoke rose. The smoke formed a message in the light.

## ONLY THE MIRROR OF A SPELL CAN DISPELL

"The mirror of a spell?"

"Like a mirror image. We need to find another enchanter, maybe?" Evie speculated. "To undo what was done in that sea of spirits."

"That makes sense," Arthur said. "Your turn."

Evie's fear dictated the question. Her breath snatched as she thought about what the answer would be before it even came. "Where is La Diablesse and her companion?"

The candle melted down further, the flame dimming but smoke still rising to form the response.

## THE HEARTLESS ARE SEARCHING FOR YOU

Evie and Arthur's eyes met – fears reflected, as they now knew for certain that they were targets.

"That must be a name they're going by," said Arthur. "Jujo said something about 'orders'. So there must be someone even scarier than La Diablesse in charge of their group!"

The thought gave Evie chills. "We knew it wouldn't be long before they discovered your trick of switching the larimar for the stolen necklace," she said worriedly. She fidgeted, her mind sweeping back to La Diablesse and her other-worldly shadow magic. "We can't stay here. We need to come up with a plan and keep moving. Just the two of us." She felt a stab of guilt at leaving Ms Bell alone, but she didn't want to put her life at risk again. "And it's not just for our sakes now. Whatever the devil woman and her psychic aide are planning to do with the larimar, you can bet it's not good."

"Mi know," Arthur said shortly. "But we can't just run out without thinking. We've got a powerful magic gemstone that we don't fully understand, and we have no magic ourselves."

A thought came back to Evie – something La Diablesse had said. "Maybe…maybe I do have magic in me."

Arthur tilted his head, whiskers twitching. "A-what you say?"

"When I tried to get the larimar back, I clashed with La Diablesse. The blast took her off her feet, remember? And she thought I had magic too. Mi thought it was just the larimar's power, but what if she was right?"

"Mi laaaawd," Arthur drawled. "And remember back at the beach with the duppies too! So what kind of magic you think you have?"

Evie wasn't sure. There was a small portion of candle left. Perhaps enough for one last question. But there were more important answers to be had.

"Who are my parents?" she asked.

The candle melted down and the last of its flame flickered. Smoke rose from the dying light.

### FOLLOW THOSE WHO LIVE FOR DEATH

As the last of the wax melted down, the candle holder itself turned to dust.

"Wait, noooo! Mi didn't know it would turn to ashes!" Arthur moaned. "That woulda been plenty useful for us, yuh know."

"Follow those who live for death? What does that mean?" Evie muttered. "Those who live for death... Killers?... No, wait! A spirit waker, right?"

"Mi don't know. But mi have a plan." Arthur tilted his hat back between his pointy ears. "There's a dive bar in town called The Soulless Sailor."

"The Soulless Sailor?"

"It's a roughneck tavern where the regulars are mostly from the magic underworld. It won't be open till afternoon, but the owner, Mr Bennett, lives above it. He's an enchanter, and he always has his ear to the ground. We might be able to find out more about what happened at Myal last night." He jiggled the sack of stolen magical items. "And if we're gonna be on the move, we'll need money. Let's hope for a quick sale."

Evie shook her head. "We saw that the Heartless are controlling the duppies, and we know they're attracted to magic. So we can't risk taking all o' that with us. The larimar is dangerous enough."

Arthur opened his mouth as if to protest before groaning. "You're right. Mi hope to live out the rest of my days without ever seeing one of them things again."

"But if Mr Bennett is an enchanter, maybe he can help dispel the magic that changed you. And he could help us find a spirit waker who can ward off the duppies, and help me reach my parents while the moon is still full. If we can find out why my parents had the larimar in the first place, perhaps we'll understand why the Heartless want it so badly and how we can protect it from them."

"All right. Let's head to The Soulless Sailor," said Arthur.

Evie climbed to her feet, galvanized. "Let's stay sharp. Stay alive!"

"Yeah man. Make a pact?"

Arthur licked his paw and held it out. Evie spat on her right hand and thrust it out for a firm shake.

After quickly gathering whatever food supplies they could – delicious bulla cakes made from ginger, nutmeg and molasses, and a couple of cold saltfish patties – Evie insisted that she write to Ms Bell to explain why they were leaving. She couldn't just disappear and leave her feeling abandoned again.

Evie found a fountain pen and tore a scrap of blank paper from a notebook.

*Mama,*

*I have to go. I promise you I'll be back, so please don't try to find me cos it might not be safe for you. But don't worry, Arthur is with me. It's like you said, to make a future for myself I need to finally learn my past.*

*And we need to get Arthur back in his body, too. Please look after it till then.*

Love, Evie

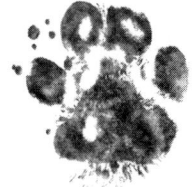

and Arthur

P.S. Please tell Rodney we're sorry for taking some of his food for the road.

P.P.S. We just had a bite of his saltfish patty and it's REALLY GOOD! He's a great cook. But we are really sorry, though.

# Chapter Eleven

# JANCROW

## Evie

Ochi had transformed from beach town to ghost town as Evie and Arthur stepped out into the streets. Word must have gotten around to the non-mages – the majority of people living or visiting there – about the duppies and the destruction at the Carnival of Magic. Around a couple of hotel tower blocks they caught peering faces at the windows, and heard snippets of animated chatter from people hiding away. Perhaps some folk had even suffered the misfortune of seeing the duppies or running into possessed mages themselves.

The roads, usually filled with imported cars from America, were quiet but for a couple of nervous-looking taxi drivers hoping for an opportunity to ferry people out of town. There were no higglers out in force selling their wares at their colourful shopfronts and market stalls. Everything had been abandoned. Evie and Arthur would need to be cautious too.

"We're gonna ha'fi find you a disguise or something," said Arthur, trotting along the pavement beside Evie. "Can't be walking around wearing the same thing as the last time the Heartless saw you."

"Says the cat wearing the hat!"

"Cho! Mi want to still feel something like a human, you know!"

Evie scoffed. "Well then let's just, you know, *borrow* some clothes." She eyed an abandoned clothes stall.

Arthur narrowed his gleaming yellow eyes. "Oh *noooow* you want me to do some thieving, hmm?"

"If it means staying alive versus running into duppies and devil women then yes, brudda!"

Arthur chuckled, drawing a smile from Evie herself. "All right, sistah. Then let's take the back alleys to The Soulless Sailor and stay outta sight."

"Mm. Too many eyeballs on us," Evie agreed, spotting a curtain twitching inside a closed hardware shop.

"On three…" said Arthur.

They sprinted to the clothes stall and Evie grabbed a set of denim dungaree shorts and a plain white tee of about her size. She didn't like that she was stealing, but she had to stay hidden from the Heartless. With the clothes in her grasp, she followed Arthur's lead, hightailing it to a narrow alleyway.

Evie hid with her back to the wall, panting and wiping her forehead. It was already warm despite the fact the sun had only risen a couple of hours ago. She made Arthur turn away and quickly changed into the "borrowed" clothes, discarding the dress she'd been wearing in a gap between dilapidated buildings.

A frantic clatter on a metal sheet roof above made Evie freeze with fright. But it wasn't a human who'd caught them. With a sudden beating of wings and a beastly croak, a large black-feathered bird hopped around the roof.

"What in the...? A jancrow!" Arthur exclaimed on recognizing the huge turkey vulture.

"What's a jancrow doing in the city instead of the hills?"

"Mi don't know, but mi nah like it at all!" Arthur broke into a trot. "Out in Saint Andrew Parish we called them harbingers of death."

"I mean... It *sounds* like death," Evie concurred, fully on edge when the vulture croaked again. They fled down the alleyway, but they found that the path ahead of them was not empty as before. At a distance was a man in a trilby hat, shadows from the brim covering his face. The man was swathed in a silken navy-blue jacket and he leaned on a cane with one hand. Evie and Arthur slowed to a walk. But when the man remained stone-still, they stopped entirely.

"An enchanter?" said Evie, taking a cue from the fancy blue of his attire. He looked like a reveller from the carnival the night before.

"Wait," Arthur began. "That's Mr Bennett. Ay! Mr Bennett." The enchanter didn't move or respond in the slightest.

"Something's…not right." Arthur backed up, fur bristling.

Evie sensed it too. Her heart raced, the overwhelming sensation of drowning in the sea of spirits returning.

Mr Bennett stayed still – a smile now the only thing visible from the shadows of his face. Then a high-pitched titter escaped his mouth, turning into a demonic laugh.

"He's possessed!" Evie cried. "Run!"

Mr Bennett's laughter trebled and he finally moved – swift and sharp. His feet levitated above the dusty ground and he flew past the pair to block their path of escape. Now he was upside down, floating on a cushion of air, face to face with Evie, and his pinprick pupils stared emptily into hers. She stumbled and backed away as his laughter continued.

"Mi lawd!" Arthur squeaked. "What do we do?"

"The larimar!" Evie cried, fumbling about her collar in the hope that she could somehow activate the gem's magic.

Arthur hissed pitiably at the duppy-possessed Mr Bennett before leaping at him with claws bared. "Snap out of it, mistah!"

The enchanter let out a growl in retaliation. A dense wave of air blew Arthur away and knocked Evie off her feet. Her head hit the concrete and pain exploded at the base of her skull, a dizzying light clouding her vision. When she regained her senses, her head still throbbing, she found the air enchanter looking hungrily at her – eyes like oblivion and mouth warped into a devious smile.

"Yeeeeeeeeeeeeeeeeeeeeees," Mr Bennett hissed. He raised his cane over his head like a club.

Evie stared up from the ground in helpless horror. In those seconds that seemed to last a lifetime, an azure glow shone brighter and brighter before her eyes. The larimar had risen on its chain from underneath her shirt. Evie felt her own skin tingling, just like at Myal. Mr Bennett hesitated. As he brought down his cane to strike, the larimar emitted a blast of energy which knocked him staggering back. The duppy screeched, vacating Mr Bennett's body and writhing on the ground, revealing every broken tooth in its warped mouth. Mr Bennett collapsed sideways, free of the evil spirit but unconscious.

Still dazed, but with enough clarity to realize this was the time to escape, Evie looked around for Arthur. Their eyes met.

"Run!" she cried.

He led and she followed, the duppy's demonic cries ringing in their ears. But they didn't get far.

Two figures draped in muted whites and black strode towards them, one young man with a bowl cut, one older with long flowing hair. Evie recognized them from Myal with an almighty start, stumbling to a halt on the path. There was no way she'd forget such brutal intensity, nor those deadly curved swords which hung from their hips. And it was impossible for Evie to know whether those blades were intended for the duppy alone or for them as well.

# Chapter Twelve

# THE SUMMONING

## Evie

Between the weakened duppy and the two figures wielding swords, Evie and Arthur were left with nowhere to run. Arthur pressed against Evie's leg, letting her know that, despite it all, at least they were together.

As the strangers reached for their swords, the duppy that had possessed Mr Bennett rose from the ground and screeched.

"Please, please, please," Evie muttered, squeezing the larimar in her hands again. The larimar glowed in response, but this time the light built until it was blinding. Evie closed her eyes, feeling the gemstone pulse strangely in her grip, and static ripple through her body. It was only when the sensation died away and she heard a wondrous gasp that she opened her eyes.

"What in the name of…?" The voice belonged to a woman,

not the sword-wielding pair. Evie gaped in stunned silence as a small, elderly woman in a kente cloth dress with blue accents, and a royal-blue headwrap stood confusedly in front of her. "Mi nah dead?"

"E-Evie...?" Arthur uttered, clearly unsure of what he was even trying to ask her. Not that she had any answers. She blinked as if to be certain she wasn't seeing things.

The Taíno pair looked astounded.

"Master Mucaro!" The younger of the two gawked. "Is that...? It can't be!"

"Sekesu," Mucaro answered, in disbelief.

Evie's mind felt like a full bathtub about to overflow. Did that man just say *Sekesu*? As in Sekesu – one of the Four Heroes of Xaymaca? Queen Nanny's big sister?! And she'd popped out of the larimar like she was calling round for a cup of tea.

"No way...!" said Arthur. "Evie! Did you just summon Sekesu's spirit with that thing?"

Evie held the pendant in her hand, looking from the iridescent gem to the tiny woman in front of her.

"So you called me? A-who are you?" Sekesu asked in her overly loud and irritable voice.

"I-I—"

Evie's muttering was interrupted by the duppy. With the blinding light of the gemstone having faded, it sprang into an attack.

"What a mess is this you bring me into?" Sekesu scolded. With the prowess of a master enchanter, she raised a wall of earth from the ground to shield Evie, Arthur and herself from the duppy.

"Cai!" The elder Taíno, Mucaro, had the manner of a drill sergeant as he sprinted towards the battle.

"Yes, master!" the boy replied, unsheathing his sword and dashing after him.

Sekesu raised another earth wall in defence, but as Cai leaped over it, Evie realized for certain that they weren't his target – his sights were set only on the duppy. He snapped his fingers and a flame appeared in his palm. Meanwhile, Sekesu slapped her ghostly palms on the ground, dispelling her defensive walls and causing the ground they stood on to rise instead. They watched the duppy and Cai clash from up on the safety of the mound.

With a deep breath out, fuelling the flame in his palm, Cai blew a blazing fire that encompassed the duppy. The evil spirit grinned, emerging unscathed from the blaze, but its hideous smile disappeared upon realizing too late that the real attack was coming from behind. Cai's flames were a diversion. His master had his curved sword drawn and sliced through the evil spirit so swiftly that Evie barely registered it.

The duppy dissipated before their eyes, like sand passing through some unseen hourglass. The evil spirit let out a final unearthly scream as it slipped back to the spirit world. As the din faded, a now conscious Mr Bennett's groans could be heard, as he sat himself up in his dapper blue suit. And then, as though remembering a terrible dream, he moaned, eyes wide and hand clutching at his heart. Arthur leaped down from the mound and scampered towards him.

"Mr Bennett. Talk to me – you all right?" he asked, completely forgetting he was a cat until the air enchanter drew back in fright. "It's me, brudda. Arthur!"

"Steady," said Mucaro, quickly approaching. He sheathed his sword and placed his hands on Mr Bennett's back. His palms, and the markings on his face and arms, emitted a green aura – he was a healer. "A duppy possessed your body so you probably feel terrible right now. But you're free."

"B-Blackheart Man," Mr Bennett whimpered, still staring warily at Arthur. "He's here."

Evie's heart clapped like a palm drum. Blackheart… All of the horror stories Ms Bell and the other grown-ups told misbehaving children on the island came back to her. *Don't be naughty or Blackheart Man will find a way into your tainted soul. Don't walk around too late after dark or the Blackheart Man will pluck out your heart and nyam it for his dinner.*

First La Diablesse, and now…

"Blackheart Man!" Mr Bennett wailed louder this time. "Him raise a duppy army!"

Cai, who'd had his piercing, treacle-coloured eyes on Evie and Arthur up to that point, turned his head swiftly in the air enchanter's direction. "That settles it then, master. The Heartless *were* behind last night!"

"*The Heartless…* Black*heart*!" Evie thought aloud, connecting the dots. She turned to Arthur. "Blackheart Man.

**88**

He must be the one giving orders to La Diablesse and Jujo."

"You were there at the Myal." Cai pressed Mr Bennett. "What do you remember?"

"Mi could hear him. Hear his voice through the evil duppy," Mr Bennett said. "He offered me power the likes of which mi never seen. Told me my magic deserved to be unleashed not restrained."

Evie couldn't believe that the greatest threat she had ever known was coming from folklore monsters that she'd thought were fiction.

"Mi…mi let him in. In my heart and mind, mi let him take control. Mi wanted to see what mi truly capable of. But then my body was not mine any more." Mr Bennett shook his head ashamedly. "That duppy. That spirit was corrupted so bad, mi never felt such evil!"

Mucaro rose to his feet, his expression severe. "You have people in town you can stay with?"

Mr Bennett lightly shook his head. "It's usually mages coming to *me* when they're in a bad spot. My bar is something of a sanctuary." He gestured to a saloon behind him painted in a duck egg colour. Evie hadn't noticed the sign for The Soulless Sailor until then. "But mi nah sure who made it out all right last night, and who got possessed by them fiends like I did."

"Then stay inside and stay safe in case any other survivors come your way. In fact," Mucaro glanced in Evie, Arthur and Sekesu's direction, "perhaps we should all get off these streets for a moment. We're in danger until the duppies are vanquished.

Until Blackheart Man and his Heartless mages are stopped."

"Be my guest," said Mr Bennett, scrambling to his feet and rifling through his jacket pockets for keys as he approached the saloon door.

Evie's attention switched back to Sekesu. The spirit had backed away, surveying her drastically unfamiliar surroundings and each one of them in turn. As shocked as everyone was to see her, that must have paled in comparison to how Sekesu felt.

"What is happening here?" she demanded. "What year is this?"

"1962, ma'am," said Cai. "You've been gone for two hundred years."

The already ghostly face of the hero became more haunting still. "Good lawd a-mercy… Two hundred?"

"And for all o' those years," said Mucaro, turning on his heel to face Evie, "not one mage has had power enough to be able to summon the spirit of one of the Four Heroes. Until this girl here."

## Chapter Thirteen

# THE SOULLESS SAILOR

## Cai

The spirit of a long-dead national treasure was not on the list of things Cai expected to see before breakfast. Yet there she was – Sekesu the Enchanter – shimmering as she entered the dank saloon. Curiouser still was the peculiar girl in dungarees, and her even more peculiar cat wearing a porkpie hat! Had this girl *really* summoned Sekesu?

Shutter blinds were drawn inside the saloon so that only a slither of daylight entered through the open door. Cai was hit by a faint smell of incense, which had likely been used to try and mask the other stale smells lurking underneath.

Mr Bennett pulled a light switch and a couple of bare bulbs flickered to life, revealing the dive bar in its entirety. It wasn't huge – only a small serving bar and five tables with bar stools turned upside down on top. Though going by the stickiness of the floor, it hadn't been mopped in days.

A tatty Xaymacan flag and an enchanter's emblem – a dark half moon in the sun – hung from separate, paint-flaking walls. Mr Bennett locked and bolted the front door behind the group: Cai, Master Mucaro, Sekesu's spirit, the girl…and the brown-black cat in the hat. Then he began removing bar stools from the tables for them to sit on. But only Mucaro and the girl took a seat, Cai choosing to stand guard by the locked door (because a barrel bolt would be useless if the Heartless came calling).

Mr Bennett offered his guests a drink and, when there were no takers, shrugged and poured a rum for himself instead. The shutter blinds remained closed, so as not to draw attention inside.

Mucaro's gaze hadn't left the girl since they'd entered. "Who are you?" he ordered rather than asked.

"N-nobody," the girl croaked. Just what was she hiding?

Mucaro eyed Sekesu warily. "You don't summon the spirit of one of the Four Heroes of Xaymaca if you're 'nobody'."

"And, and, and," Cai chimed in, wagging a finger in the air, "you don't have one of the Four Heroes' gemstones if you're 'nobody' either. No, sir!"

"Just a minute now," Sekesu said, turning to the girl. She looked as bewildered as her but with a dash of annoyance too. "You have my larimar? You called me here just to box up a duppy when I was enjoying a nice siesta in the afterlife? Cho!"

"Well, mi didn't know about…" the girl babbled. "Mi nah even understand how—"

"So, what, this old lady was just…living in the larimar the whole time?"

A boy's voice suddenly came from nowhere, startling Cai. Sekesu jerked back, and it took a moment for Cai to process that the sudden interjection had come from the cat wearing a hat!

"Less of the 'old', thank you!" Sekesu recovered from her surprise to snap back.

"Master…" Cai pointed with his akrafena. "The cat just spoke!"

"Thanks, Cai – I see that."

Cai scrambled for answers. He'd never seen such a thing in all his thirteen years. "Is it enchanted? Is this the larimar's power?"

"These are the questions we need to ask of *them*," Mucaro replied.

"That's not the power of my magic," said Sekesu. "Mi an earth enchanter…well mi *was* an earth enchanter when mi was alive! Mi can't use my magic on anything with a spirit, only earth, stone, wood and plant life."

"So if it isn't an enchantment that's making the cat speak—"

"The 'cat' is called Arthur, brudda," the cat said irritably. This day was getting stranger by the minute.

"But wait…" said Mucaro, his dark eyes suddenly flickering with realization. "You're a human spirit, aren't you? This is the work of a spirit waker."

Somehow this possibility hadn't even entered Cai's mind.

A human spirit trapped in the body of a cat? What a dire fate. Spirit waker magic was scarily powerful!

Sekesu's eyes grew even wider as she turned back to Arthur. "Mi laaaaawd!"

"Mi know!" Arthur moaned.

"Mi ha'fi ask again," Mucaro pressed. "Who are you?"

"Wait. Time out, time out!" Arthur called, looking from Mucaro to Cai. "First, can you put away your damned spirit sword? Mi feel like mi losing one of my nine lives just looking at that thing!"

"We're not your enemy. I don't think you're ours either," the girl added. "But that doesn't mean we can trust you. So tell us who *you* are and what you want."

The cheek of it! As if she were in a position to order *them* about. Cai glanced at Mucaro for instruction.

"Sheath your akrafena, Cai," Mucaro said after a moment.

Cai was surprised, but he supposed they needed answers, and the best way to get them was to cooperate. He slipped his sword into its leather sheath.

"My name is Cairi. It means 'little island' in my ancestors' tongue, in case you're interested." Cai quickly gathered from the sour look on the girl's face that she was not. "But, anyway, everyone calls me Cai. I'm a fire enchanter and Master Mucaro is a healer. But we're both shamans," he said proudly. "We're a special squadron of mages who make sure evil spirits are sent back to the spirit world."

"Raaahtid!" Mr Bennett exclaimed, choking on his stiff

drink mid sip. "Mi shoulda known that's who you is!"

The girl and her cat exchanged a glance, as though they'd just realized something…

# Evie

Evie and Arthur had spent so much time around each other that, just from one look, Evie knew Arthur had recalled the same memory. It was something La Diablesse had said to her partner Jujo as they'd left The Mangrove:

*Let's go, then, before the shamans find out where we are.*

"So Blackheart Man and the Heartless summon duppies, while you shamans vanquish them. You're enemies."

"That's right," Cai answered. "Our squadrons have been battling Blackheart and his followers for years now."

"But most importantly our squadron guides the dead from this world to the spirit world," Mucaro explained. "Cai is my apprentice."

"But I'm very close to being a full shaman," Cai added quickly, seeming put out.

Arthur's fur stood on end and he backed up a touch so that he almost fell off the bar completely. "You're grim reapers?"

Cai rolled his eyes. "No, not grim reapers – shamans! This is reality…um…Artemis."

"It's Arthur, bowlhead!"

Mucaro cleared his throat to regain control of the

conversation, and gestured to Evie. "You have something that was entrusted to the original Maroons of Xaymaca – those who awakened ancestral magic and set up their own towns free from the British colonizers." He turned his attention to the spirit of Sekesu. "Something that belonged to Sekesu here – the larimar."

Evie automatically reached a hand to her chest as though to check the gemstone were still there.

"A-true," Sekesu said. "I was a Maroon, and before I passed away I channelled my magic into the larimar. It was meant to stay with the Maroon chiefs, and to be used only when Xaymaca needed powerful magic to defend itself again. How did you come to have it?"

Evie clung to the fading memory of her parents. But the picture she tried to focus on was in tatters, and she could feel frustrated tears coming. She wished she could answer Sekesu's question fully. But however she had tried to remember her parents, it was clear it was far from the truth of who they were. She, too, needed answers. Just who were her parents that they had possessed such a powerful artefact entrusted to hidden communities in the mountains?

"I was found with this when I was four years old. I can remember my parents giving it to me...before they set me adrift at sea." She cleared her throat lightly. The more she revisited this moment, the clearer it became how many pieces of herself were missing. "There was a shipwreck. I was the only survivor. The larimar saved my life." Then a revelation hit Evie like sunlight breaking through the darkness of an eclipse. She turned to the spirit beside her. "*You* saved my life."

Sekesu's mouth opened and closed again – a moment of pensiveness giving way to annoyance. "Mi dead. Mi nah remember dat!" she said. "It's the magic that saved you."

Evie was taken aback, but a closer look at Sekesu's face suggested her words weren't in anger but confusion.

"Your name?" Mucaro interjected.

"Evie."

"My name is Mucaro. We've travelled from Accompong Town in the west."

Sekesu's eyebrows raised at the mention. "Accompong? Then the Maroon towns are still standing strong after all this time?"

"Accompong, Cudjoe's Town, Sekesu's Town, Quao's Hall and Nanny Town are all standing. Not all o' them strong, though…" said Cai, immediately dimming the joy that had lit up Sekesu's face.

"Now then…" Mucaro's brows ran together. "The larimar should be protected by the Maroons. We'll need it back from you."

"The larimar holds too much power fi one girl to have," Sekesu said.

Evie shifted back off her stool defensively – her heartbeat soaring as all eyes peered at her expectantly. She'd just gotten the gemstone back, and now people wanted to take it from her again?

"But it's not just the larimar mi worried about," said Mucaro, stern eyes piercing through her. "You've summoned Sekesu. So you realize, don't you, that the duppies will come for you too? Because you've awakened your magic."

Evie recalled how the evil spirits had only possessed mages at Myal – drawn to their powers and making them their own. She swallowed hard and nodded. So La Diablesse had been right. She *did* have magic... She had *magic*! After all the years of seeing it, but not wielding it, now she would feel magic all around. This meant the static sensation she'd felt wasn't the larimar at all; it was her own magic stirring! But when had her magic awakened? No...it had to have happened with...

*The spirit waker at Myal!*

"And your magic is the rarest of all," Mucaro continued. "Do you understand what you are?"

The truth was laid out in front of her, overwhelmingly so. *She* had summoned a spirit from the realm of the dead. Slowly she nodded again, a fresh wave of fear consuming her – how could she hope to control such powerful magic? "A spirit waker..."

"Evie..." Arthur gasped. "H-how...?"

"Myal," Evie answered. "The old spirit waker who couldn't help me reach my parents. He seemed to believe they were mages. He musta sensed ancestral magic in me and awoken it."

"My gosh!"

But why, Evie wondered, had the spirit waker not told her what he'd done?

Sekesu stared intently at Evie with her large dark eyes, as though she was a riddle. But she said nothing.

Mucaro got to his feet. "So we ha'fi get you, the larimar and of course Sekesu to safety. We'll protect you."

"We will?" Cai squawked. "I mean, we will," he said with more conviction under Mucaro's glare.

"And me, nuh?" Arthur interjected. "We come as a pair, yuh know!"

"Right." Mucaro nodded. "We need to return the larimar to the Maroons in Sekesu's Town. That's over in Portland Parish. It won't be a straightforward journey, but with Sekesu's magic as well as our own, our chances of evading Blackheart Man and the Heartless are much better. To think we have the spirit of a mighty Xaymacan hero with us."

"Mi beg you all, don't challenge Blackheart Man alone," Mr Bennett implored. His expression sent a chill through Evie as his eyes scanned every face in the room. "He looks straight into your soul and awakens your ugliest thoughts and desires. He'll make it so you're happy to let darkness in."

"Mi can't believe someone exists who's twisted spirit waker magic like this," said Sekesu, looking entirely crushed by Mr Bennett's words.

The thought of going up against someone who'd mastered spirit waker magic to such devastating effect made Evie fret even more about getting a handle on her own magic.

"Can mi help you in any way?" Mr Bennett asked Mucaro. "I owe you my life."

"Do you have a telephone?" Mucaro asked. "Mi need to call our squadron from Accompong to handle any remaining possessed mages out here. And mi ha'fi call ahead to the chief in Sekesu's Town. Dem need to know we have their larimar, and a spirit waker who must be protected at all costs."

Mr Bennett ushered him through a beaded drape covering a doorway behind the bar.

It was as though Evie had been looking at a trick image and her eyes had adjusted to see the hidden picture. *Follow those who live for death,* the magic candle had told them when she'd asked who her parents were. The shamans' job was to guide the deceased to the spirit world. It was clear to her now. If she followed Mucaro and Cai, she'd find out who her parents were. And if she could learn to control her spirit waker magic, she'd surely, finally, be able to reach them too.

## Chapter Fourteen

# THE XAYMACA EXPRESS

## Evie

The two shamans took positions front and back of the motley group, guarding Evie, and Sekesu's spirit, with Arthur padding along beside them as they skulked through the back roads of the deserted town towards the coast. Mr Bennett's warning had Evie on edge, but there was no sign of the Heartless, or duppies, or possessed mages for now.

"Where exactly are we headed?" Arthur asked, his voice a harsh whisper. Cai shushed him, to which the boy-cat kissed his teeth in reply, following up with a hiss for good measure.

"To grab a lift outta here," Mucaro whispered back. "We've some distance to cover to get to Sekesu's Town. But there's a shaman rest house on the way where we can lay low."

"Where's that?" Evie asked, feeling slightly more comfortable as they discussed the plan.

"Our Taíno ancestors called it Guayguata," Cai answered, apparently never one to miss out on dishing out facts. "But you'll know it as Annotto Bay."

That was still in her home parish of Saint Mary, just bordering Portland where Sekesu's Town lay. Evie had seen the bay on a map at The Mangrove, and always dreamed about travelling across all fourteen parishes and seeing the whole island. Never did she think the first time she left Ochi would be under such dire circumstances.

"Once we get there, I'll call the captains at Sekesu's Town again, to secure a pickup for us," Mucaro explained. "Let's hurry now."

Before long Evie noticed they were headed towards a plume of smoke beyond the palm trees and breeze-block houses. Mucaro turned into an open roadway where a large sign read *Xaymaca Railway Corporation*. They had gone minutes without seeing another soul, but suddenly they found themselves joining a great crowd fighting over each other for a way out of town.

"Hold on." Evie gaped. "Are we taking a train?!"

"You did never take one before?" Mucaro asked.

Any attempt Evie had made to disguise her excitement fell flat. Even more so when the wondrous black steam engine and its many metal carriages slid into view against the backdrop of the sparkling ocean.

"Woooaah!" Arthur leaped up into Evie's arms to get a better look.

"What a-madness is this?" Sekesu looked somewhat frightened by the gigantic machine. The steam pouring from its huge funnel must have looked devilish to her.

Cai cleared his throat. His eyes were gleaming. "Another marvel of modern engineering, Ms Sekesu. This is a…steam train."

Evie sighed inwardly at the way he'd slowed down on these words, as though talking to a child rather than a 250-plus-year-old magical spirit who also happened to be one of the nation's saviours.

"This steam-powered machine is a more sociable way to travel with other people across the island, unlike the automobiles you've seen around! The Xaymaca Express runs on tracks rather than road, and it stops at fifty different places. They started building the network in 1845 – that's, what, a good eighty odd years after your death?" Finally, Cai paused for breath, eyes wide as though he'd blown his own mind with the information he'd shared. "Mi never did think about how much has changed so fast this century!"

Mucaro harrumphed at this, twiddling his clunky neck beads. "It's a shame, still, that Xaymaca went racing towards modernization and industry at the cost of magic and the spirit."

"But how you mean?" Sekesu asked with a frown. "This thing nah magic?"

"No, ma'am. Come now, let's get aboard. We might ha'fi get our elbows out here."

"Why don't you wave your spirit swords around? That oughta do it," Arthur offered, hopping back down from Evie's arms.

"What about Sekesu?" Evie asked. "We can't just get on the train with a spirit!"

"Only those with magic can see her, if she chooses, and mages only make up about thirty per cent of the population nowadays anyway," said Cai.

"But wait. Mi have no magic so how come mi can see her, then?" Arthur asked. Know-it-all Cai looked stumped, and Evie smiled just a little at this.

"Hold on a moment! Did you say thirty per cent?" Sekesu asked.

"Yes," said Cai, glad to change the subject.

"What happened?!" Sekesu looked distraught. "Ancestral magic should have flourished after our time."

"Mi promise we'll speak more once we settle into our compartment," Mucaro answered. "Let's board now."

At the ticketing booth, Mucaro proceeded to order from a frazzled-looking man who seemed in need of both a break and a tall glass of water. There was no air circulating through his booth and sweat dripped profusely from his crinkled forehead.

"Where you a-go?" the ticketer asked.

"Annotto Bay."

The ticketer looked straight through Sekesu, eyeing Evie,

Cai and the cat with the hat, not even trying to disguise his bewilderment. "Both o' dem pickney and the puss with you?"

Evie kissed her teeth loudly, taking offence at being called "pickney" when she was a teenager now. Mucaro blinked at her before turning back to the guard.

"Regretfully, yes."

Onboard the train, Evie and Arthur were awestruck as they breezed through the fancy carriage with its mahogany decking and plush red cushioned seats.

A young, gangly porter wearing a peaked hat to match his grey buttoned suit led the way to their compartment. He politely opened the door for them, and Evie and Arthur rocketed in, taking their seats on one side of a table while Mucaro and Cai slid onto the seats opposite them. Sekesu's spirit hovered, staring out of the window and all around the cosy compartment.

Once the porter had bowed and left them, Evie leaned into Arthur. "Geez, that brudda's moustache is coming through even worse than yours."

"Yuh too cold, Evie!"

Sekesu remained entranced as the train set off with a whistle. "And this is not an enchantment, nuh?"

"No, ma'am." Cai smiled at her awe. "Just engineering. Don't worry, you're completely safe. The Corporation's record is near spotless. Well, aside from that major derailing in Kendal five years ago where about two hundred people died. Master says that was a busy week for us!"

There was silence as the train picked up speed and Cai glanced from ashen face to ashen face.

"*Why* would you bring that up *now*?" said Arthur, exasperated.

A waiter entered the compartment and greeted the group. "Would you like to order anything from the menu?"

Mucaro cleared his throat and gestured to the leather-backed books in front of them all. "Select whatever you want."

Evie's eyes widened. "Whatever we want?!"

"Um…" Clearly Mucaro regretted his choice of words, so Evie quickly ordered before he had a chance to stop her.

"I want the callaloo rice with rundown and a little bit of mutton with bammy to soak it up, plantain aaaaand a bowl of festivals." Arthur nudged her swiftly. "Make that a heap o' mutton rather than a little bit." She put down the menu, already salivating, and glanced at the stunned faces of both the shamans and the waiter. "Please," she added in her politest voice.

As the train made its first stop to pick up more passengers before lurching off again, Evie marvelled at the experience. She pressed her hands and face up to the large glass window and watched the glistening ocean before it eventually turned to rolling green hills. She was only half listening while Mucaro spoke, until her attention was caught by the mention of the larimar.

"Mi could tell you about the gemstones myself, but that seems a waste when we now have one of the heroes right here with us," said Mucaro. All eyes turned to Sekesu, who drifted away from the window at the sound of her name. "Ms Sekesu, history has remembered you and your kin as the Four Heroes of Xaymaca: Queen Nanny the Spirit Waker, Quao the Healer, Cudjoe the Diviner and you – Sekesu the Enchanter. Perhaps you could tell us about the creation of the stones?"

Sekesu looked proud. "Well…first we ha'fi go back to 1494 when the Spanish invaded the island and all but wiped out the Taíno people. And then in 1655 the British attacked *them* to take Xaymaca for themselves. In the upheaval, the surviving Taíno people fled to the mountains, along with many enslaved Africans who'd been forced to labour on the Spanish plantations. The escapees were called 'Maroons', from the Spanish word 'cimarron' meaning wild and unruly!"

"Oooh," Evie uttered. She'd never known that's where the term had come from. Cai snorted, making it very clear that he had.

"Anyway," Sekesu continued, "two Maroon factions were formed, one in the east and one in the west of the island. Hidden towns were created where the spirit of the ancestors could thrive, free from the Europeans. Escaped slaves joined the Maroons over time, and the factions battled the British forces for decades to keep their freedom. But it wasn't until one young woman – a spirit waker – woke up the sleeping magic within us all, that the tide truly turned against the British."

"Queen Nanny…" Evie marvelled.

"Mmhmm, my younger sister. She, Cudjoe, Quao and I led our warriors, and with ancestral magic we sent the British home with their tails between their legs! By 1739 we'd liberated the whole island." Sekesu looked at each face around the table as though she was telling a story around a fire. She knew how to hold an audience. "The four of us understood we'd likely not live to see the nation blossom into its own. We'd ha'fi entrust it to the generations to come. But we decided that we'd leave the essence of our magic with our communities, as a day would likely come when they'd ha'fi fight hard for their freedom again."

"You mean if the British came back?" Evie asked.

"Anyone!" Sekesu replied. "Nanny fell sick. Healers couldn't do anything for her. We knew she didn't have long. So mi created a natural gemstone that she poured all her powers into – an amethyst – so that her magic would outlive her." The memory slowed Sekesu down. She took a sorrowful pause and then continued.

"Before Quao and Cudjoe passed away some years later, mi did the same with a coral for Cudjoe and an emerald for Quao." She turned her gaze to Evie. "Mi was the last of us to leave this earth. I poured my magic, and a fragment of my spirit, into the larimar you have around your neck, dearie."

Evie marvelled at the fact that a small piece of Xaymaca's hero had really been with her all through her life. Sekesu had been a part of the only home she'd known. For that, she felt gratitude.

"So…" Mucaro's gravitas was such that he was able to take control of the conversation again with a single word. "The magic gemstones were kept secret from those outside of the original Maroon towns, and protected for generations in the communities of each hero. The amethyst was kept in Nanny Town in the Blue Mountains; the coral in Accompong just below Cockpit Country; the emerald in Quao's Hall in St Mary, and the larimar in Sekesu's Town in Portland."

"*Were* kept? Mi have a bad feeling why you use past tense for all o' them," said Arthur.

"Well, in the past nine years, two of the four gemstones have been stolen."

"It was the Heartless, nuh?" Evie asked. "La Diablesse and her partner Jujo had a red gemstone on them. It musta been the coral, then."

Cai looked ill at ease and flicked his eyes towards Mucaro. But his master remained as impassive as ever. "Correct. Blackheart's goal is to gather all four gemstones. Just as you've summoned Sekesu, he intends to find a way to do the same with all of the Four Heroes, and to control their spirits. With their combined magic, he plans to blow apart the barrier separating the realm of the living and the realm of the dead."

Evie gasped in sheer awe. It was the wildest of goals. She

remembered what Jujo had said about wanting to understand whether Obeah could be a bridge between worlds and, alongside shock, she couldn't deny a flutter of fascination. Her parents... *Would it be so bad?* The thought crossed her mind. But guilt swallowed it up immediately. What would it mean to break through the barrier? What would happen to the living?

"Why would he do that?" she asked.

"He believes it's his route to immortality – defying death to exist beyond a physical body and become a god," Mucaro explained. "But, Evie, imagine existing as neither human nor spirit in a world without joy, feeling, love, everything that it means to be alive! Imagine what he could do with a world full of duppies under his command, and no way to be rid of them."

Evie's heart sank. Of course there was malice to the Heartless's plan. What had she been thinking after everything La Diablesse had inflicted on her? "So was Sekesu's larimar stolen too?" Evie asked, trying to piece together her parents' involvement in the story.

"Actually, the larimar was considered lost until today," said Cai. "A group from Sekesu's Town tried to take it to an undisclosed location for security, but they never returned and were presumed dead. It was the emerald that Blackheart Man and the Heartless stole from Quao's Hall."

"This larimar was lost?" Evie muttered to herself.

"And that's why we need to return it to Sekesu's Town," Mucaro explained. "It was always meant to be protected by the most powerful mages of that community. The Heartless no longer have the advantage of surprise if they try to attack. In fact, *we* do. The Maroons are ready, especially with Sekesu herself summoned to our side."

The thought of fighting alongside one of the historic heroes of Xaymaca filled Evie with pride. But Sekesu herself looked weary. This was a tumultuous new world she found herself in. She'd been laid to rest having already protected her people, and here she was having to fight once again.

"After we've returned the larimar, we'll journey on to Nanny Town. We'll join our shaman sisters and brothers to fortify the town and protect Nanny's amethyst. We must stop the Heartless from getting hold of *that* gemstone at all costs."

Evie and Arthur shared a glance. "Mi know Nanny is the Mother of Magic in Xaymaca, but what makes her gemstone more important?" Evie asked.

"Each of the four gemstones will increase the power of a mage of that same type, because it contains the magic of the Four Heroes. The larimar would enhance Cai's enchanter abilities, for example. So you can imagine if the amethyst, the spirit waker stone, were to fall into the wrong hands…"

"Mi see now," said Evie, realizing what it would mean if Blackheart Man were to capture it, with all of his evil spirit waker magic.

"You, too, are a spirit waker," said Mucaro. "Now, spirit wakers can act as mediums to the spirit world. They can also wake the ancestral magic in others, just as Nanny was able to do for the Maroon warriors. Just as the spirit waker you met at

Myal did for you. We shamans even believe that reincarnation is possible through spirit wakers, as death is never truly finite. Spirits can be reborn in the living world."

"Incredible…" Evie was continually staggered by the power of Obeah. How would she ever come to understand this gift of magic or have the confidence to wield it?

"But as we've seen today, Blackheart Man has twisted *his* spirit waker abilities into something wretched," said Cai, with more than a touch of venom in his voice.

Mucaro continued. "The role of shamans is to guide the spirits of the dead from this world, before they become corrupted. But Blackheart Man brings corrupted spirits back to this world as duppies to wreak havoc."

"What does this mean for my body switch?" Arthur asked. "You said a spirit waker did this to me. But we never encountered Blackheart Man."

"Well, we have seen a spirit waker with power enough to summon Sekesu today," said Cai, drumming his fingers on the table. "Isn't it possible that the person who put you in that body is sitting right next to you?"

## Chapter Fifteen

# CERASEE TEA

### Evie

"Wait a minute, now!" Evie blurted. "That's nonsense!"

"Is it?" Cai challenged. "You said yourself that you didn't encounter Blackheart Man. And you're not in control of your magic."

"But… How mi even…?" She didn't know which was worse, having power enough to be able to do such a thing or the way this shaman boy was accusing her of it. She'd lost her composure now, and Arthur's probing stare made her even more upset.

"You don't know everything, and it's not like I'd ever hex him on purpose!" Evie folded her arms defensively and gave ·Cai the Queen Nanny of glares.

"You could work on your tact a little more, Cai." Mucaro patted the boy's shoulder. "I don't think Cai meant to accuse you of anything, Evie."

"Well, she don't know what she's doing and all, so—"

"What I think Cai meant to ask is," Mucaro spoke slowly but firmly, levelling a stare of his own at his apprentice, "what can you tell us about your encounter with the Heartless?"

Evie and Arthur told them everything – from the Mangrove Hotel to sneaking out to Myal, the unleashed duppies and being followed back by La Diablesse and Jujo. Evie faltered when she reached the point where the devil woman took her spirit to the brink of the realm of the dead.

"La Diablesse had the coral and the larimar. One minute mi in the hotel and the next mi in that place – like a sea of spirits."

"Wait – you went *there*?!" Cai asked. "That's the space between life and death. Only shamans are supposed to be able to journey there. So how…?"

"Well." Mucaro looked agitated, flicking at the clunky set of beads around his neck. "Sadly, the Heartless have one of us on their side, so it makes sense that they know our secrets."

Evie swallowed, eyes flitting between the two shamans. A traitor shaman was with the Heartless? Who was it that Mucaro was talking about? When no further explanation came, she let her mind drift back there, to that space between life and death. "Mi felt so close to death," she continued. "Mi could feel and see the spirits of the dead all around me. There was a light – a break in the water. For a moment mi…mi wanted to go towards it. La Diablesse had me in her grasp…"

"Take your time," said Mucaro soothingly.

"Then mi hear Arthur's voice calling me, and before mi know it, mi back."

Arthur took over. "From where I was standing, it looked like the two o' them were frozen in time. Mi switched the larimar with another piece of jewellery first, but then mi tried to break the demon woman's hold and snap Evie back to life. But mi tripped when the hotel cat darted past outta nowhere."

"And so you and the cat must have gone to that plane too, when you connected with Evie and La Diablesse?!" Cai deduced.

"Yeah man. Just for a moment. But my spirit came back in the cat! The cat ended up in my body and mi nah understand how."

"Evie, it's possible that you latched onto the spirits of those you know and love to resist the pull of death." Sekesu spoke again. "Arthur's voice called your spirit back to this world. Then your natural inclination was to protect him too. You brought your spirit and Arthur's back intuitively, but didn't count on the cat spirit being with him."

"Man, Evie…" Arthur was mind-boggled. "What a power yuh have!"

"But then, how do I undo it?" Evie asked Sekesu.

"Mi don't know," Sekesu admitted. "Mi an enchanter not a spirit waker. But what mi can do is help you understand magic. It's one thing awakening it but it's a whole other thing controlling it."

Relief washed over Evie. She hadn't realized how badly she needed this support until it was offered to her. *She* was a spirit waker. She was fearful but she wanted to understand. If she practised her strand of magic, not only could she get Arthur's spirit back to his body, but she could one day commune with her parents. "Thank you, Sekesu."

"And with all your potential – with the power you've shown us – if we can help you to control your magic and that of Nanny's amethyst stone, Blackheart Man will surely meet his match," Mucaro enthused. "You could have the power to undo every one o' dem duppy summons. That's why we ha'fi get you into the safety of the Maroons."

Evie glanced at Sekesu for more reassurance, struggling to bear the weight of that much expectation. The spirit regarded her with a light crease in her brow. But she quickly nodded and offered Evie a determined grunt. Evie felt Cai's eyes on her too. He turned away, but not before she'd noticed the scepticism etched on his face.

Soon the group were sitting in front of a feast fit for a queen – a welcome respite. The waiter wheeled his trolley into the compartment, placing plates on the table, each covered with a shiny metal cloche. He lifted the cloche for each dish, and Evie and Arthur released a squeal of delight every time. A mountain of food awaited, and they were plenty ready for the conquest.

There was silence for a while, with the exception of Evie and Arthur's ravenous guzzling and lip-smacking. Mucaro was the first to break it.

"What's the matter, Cai?"

Cai's eyes were still fixed on Evie. There was something strangely familiar about those treacle-coloured eyes. "Mi not feeling so hungry right now." His stomach let out a long noisy complaint to the contrary, and his face flushed red. "Well, perhaps a little." He scanned the dishes in front of him and a furrow appeared beneath his dark fringe. "What happened to my chicken wings? There were five pieces before. I counted."

"Wasn't me," said Evie.

"Me neither," Arthur followed.

"You didn't even order any wings yourself!" Cai complained.

"You didn't want to eat a thing a moment ago!" Evie shot back.

"It's the principle. Cho!" He reached inside his robes and pulled out a small rolled-up paper bag. He opened it and poured chillies onto his meal.

Evie raised an eyebrow when the pouring became prolonged. "What's all that?"

"Scotch bonnets," Cai said, lacing his food with them.

"How much chilli you need?" said Evie in disgust.

"As a fire enchanter, quite a lot. Mi need to stay fuelled."

"Think of it like an elite athlete," said Mucaro. "You aren't going to perform to your best if you don't fuel your body with nutritious food and stay hydrated. The same is true for your magic."

"So what do spirit wakers eat?" Evie asked, not wanting to stop gorging on her spread.

"Why don't you try some cerasee tea?" Sekesu suggested. "It detoxifies the body. A healthy body means a stronger spirit, for summoning, projecting outta your body and more easily returning to it."

"Mi have just the thing," said Mucaro, opening his robe and revealing a long hand-sewn sash of pockets filled with herbs.

"What the...?" Evie gaped at the extent of his herb stash.

"I'm a healer," Mucaro said, "so mi *always* come prepared." He rifled through the pockets and a bag of white starch dropped out onto the table.

"That's the tea?" Evie asked.

"It most certainly is not!" said Cai with an edge to his voice, while Mucaro quickly placed the bag back.

Evie looked from one shaman to the other questioningly. "So...what was that?"

"Arrowroot," Mucaro answered cagily.

"It will grant you temporary super-strength," said Cai, unable to resist providing information.

"Oooh!" Evie replied brightly.

"But you won't be able to move a muscle for hours afterwards so...double-edged sword."

"Oh."

"Here you go," said Mucaro, withdrawing a bag of cerasee leaves and stems.

Once the herbs had brewed in boiling water, Evie took a tentative sip and gagged. "Tastes like someone wrung out a dutty sock!"

Sekesu laughed then, high-pitched like an overexcited gull: "Keeheeheehee!" It was so unexpected that Evie and Arthur burst into laughter too – Evie trying not to spray cerasee tea all over the table. "Mi suppose it's an acquired taste."

"Another wing's gone! Who took it?" Cai barked.

"Cairi…" Mucaro motioned for him to calm down.

"Them nyam up mi food, master!"

"Mi know, mi know. It's all right."

Evie struggled to hold back another fit of laughter and cast a knowing glance at Arthur. But Arthur was stock still and there was steam pouring from his tiny face.

"Arthur? You all right?"

The cat grunted and managed a single nod. But his fur was so wet he looked like he'd been for a swim. Within seconds, he was hooting and hollering, the heat becoming too much.

"It was you, mangy cat!" Cai sat back and cackled, wholly satisfied that spicy justice had been served. "That's what yuh get!"

After almost an hour and a half's journey, the train's brakes squealed – metal complaining against metal – as it slowed down to make another scheduled stop.

"We're here," said Mucaro, and sure enough a sign for Annotto Bay hung over the platform outside.

More passengers would be boarding the train here as well as leaving it, so Mucaro insisted that everyone wait in the compartment while he stepped out to survey the station. The Heartless might have been following them – waiting for the chance to attack and take the larimar. When Mucaro called all clear, the others followed behind Cai.

Just like in Ocho Rios, Annotto Bay's station was right on the coast. It wasn't as busy as Evie's hometown usually was, and she wondered whether news about the unleashed duppies had reached here.

Mucaro led the way down a wide, palm-tree-lined road. It was on this quiet stretch that they stumbled across a near translucent middle-aged woman. She hovered like a shadow made of crystalline light, in a long dress with a headscarf wrapped tightly round her head. In a second, Mucaro and Cai had reached for the akrafena swords at their hips. Arthur pressed his body low to the ground, ready to run. That was all Evie needed to confirm her fears.

"D-duppy!" she gasped.

## Chapter Sixteen

# THOSE WHO LIVE
# FOR DEATH

## Evie

Cai turned to Evie, eyebrows reaching so high they were lost under his fringe. "That's a regular dead person not a duppy!" he corrected. "Master, let me see to this. I can do it."

"It isn't your time yet," Mucaro quickly answered.

"But—"

"That's an order, Cai. Protect our guests. I will ferry this spirit."

Mucaro unsheathed his akrafena and the ghost of the woman let out an alarmed cry, falling to her knees as the shaman approached. Evie was confused. Weren't Mucaro and Cai both shamans? So if ferrying spirits to the realm of the dead was their primary role, why was Mucaro so insistent that his pupil sit it out?

"Look and listen, Evie," said Sekesu. "But don't think of the spirit as something other-worldly. You are a spirit waker so part of you is of that realm too."

Seeing the baffled look on Evie's face, Sekesu nodded to herself and continued. "You've drunk cerasee tea, and its effects should still be potent enough to help you. Read the spirit of the deceased in front of you, and read Mucaro's spirit too. Feel what their spirits are communicating without words."

"How mi do that?"

"My magic felt like...like a waking limb the first time," said Sekesu. "Mi realized mi had a connection to the earth that couldn't be seen. But mi could feel it like an invisible limb. You ha'fi feel your own connection to the spirits of everyone around you."

Evie tried to rid herself of the thoughts that were racing through her mind. She tried to remember the static-like feeling of her magic. That must have been the connection of her magic to the great energy, Obeah.

"Breathe deeply, slowly," Sekesu guided.

Evie slipped into a state of quiet. The static tingle became an invisible touch – a foothold in the spirit world. It was as though she was in two places at once. The sensation excited her so much that she nearly lost focus. But she kept with it.

The ghost of the woman in the road now looked at Evie, understanding that she was a spirit waker. Her fear was palpable. The spirit knew that Mucaro was there to take her.

*I'm not ready,* the spirit said. *Please spare my soul.*

But Evie couldn't communicate back. This was still a world unfamiliar to her. She focused instead on Mucaro's spirit. But Mucaro didn't seem to acknowledge the woman's fear. There were no soothing words for the dead. It was routine for him. Evie listened with her spirit.

*I must lead you to the spirit world,* Mucaro's spirit said. *Before you can unleash hell here.*

Evie's consciousness snapped back into her body and she shivered. The spirit was being treated like a criminal. How exactly would she unleash hell?

"Your eyes were glowing violet!" Arthur told her.

"That is spirit sight," said Sekesu with a sage nod. "That's what my sister was able to use to awaken our magic."

But rather than feeling excited, Evie felt troubled by what she'd seen and heard. "Does…everyone have to face you when they die?" she asked Cai. She thought about her own parents' passing and felt afraid on their behalf, as she watched Mucaro with the spirit – one hand on her shoulder and muttering some private words of ritual rather than of comfort.

"Not everyone," said Cai. "Some spirits are able to find their own way from this world – some are more accepting of death than others." Cai was also watching his master perform the ritual. With his akrafena, Mucaro slashed through the fabric of their world and then his body fell still as a statue. The woman's spirit had disappeared, and Evie realized that Mucaro's spirit had travelled with it. It was just his body, an empty vessel, that remained in front of them.

"But you'll stop like this for every spirit you come across?" Evie asked. It felt so brutal, to meet your end at the hands of a fearsome figure with an even more fearsome-looking blade. Even if you *were* already dead.

Cai nodded. "That's the job of the shaman."

"But you're not a true shaman yet, are you?" Sekesu probed. She, too, had noticed the disagreement between Cai and his master.

"No," Cai mumbled. "To become a true shaman you need to lead a spirit to the realm of the dead. Alone." His eyes lowered and his brows knitted together. Clearly it was a touchy subject. "You've been there, both of you, to that space between our world and death. You died, Sekesu. And you," he motioned to Evie, "you called it the 'sea of spirits'."

"Yeah," Evie answered, her hairs standing on end.

"Only our spirits travel there." Cai pointed to his master. "And to resist the pull of the realm of the dead takes immense focus and training. That's what we ha'fi go through first before we become true shamans."

"So that's why you're partnered with Mucaro – as training?" asked Arthur.

"Yes. Master will let me lead when he believes I'm ready."

Evie studied Cai's jutting jaw and intense stare. She understood him better somehow. "But you think you're ready now, don't you?"

Cai's eyes flicked up. "Mi know so," he said, a hint of impatience betraying his soldier-like demeanour. "But mi trust in the master's plans. There's an order to everything. There has to be."

Mucaro's body remained still, an empty vessel kneeling on the dusty ground.

"What would happen if you didn't take spirits to that place?" Evie asked. "If you left ghosts to roam until they found their way?"

"They'd become duppies if we didn't," said Cai, his frown now canyon deep. "All the stories about evil spirits you've heard – that's how it happens."

Evie's heart galloped. That was how evil spirits were born? Just normal people who had died and couldn't pass over?

"Our spirits aren't meant to stay in this world outside of our bodies," Cai explained. "They become corrupted – stuck in this world with all its sensory treasures but not having bodies to experience them."

So that was why Mucaro was so adamant that the deceased woman would "unleash hell". A troubling thought crossed Evie's mind and she turned to Sekesu. The spirit of the earth enchanter seemed to understand her instinctually.

"My spirit won't be able to stay here for long either," Sekesu said. "You brought me back here but if mi stay, mi become corrupted too."

Evie and Arthur gasped in unison.

"But we need you to defeat Blackheart Man and La Diablesse!" said Evie. "How long do you have?"

"There isn't a set science to it," said Cai. "It depends on

many things, like how much still ties a spirit to this world: loved ones and possessions for example." He glanced over at Sekesu concernedly. "We need your power to win the fight. At least in your case there's no one alive tying you to this world. But it must be quite a shock seeing this future. And the more you experience of this new world…"

"The more mi want to see," Sekesu finished. "So just as I've been summoned here, I'll need to be sent back to the spirit world."

The weight of further expectation sat uncomfortably on Evie's shoulders as the hero gazed at her. "But mi nah understand how mi even called you here!" she said.

Sekesu smiled. "And that's where mi can help you."

Mucaro's body lurched back to life as his spirit returned. He rose from the ground and sheathed his akrafena. "All right, let's carry on," he said. "The safehouse is just down the road."

"Yeah. That's quite enough chatter," Cai added.

"You're the one who's been doing most o' the talking!" Evie scoffed.

"Right, answering *your* questions."

"Hush up, both of you, and let's get walking," said Arthur, scurrying along after Mucaro. "There's enough hot air already without you two quarrelling!"

# Chapter Seventeen

# SPIRIT SIGHT

## Evie

Before long, the group reached a blue mahoe-wood inn on a mound, painted pink and white. The sign at the foot of the hill read *The Rest Easy*. There were large blue mahoe trees all around, obscuring the lowest part of the building. They were making their way across the tree-covered lawn when Cai spoke up.

"Now, there are booby traps and snares everywhere in case of an attack, so tread carefu—"

No sooner had Cai spoken than a large log swung from above – almost launching Arthur into the sky, had he not darted away by a whisker. He landed in a crouch but the ground crumbled beneath him, and he leaped to safety with a yelp. Soil and dried mahoe leaves fell into the man-sized pitfall while Evie caught her breath.

"—carefully," Cai finished, looking perturbed.

"Raaahtid! You couldn't have told us that *before* we come marching in unuh yard?" Arthur cried.

Cai's mouth twitched, as he tried to hide his amusement. "Well...it's a good job you have the reflexes of a cat now, mi suppose."

"Cho!"

From that point onwards, the group moved together, Evie and Arthur hesitantly following Mucaro and Cai's lead while Sekesu drifted beside them.

"Here we are, then," said Mucaro as they climbed the white steps to the front door. "I'm going to make the call to Sekesu's Town. Stay inside the building, all o' you." He unlocked the front door and pushed it inwards with a long creak. "We have beds in the back rooms and some food in the pantry."

Being back somewhere homely made Evie think of Ms Bell. She wondered how her guardian had reacted when she found her letter. Whether she would be all right – especially with a cat-boy to contend with. When would she see her again, and what would she think of Evie now, as a spirit waker?

"Why don't we use this time to work on your magic, young miss?" Sekesu suggested. "The sooner you're in full control the better."

Evie grinned. "Yeah man!"

Arthur coughed conspicuously. "You just going to leave me here with bowlhead?"

"You should be so lucky," Cai snapped. "Mi got better things to do than cat-sit, yuh know."

"That's right. You should go and train your spirit too," said Mucaro with one finger in the telephone's rotary wheel. "Your performance could have been much stronger against the air enchanter. I expect more from you, and you should demand it of yourself."

"I do, master," Cai replied. "I promise I'll do better next time!"

Evie didn't miss the disappointment on the young fire enchanter's face. It was no wonder he was so highly strung, the way Mucaro drilled him. She glanced at Arthur apologetically and he sighed.

"Go, go. The sooner you master your magic the sooner mi can stop being a cat."

Now it was Evie's turn to feel pressured.

Sekesu had already drifted away. "Come then, come then!"

Evie followed the enchanter towards the nearest reception room. Cai's prying eyes followed them as they left, but he pretended not to be looking the moment Evie glanced in his direction. Between him and the bars on the outside of the windows, Evie wasn't sure whether she felt like a guest or a prisoner. Then again, maybe a prison was the safest place for her with the Heartless in pursuit.

Evie sat cross-legged on the tiled floor of the side room. It hadn't been cleaned in a long time judging by the dust that had gathered there and on the seafoam-coloured seats. A wilting bunch of orchids sat in a vase of browning water, and a couple of dead flies were dotted by the barred window. She focused instead on the black and white photographs of Maroon communities that lined the walls. Evie knew instantly that a photograph of people gathered round a large tree had been taken at Accompong Town. She'd heard much about the revered Kindah Tree. Mages called it the "One Family Tree", where the Four Heroes and other Maroon leaders had plotted out their fight against the British soldiers. Maybe she'd be able to visit one day when she felt worthy of the honour.

Sekesu reached for the larimar at Evie's neck, pulling her out of her daydream. Sekesu's fingers appeared to brush through it before the gemstone flicked to the left.

"Ehhhh!?" Evie gawked. "How yuh do that without a body?"

"How yuh think?" Sekesu replied with a contented grin. "Always remember that Obeah binds *everything* – things that you can see and things that you can't. Mi have the power to touch the larimar – manipulate it – but mi can't *feel* it. In this spirit form, mi can no longer feel the physical world, even if mi have the power to change things in it."

The feeling of being a part of this supernatural energy and being able to manipulate it gave Evie a fresh focus and excitement. Here she was, learning from one of history's great mages. When she'd longed for magic back at The Mangrove Hotel, she never could have imagined such a thing.

"You had the larimar for a long time, so it makes sense that we have a connection too. That's how you summoned me, even though you didn't understand that we were bound," Sekesu said.

Evie felt great warmth, understanding that they had been connected between worlds, even if the two of them hadn't grasped it. "Mi know your magic well," she said, thinking fondly of The Mangrove Hotel. "It's been a beautiful part of my life."

"Life *is* beautiful, Evie." There was a sombre edge to Sekesu's voice. "Despite the darkness that's looming. That's why mi help you fight for it."

Evie tried hard to shake away thoughts of the Heartless, and what a world of duppies and death would look like if they got hold of all four gemstones and tore through the barrier between worlds.

"One thing you ha'fi understand, dearie, is that this world is giving far more than it's taking. All of nature has much to offer us. Our ancestors understood that, and we students of Obeah do our best to understand too."

With her hands at heart level, fingertips together in a shape like a mountain, Sekesu closed her eyes and the dying orchids in the flower vase sprang back to life, reborn. An astonished murmur escaped Evie's open mouth. "Nature can be healing just as it can also destroy. Magic is the same."

"Woah," was all Evie could utter.

Sekesu relaxed and placed her hands back on her lap. The flowers wilted once more. "And it's up to everybody who connects with Obeah to decide whether they want their magic to heal and create, or to destroy and cause suffering. Not everyone is able to unlock the ancestral magic that freed this island. But for those who can, a choice has to be made."

Sekesu gave the same cautionary stare as Ms Bell when Evie talked back too much. But, also like Ms Bell, Evie now understood that this was coming from a place of concern, love and care.

"Magic may have awakened in you, but only you can decide how you use it. You've seen its misuse with the poor man who got himself possessed by Blackheart's duppies. You've seen it used against you by the Heartless. They tried to take away the larimar – your link to your parents in the spirit world. You have every right to be upset and frustrated – to want to use this magic selfishly. But there is another way."

Evie couldn't help but feel there was something familiar in this spirit in front of her. Was it because a part of Sekesu's spirit had been inside the larimar? There was calm, not only in the words she'd spoken, but in her aura. A warmth that took away Evie's impatience and the sadness that had built up since Myal.

"Please show me."

"Mm." Sekesu grunted her acceptance. "Obeah is all around us. It nuh matter what kind of magic you're blessed with; we all tap into it the same way."

"Like how I used spirit sight earlier?" Evie asked.

"Right." Sekesu nodded. "It's a sixth sense. Knowing what type of magic you have means it's easier to find your threads of connection. My threads are plants, trees, the earth under our feet. Mi can feel it stronger than anything. Your threads will be a connection with the spirits of every person, living or dead."

"Woah," Evie uttered again. "So mi can somehow speak with everyone's spirit?"

"Try it." Sekesu lifted her chin, the hint of a smile on her ghostly features. "Tell me how many spirits you can feel around us."

"O-okay," said Evie, determined to get a handle on things.

"Take your time," Sekesu replied, sensing her eagerness. "Close your eyes if it helps."

Evie started off with her eyes closed, but when she found the darkness to be more of a distraction, with her thoughts drifting, she opened them again. She thought back to the spirit they'd seen on the road who Mucaro took to the space between worlds. Evie was able to read the spirit and understand her feelings, even though she was unable to communicate back. That was the state of connection she needed to harness at will.

*Find my threads of connection…things you can't see…*

She thought of herself as one with the great energy. And slowly she felt it all. The intensity of two spirits in training; there was Cai, spirit burning bright and determined. There was Mucaro, tense and indignant. Then she found Arthur… climbing shelves to guzzle food from the pantry. His spirit was in flux. She felt guilt that he was alone for the first time since they'd left the mangrove. But there were others too – unknown passers-by outside of the safehouse.

"I can feel several spirits around us."

"Good." Sekesu nodded. "You're a natural at spirit sight. Let's keep it up. Mi not an expert on spirit wakers, but here's what my sister told me. She was able to see into the spirits of all of us. Many things were revealed to her: our strengths, weaknesses, fears, intentions… That was also how she was able to see where magic lay dormant and help people to tap into it."

Evie felt overawed that she had this kind of power at her fingertips. But a sudden thought intruded, bringing a fresh wave of anxiety. This was why Blackheart Man was to be feared. He could see in this way too. He had spirit sight, and in his hands it was dangerous, just as Mr Bennett had warned them. How could she defeat him with all his power *and* experience?

"Now, bring your focus back and tell me what you read from this spirit of mine."

Evie studied the spirit in front of her. She took in Sekesu's distinguished features but also the energy she projected. Her spirit was stable and incredibly powerful. It felt magnetic. This was the resolve of someone who had seen and performed great feats during their lifetime.

Once Sekesu's energy took shape in Evie's mind, she heard a voice calling.

*Come forth and embrace the magic of your ancestors*, Sekesu was saying. *The magic of the Maroons. The magic of Nanny. Embrace it as your own.*

"I can see," Evie half-whispered.

*Keep your focus*, Sekesu implored.

Sekesu needn't have worried. Evie was locked into spirit sight, and she realized that she could see even further. Sekesu was strong, but she was also afraid. This future world she found herself in was not the island full of magic she'd anticipated before she'd passed away. And she worried that the strongest magic now lay in the hands of the darkest mages: the Heartless. That was why she'd warned Evie from using her magic for the wrong reasons.

"That's enough for now," said Sekesu abruptly, and a sudden jerk of her body snapped Evie from her trance.

Evie suddenly felt conscious that she'd been too intrusive. "I'm sorry. The…connection I felt was so strong—"

"It's all right," Sekesu answered quickly. Evie certainly hoped so. But she felt proud that she had done what she'd set out to do. She'd found her connection and used spirit sight.

"So this must be how being a medium works too, nuh?" Evie asked Sekesu hopefully, sensing the ability to communicate with her parents in the spirit world was finally within reach. "I become the bridge, connecting the spirit of someone in this world with a spirit in the realm of the dead."

"Yes, but that is a technique that will require a lot of work to master," Sekesu cautioned. "First things first, mm? Why don't you try locating more spirits outside again? That'll be a useful tool in a combat scenario, to find out exactly who is around you. And once you sense their spirit, you should be able to gauge how near or far they are and what their intentions might be."

"Mi can do all that?" said Evie incredulously.

"If you hush up and focus, dearie, yuh might!"

# Chapter Eighteen

# NIGHT WATCH

## Evie

Around an hour later, when Evie emerged from the side room, she found a spread of snacks: cornbread, spiced bun and cheese had been laid out for them all. Arthur lay on his side with his hat tilted over his face. He'd clearly already had his fill to the point of napping it off.

Through the front window, they could see Mucaro keeping watch on the veranda. As Evie got closer she noticed that Cai was still training on the lawn. Mucaro barked instructions and his apprentice responded in kind. Evie felt like she could break a sweat just watching him. She thought she'd had it tough following orders and tending to guests at The Mangrove Hotel. She couldn't imagine the strain of having to deal with the dead day in and day out, never mind with a master telling you what to do and when.

"You're back. How'd it go?" Arthur asked, lifting his hat to peer at her.

"You won't believe it!" said Evie, piling up a plate with bun and cheese. "Mi can read people's spirits. Mi can actually see into the depths of your soul, Arthur."

"How you mean?"

Evie grinned, taking a chomp out of her snack, then struggling to speak with a full mouth. "Mi can see people's intentions and communicate without speaking, spirit to spirit."

Arthur blinked and got to all fours. "Wait, yuh doing it now?"

Evie laughed. "No. But you know what we could try?" Arthur slow-blinked without answering. "Sending your spirit back to your body! It's all about being the bridge to connect spirits. I should be able to connect your spirit and Clinton's so that you switch back to your bodies."

"Really?" A rush of excitement caused Arthur's voice to peak. "You think you can?"

"Well, let's try it."

"Yeah man, why not?" Arthur's tail batted the floor, side to side. "But wait. If I go back to my real body…you'll be here by yourself."

Evie watched her friend closely. She'd already thought about this and resolved to do it, having seen how agitated Arthur's spirit was earlier. "We started this journey with two goals," she said. "To find out about my parents and to return you to your body. We should try and achieve one o' them now."

Arthur went quiet so Evie forced a smile.

"And you'll come back," she insisted. "I know you'll find a way back, and we can all go on to Nanny Town together."

"If yuh sure," Arthur replied.

Evie pushed her plate aside with a scrape over the rosewood tabletop. She sat facing Arthur and saw past his furry exterior, to the spirit of the boy with the cheeky grin she knew so well. His spirit was ablaze with hope to return to his real body, and even admiration for Evie. Then she tried to reach his real body containing Clinton's spirit – to find a point of connection. But minutes passed and she drew nothing.

"Maybe…maybe you're just tired after practising with Sekesu," Arthur offered. And she was, but she wasn't so sure that was the reason. She had another theory.

"Your spirits are too far apart," she said. "Mi don't think mi can do it until you and Clinton are together." She didn't even know if she could do it at all yet. She watched Arthur's spirit deflate – the fire that had been there a moment earlier extinguished – and her guilt mounted. "Or…what if Nanny's amethyst stone can be used to get you back?"

Arthur looked at her questioningly. "You mean to boost your magic?"

"Right. With her spirit waker magic added to my own, surely we could return your spirit to your body, no problem."

"Mi suppose," he replied, but his enthusiasm had drained away. "Mi been cooped up in here too long. Think I'll go stretch my legs."

Evie opened her mouth to find words of reassurance but closed it again, as she wasn't even sure of herself. Then Arthur was gone, out of the open window, and she was alone with her thoughts.

Full up from her meal, and tired from her session with Sekesu, Evie went to rest until the Maroons of Sekesu's Town came to collect them. The back room was a cheap wooden lodge with two metal bunk beds. Evie took one of the high bunks so that she was less likely to be disturbed if someone entered. Two small windows were kept ajar even though the air coming in wasn't especially cool.

At a certain point in the evening, Evie woke in a daze to the sound of muffled but unmistakable crying. It took her a moment to remember exactly where she was. Turning over in her bed and peering over the mattress in near darkness, she gauged that the quiet sobs were coming from a lower bunk. To her surprise, it was Cai, the outline of his bowl cut unmistakable. At the sound of Evie stirring, he looked up, then wiped his face and rolled over to face the wall. He must not have realized Evie was there. The uncomfortable silence between them grew heavier until it felt like Evie was pinned under its weight.

"Cai?" Evie began.

"What yuh want?"

"Nothing, mi just…" Evie faltered. "Mi just want to check everything's okay."

"It's fine. Please go back to sleep."

And though Evie wondered privately what had upset him so much, he refused to say anything more.

Now that she was awake, Evie needed to pee. The outhouse was across the lawn, round the back of the lodge, so she wriggled down to the floor as quietly as she could and tiptoed towards the door, feeling for her sandals.

The moon was low and full above the trees, light entering through a narrow cabin window. Singing crickets and even higher-pitched tree frogs joined in a raucous symphony. As Evie pulled open the door and stepped outside, she could hear low voices coming from nearby.

"...never could have dreamed what a complication was coming my way." Arthur's silhouette sat on a fence, his tail swinging agitatedly. Mucaro, still on watch duty, stood beside him.

"In all my years of practising magic, I've only come across one person capable of projecting his spirit into another living thing," said Mucaro. "Blackheart Man."

Arthur didn't respond.

"But unlike Blackheart, Evie isn't in full control of her powers. Sekesu's teaching will be good for her. And if she reaches her potential, then we're saved. Once we get to Nanny Town and she summons Queen Nanny's spirit, as she did Sekesu, the battle is won. And you, Arthur, being in that body makes you valuable in this fight. If the enemy doesn't know this has happened, you can go unseen..."

"Mi just want to leave this island, make my riches and live in peace," Arthur said. "I'm not a hero and mi don't want to fight."

A range of emotions stirred in Evie all at once. What if she couldn't do what was needed? The Heartless wouldn't just sit and wait for her to reach her potential. What if they found her before she'd gained full control over her powers? And her best friend – he'd once more declared what was really important to him, and it wasn't staying beside her. It felt as though someone was taking scissors to a rope being held between them.

"Hmm," Mucaro uttered eventually. "But you saved Evie from La Diablesse at the hotel, without thinking of yourself. If she means that much to you, then perhaps you'll discover that you're more heroic than you know."

Evie waited for Arthur's reply, a hint that perhaps he was rethinking his words. But when he remained silent, she carried on disappointedly towards the silhouette of the outhouse.

It was in leaving the wooden toilet and navigating the narrow pathway back to the house that Evie heard a rustling from above that only ceased when she came to a stop. She looked up but saw nothing in the darkness. Evie continued along the path but felt that something was very wrong.

Cai was back outside and fully dressed, speaking with his master, while Arthur remained in the same position on the fence. Sekesu was nowhere to be seen, but there was definitely another presence among them. It wasn't anything like Sekesu's aura, though. Evie looked over her shoulder, finding her thread of connection to the spirits once again. She could feel a spirit other than her four companions. Peering back into the breadfruit tree, she found it. And the spirit was staring straight back at her.

She took a step back, breath snatching. "J-jancrow!"

Both shamans reacted as though she'd pricked them with a needle.

"What did you say?" Mucaro asked.

Evie pointed to the tree. "Another jancrow!"

"What do you mean 'another'?" Cai demanded. "No, no, no. We've been followed!"

He rushed towards the tree, drawing his akrafena. Mucaro dashed after him and the beating of wings leaving the tree could be heard. Cai shot a funnel of fire after the bird and it cawed in pain, tumbling towards the ground, alight like a fallen phoenix. Mucaro levelled an akrafena at it. The bird's cawing turned into rapturous high-pitched laughter.

"Mi see yuh! Blackheart soon come!" the jancrow cawed. "Blackheart soon come. Yuh dead!" The laughter continued, sharp steely notes cutting through the darkness of night. Mucaro skewered the bird into silence, then bellowed in frustration. It was the first time Evie had seen him lose his composure, and it rattled her.

"When did you see a jancrow before?" he asked, an urgency to his voice.

"Back in Ochi," Evie muttered guiltily. "I'm sorry, it was just before we met you. I—"

"Evie, Blackheart can project his spirit into jancrows and use them as vessels. And he can trap the spirits of others in them and control them, just like this."

"He uses them as his spies. We've been followed from the start!" said Cai in frustration.

Mucaro was the one to break Evie from her inertia. "Let's go, now. Find Sekesu. We can't stay here any longer."

That was when the first piercing howl rang out in the distance, answered a moment later by another.

# Chapter Nineteen

# THE SAFEHOUSE SIEGE

## Cai

Cai's akrafena blade caught a faint glint of moonlight. The howling gave him chills. He knew that they were meant for just that reason – to intimidate. But the creatures stalking them had just as much bite as they did bark. They were deadly.

"Lagahoos!" said Mucaro, before cursing under his breath.

"Mi laaaawd, lagahoos are real too?" Arthur fretted.

They were real, all right. But they weren't anything like the shapeshifting werewolf-type monsters of lore. They were spirit wakers who channelled beast spirits and used their feral attributes to enhance their own strength.

"Oh, this is *not* a good time to be a feline!" Arthur croaked.

"Go find Sekesu, Arthur!" Cai ordered. "You're the fastest."

"There are four spirits out there. Mi can see," Evie called.

Regardless of how Cai felt about this bull-headed girl, he was grateful in that moment that she'd found a level of control over her spirit waker abilities. They had Sekesu to thank for that.

"That's useful for us to know," said Mucaro. "Let's think about our position here. We need a clear line of escape as well as defence."

Cai took Evie's arm with his free hand and pulled her back with him as he sidestepped. He could feel her initially resist before thinking better of it. Why did she have to be so stubborn? It was her life he was trying to save anyway!

A pair of red eyes glowed in the darkness of the brush, and Cai watched with trepidation. The wolf-man was massive, at least two metres tall. His ebony torso was like that of a wrestler and covered in patchy fur. His huge mouth revealed bared fangs rising upwards in a bloodthirsty smile. The lagahoo took a couple of rapid steps, and a trap was triggered, a great log swinging down towards it. Cai readied himself – once the log had struck and caught the wolf-man off guard, he would swoop in with his akrafena to end it.

But with incredible reactions, the lagahoo swiped with a muscular arm, and his clawed hand splintered the log apart. Cai could only stare aghast at the brute force of this beast. His heart sank even further as another figure emerged from the darkness slightly apart from the lagahoo. A young man whose face he hadn't seen in years.

"Jujo…"

"Focus, Cairi!" Mucaro called. "Your enemy is in front of you. You can best him. He *will* atone for his crimes."

A stunned Jujo returned Cai's stare. His eyes flicked down to the feather necklace around Cai's neck. His shock was unmistakable, even though he quickly masked it. If Jujo hadn't recognized his younger brother before, he certainly had now.

"This can go easy or hard for you," Jujo called. "Just give us the larimar and no blood needs to be spilled today."

"You know we won't do that," Mucaro answered.

Jujo scowled, drawing his own akrafena from his hip. "Of course you won't."

The lagahoo by his side turned to him as if for permission. Jujo nodded. The wolf-man howled before tearing into a charge at Cai and Evie.

"Cai!" Evie cried.

He kept a tighter grip on his akrafena and waited a beat longer. The ground collapsed under the lagahoo as he fell into a pitfall. Cai didn't hesitate, gathering all of the fire energy he'd stored up and unleashing a ferocious blast. The dried leaves and twigs inside the deep pit set alight and the lagahoo howled again, but this time in agony.

"On your left!" Mucaro shouted, a little too late.

Cai turned with his sword raised ready to defend, but a second lagahoo, who'd hidden himself in the shadows, leaped out and clawed at the boy, sending him sprawling. Cai felt the sharp pain so strongly it took away his senses. He realized after a moment that he couldn't feel his left arm.

\* \* \*

# Evie

A whimper escaped Evie's throat. There was no doubt that Cai was down and out. She backed away towards the house, knowing that the lagahoo could finish her with a flick of a claw.

Mucaro dived in to protect his apprentice and forced the lagahoo to face him instead. The lagahoo snarled. He was just as large as the one Cai had trapped in the pit of fire, and equally fast to boot. It was Jujo, though, that Evie worried about. She'd lost sight of him completely in the chaos of the fight. She tried to pinpoint his position with spirit sight and found him in the shadows of the blue mahoe trees. But she had felt four spirits. The other was still hiding deeper in the thicket.

"Sekesu, where are you?" Evie cried in frustration.

Jujo sprinted rapidly towards Mucaro, his akrafena readied for the kill while Mucaro was distracted in his clash with the lagahoo. But suddenly, there was a flash of blue and the earth beneath Jujo's feet locked him in place. Tree branches reached out like arms and wrapped themselves around Jujo's struggling body. He looked directly at Evie as though she were the cause, but then gazed past her, his jaw dropping in disbelief. He was seeing a ghost – Sekesu's to be exact.

The earth enchanter had one hand in a fist, maintaining her hold on Jujo while she used her other to launch a pillar of earth from beneath the lagahoo. It connected with the wolf-man's jaw, stunning him and allowing Mucaro to land a decisive slash with his akrafena. The lagahoo fell to the ground.

"It can't be! Sekesu...how? Who summoned you?" Jujo's eyes flicked from the old hero to Evie. He'd figured it out. "The girl...a spirit waker!"

Even if Evie had wanted to respond, there was no chance. A gasp caught in her chest as she was locked in the grip of someone's magic, unable to move a muscle or speak a word.

*No! The fourth spirit, it belongs to...*

Mucaro was also stuck in this enchantment, his face a mask of distress. La Diablesse emerged from the trees. She had infinite shadows to play with at night – her powers were at their strongest. There was no escaping her hold.

"This is remarkable." La Diablesse took in the scene. "So this is your magic! To think that you were a spirit waker all this time."

La Diablesse studied Sekesu in awe. Sekesu was unaffected by the shadow enchantment, but hesitated to attack while Evie, Mucaro and the incapacitated Cai were trapped within it.

"Mi did never see an enchantment like this!" Sekesu said worriedly.

"I should have realized after we clashed at the hotel," La Diablesse said, ignoring the spirit now. "But you've picked the wrong side, Evie. These shamans, the Maroons, they can't help you – not if you want to have your parents back. You understand this, don't you?"

Evie couldn't answer, as La Diablesse well knew. But what did she mean, have her parents back? The devil woman drew nearer.

"Evie, there's a darkness in this woman the likes of which mi never seen," said Sekesu. "Her magic is twisted. Don't listen to her."

But Evie had no choice but to listen.

"You understand the darkness, don't you, Evie? Because you've lost loved ones too." She grew closer still and Evie saw it again – the sadness in her eyes that she'd noticed the night of the Myal. As she was stuck in her enchantment, Evie was unable to use her powers to see within La Diablesse's soul. But she didn't need to do that to see the woman's grief was real.

"She would have been about your age now…" La Diablesse said, and it was as though she had struck Evie physically with her words. Evie understood then that La Diablesse had been a mother. She had lost a daughter. "Hand over the larimar, Evie, and with the power of the Four Heroes we can do something revolutionary. We can tear down the barrier between the world of the living and the world of the dead. We can bring them back. There'll be no more death. No more loss or loneliness."

Evie again tried to make out the faces of her parents from memory, tried to remember the outlines, the scents. She panicked when the memory wouldn't fully form.

La Diablesse reached out both hands, her honeyed voice soothing to the soul. "It's okay, Evie. With your magic, too, we can achieve our goal. Together."

"That's enough!" Sekesu said. "You're not going to use my magic or my sister's to do that."

With no further warning, Sekesu attacked. La Diablesse

leaped away from the enchanted ground that tried to swallow her up. Her dress rode up, revealing the transformed leg with the cow's hoof.

"This magic has corrupted your spirit," Sekesu said. "I knew there was something demonic in you."

La Diablesse scowled and backed far away. Understanding that Sekesu's abilities were more than a match for hers, she retreated to the shadows. But she didn't notice a cat in a porkpie hat trotting over to the fiery pitfall with a long branch in its mouth. The branch set ablaze and Arthur ran with it to Cai. The shadows on the ground changed with the increased light, and the shaman boy was freed.

"Cai!" Arthur called. "You ha'fi do something to break the others free!"

Cai blew his spirit energy onto the burning branch, causing the flames to swell into an inferno, casting immense light. Mucaro broke free of La Diablesse's enchantment, swiftly grabbing Cai and Arthur. Cai screamed in agony for his damaged arm.

La Diablesse disappeared into the night and Evie's body, all at once, was hers to control again.

"They're retreating for now," Sekesu said.

Evie was surprised to see the lagahoo that Mucaro had cut down climb unsteadily to his feet, clutching at his wound, and rush off after his fellow Heartless. It was only then that Evie noticed Jujo had disappeared from the clutches of Sekesu's enchanted tree as well.

"Are you all right?" Mucaro asked, propping Cai up.

Evie was still shell-shocked and nodded absently. But she was far from all right.

"Cai..." Mucaro's voice barely disguised his concern as he took in Cai's arm.

"I think it's broken," Cai said through gritted teeth.

"I'll heal it. Ease back now – you've done plenty." The markings on Mucaro's arms glowed green, as did his palms. He turned to Arthur, whose fur was still on end after their encounter with the Heartless. "That was brilliant thinking, Arthur. Didn't mi tell you you'd be an asset?"

"That's got to be another one of my nine lives gone, nuh?" Arthur exhaled deeply.

"When did Jujo escape the tree?" Evie asked distractedly.

"The Taíno?" said Sekesu. "He's stronger than mi thought. He musta broken free when mi was focused on going for that devil woman."

"Or he discovered a weakness in your enchantment," said Cai matter-of-factly. Even in agonizing pain he pulled out all the answers. "He's a diviner."

Sekesu made a noise like a scoff but also looked somewhat impressed. Evie glanced at Cai. He appeared to be looking at his arm while Mucaro used his healing magic, but his eyes were elsewhere and glassy. During their face-off with Jujo, she'd realized why Cai's deep, dark eyes had seemed so familiar. The two were related. She wondered whether Jujo was the shaman Mucaro had mentioned, who'd turned to the side of the Heartless. That would explain what Mucaro meant when he said Jujo would "atone". She suspected there was a lot more to tell. It was written all over Cai's face.

Without warning another sound tore through the night air and put the group on edge. It took a moment for Evie to realize that it was a motor tearing up the dirt road.

"Thank heavens," Mucaro muttered.

A minibus roared up towards the house. As its headlights fell on the group the driver pipped his horn a couple of times, as though they hadn't already noticed a speeding red beast of a van hurtling towards them. The minibus screeched to a halt and a stocky man stepped out of the driver's side.

"Omar," Mucaro said.

"Master Mucaro, long time, brudda," Omar responded. "Sorry mi a bit late. You wouldn't believe the day I've had, mi say you would nah believe it…" He tailed off upon properly taking in the dishevelled group and then noticing the burning fire trap and battle-scarred ground. "Lawd… What-a gwarn here?"

## Chapter Twenty

# FRACTURES

## Cai

Cai woke up to sunlight breaking through a curtainless window. He sat up to find Mucaro sitting in an armchair beside his bed.

"What time is it?" Cai asked.

Mucaro gave his leather-strapped wristwatch a cursory glance. "Almost seven. You had a decent rest."

That was putting it lightly – in typical Mucaro fashion. Cai didn't even remember the minibus arriving at Sekesu's Town. He'd been out fast. Conversely, his master had dark bags under his eyes. He'd probably been sitting in the chair all night watching over him.

"How's your arm feel?"

Cai cautiously lifted his left arm and rotated it. "A little tender but fine, master. Thanks for healing it."

Mucaro nodded. "You'll need to make sure you don't do anything strenuous for a day or so."

Mucaro appeared to be in fine enough spirits, but Cai felt ashamed. He couldn't afford to be sidelined while the Heartless were still loose and looking to strike. He didn't want to be a burden.

"Master…I'm sorry. Mi let you down again."

Mucaro unfolded his arms, thick eyebrows raised curiously. "How you mean, let me down?"

"You had to step in and protect me. La Diablesse trapped you too, because you tried to rescue me." Cai fought back frustrated tears. "Mi try as hard as mi can and still—"

"Cai," Mucaro said, shaking his head. "You're my apprentice. It's my duty to protect *you*."

"Mi shouldn't need protecting now!" Cai shook his head, stuggling to meet his master's eyes.

"Cai, you did excellently against the first lagahoo. Anyone would find it difficult taking on two o' them. I'm only sorry that mi was focused on Jujo and didn't sense the second lagahoo earlier."

Cai glanced at Mucaro, trying to read his expression. Mucaro didn't tend to talk about Cai's brother, such was the depth of Jujo's betrayal. But even though he was rarely mentioned, Jujo had cast a long shadow over Cai and Mucaro's entire working relationship. Where Jujo had fallen from grace in joining Blackheart Man, Cai wanted to rise in glory. He wanted to rectify every wrong his brother had done. But most of all, he wanted to be strong enough to defeat Blackheart and bring his brother home.

"Jujo will face justice for turning his back on the shamans," said Mucaro as though reading his mind. "Now that you've faced your brother once, you'll know what to expect next time. You'll be ready."

Cai stepped from his bed, looking towards the door. "Evie, Sekesu and Arthur. Are they safe?"

"Perfectly," said Mucaro. "To say Sekesu's Town has been shocked by the return of the larimar and Sekesu is an understatement. But at least it's brought some joy to them, given the awful situation we find ourselves in with the Heartless."

"But Sekesu can't stay," Cai said. "Or she'll become corrupted."

"No, of course not," Mucaro answered. "And she knows this. Now that the larimar is home, it's up to Evie to master her abilities, learn how to reverse Sekesu's summoning and send her back to the spirit world."

"If Sekesu hadn't been with us last night, we would have…" Cai tailed off at the thought. "She'd be so important to us in the fight against Blackheart."

"It's true. But we can't risk a spirit of her power becoming corrupted in this world. Better that she prepares Evie so that she can use the amethyst stone. Then Evie can summon Nanny before the Heartless have the chance to. Nanny will save Xaymaca again."

"Master," Cai started. "Do you…think we can trust Evie with Nanny's amethyst? Don't you think her motivations might be more personal than for the good of the world?"

"All you can do is watch and listen, Cai," Mucaro replied. "Sometimes people need the right guidance to put them on the path to becoming their best selves. What better mentor for Evie than Sekesu?"

Cai nodded, but perhaps unconvincingly because Mucaro added, "People reveal their true selves in time. You just need to respond to the signs when they're shown."

These words hung heavy in the humid air – the inference being that Mucaro had not responded to signs quickly enough in Jujo's case. Cai knew that haunted his master more than any spirit they encountered on the road.

## Evie

In another room, elsewhere in Sekesu's Town, Evie perched on the edge of a flimsy single bed, alone with her thoughts. Arthur, curled up at the end of the bed, was fast asleep. His porkpie hat hung on a bedpost beside him.

The previous night felt like a fever dream, what with accursed jancrows, wild wolf-men and yet another encounter with La Diablesse and Jujo that they were lucky to have escaped from. She couldn't say unscathed because Cai's arm had been broken. He'd been quiet in the minibus, drifting into an uncomfortable sleep after Mucaro's healing was done. The way Omar, the Maroon captain who'd collected them, threw that van about on the bumpy, winding roads it was a wonder they didn't *all* have broken limbs as a result.

On arriving at Sekesu's Town, someone had blown an abeng – an instrument fashioned from a bull horn. She later found out that it was to announce the arrival of Sekesu's spirit – a feat which drew wonder from the township. Evie felt around her neck on instinct, but the larimar was gone now – handed over to Omar. Evie had been too tired to protest. And in any case, Sekesu told her that they would meet again in the morning. Now morning was here but it wasn't Sekesu that was on her mind. It was La Diablesse.

*She would have been about your age...*

La Diablesse – Lana – had a daughter once. She seemed desperate. Evie supposed that *she* had been desperate in her own way, in going to Myal.

*You understand the darkness, don't you, Evie? Because you've lost loved ones too...*

There *was* an unspoken understanding. The struggle to piece a life back together after it's been torn apart. Evie could hardly remember her parents. Their love and warmth was shapeless – barely a memory. And she had nothing else to cling onto. The Mangrove Hotel was gone. Arthur planned to leave the island. She didn't want to feel alone any more; she wanted a real family. Was what Mucaro had told her about destroying the barrier between life and death really true? How could anyone be so certain when it had never been attempted before?

"Evie?"

Arthur's croaky voice made her jump. "Marnin', Arthur. What is it?"

His little chest was moving fast. "We can get my spirit back to my body, can't we?"

Evie descended further into her sadness. He must have had a nightmare. In a way, he was already living a nightmare in that body. But the real question behind his words was *Can YOU get my spirit back to my body?*

"We'll try again. We'll find a way," she said, stroking the fur on his side.

A knock on the door of their room caught them both by surprise.

"Hello?" Evie answered.

The door opened slowly and a head popped through. It was a girl about their age with glowing skin, two perfect plaits and large glasses that covered about two thirds of her face and magnified her eyes.

"Um, g-good marnin'," she said shyly. "Won't you get dressed and come out for breakfast? The whole town is waiting to meet you."

## Chapter Twenty-One

# SEKESU'S TOWN

## Evie

Evie quickly washed and dressed while Arthur licked at his paw and dabbed his head before placing his porkpie hat back in its rightful place. It was a small cabin-like house they were staying in – clearly lived in, though no one else was around. Silver photo frames hung on the walls and ornaments cluttered a large table in the kitchen/living area. Someone had given up their home for them, for the night.

Evie pulled open the front door, which creaked in response. The timid girl was waiting on the tiled porch.

"Marnin'," Evie greeted.

"Do you live here?" asked Arthur.

"Yes," the girl replied, trying her hardest not to look as curious about the spirit trapped in the body of a cat as she clearly was.

"Thank you, for letting us rest here," said Evie.

"It's no trouble," the girl said, with the briefest eye contact. "My mami offered."

"I'm Evie."

"Mi know," said the girl. "Sekesu told the chief everything. Mi can hardly believe such a thing as the town's hero returning to us. It's true magic."

Evie smiled at that, and her excitement grew at being in a Maroon town full of mages and magic. They were safe.

The girl introduced herself as Clementine before the three of them walked together along a narrow, bumpy road. An earth enchanter greeted them as he sought to carefully fill in potholes with his magic. Water enchanters with their straw hats and loose vests were out in their fields drenching their crops. Evie and Arthur marvelled at it all. It was a far cry from modern cities like Kingston with their high-rises, stuffy suits and imported cars. This was serene, just slow, simple living and practical magic. There were cockerels and hens strutting about freely outside of houses. A cascade of trees lined the roads, and the beautiful Blue Mountains stood tall above it all.

"Where's Sekesu now?" Evie asked as they walked.

"At the community yard, where we'll all eat together," said Clementine. "But the chief of Sekesu's Town wants to meet you first."

Evie and Arthur glanced at one another.

"What she want to see us about?" Arthur asked cagily.

Clementine smiled reassuringly. "You don't ha'fi worry," she said. "My mami is actually very lovely."

It wasn't long before they arrived in the heart of Sekesu's Town. The rows of trees along the road became rows of small, colourful houses. They passed a laundrette and a grocery store. A group of curious older men stopped their game of dominoes to say hello to the chief's daughter and welcome the young spirit waker who'd brought Sekesu back. Then they carried on their game and Evie overheard one of them cussing out another, insisting that he'd enchanted the dice to win.

The group drifted down another small dirt road with a sign pointing towards the community yard and the Maroon Museum.

"This way," said Clementine in a small voice. They followed her towards a wooden cabin where she knocked and poked her head around the decorative front door. "They're here, Chief Marcia."

"Thank you, Clem," her mother called. Her loud voice was the polar opposite of her daughter's near whisper.

Clementine guided them inside. Omar was scribbling away at notes under a pile of folders on a corner desk. He stopped, placed his pen behind an ear and greeted them as they entered. "Good marnin', mi say good marnin' to you both."

At a larger desk, a graceful, dark-skinned woman in a stunning yellow and royal blue kente dress with matching headwrap, stood to greet them.

"Akwaaba! Welcome," she said in a voice fit for a stage. "It's an honour to meet you, Evie. And you, too, Arthur."

"H-hello," the pair replied.

"Thank you for letting us stay in your home…er, chief…Ms Marcia…" said Arthur as he doffed his hat.

"Marcia is fine, Arthur," said the chief, amused but respectful. "Mi was up late speaking with Sekesu, who's told me your story. It's extraordinary! Evie, you really had the larimar all this time and were none the wiser about what it was you held?"

Evie shook her head.

"And your parents, you say they gave it to you?"

"That's one of the earliest memories mi have," said Evie, before thinking to herself that although she repeated that phrase a lot, it was now a husk of a memory. She swallowed the thought down with an ache in her chest.

The chief looked curiously at Evie, taking in the details of her face. "We'll soon have you back with your companions for the meal, and let festivities begin," she said with gusto. "But first, we'll take you to our museum. Mi think you might be pleasantly surprised by what you find."

The cabin door swung open suddenly and a burly-looking young man walked through with a drawstring bag slung over his shoulder. His face was so placid and unassuming that it didn't quite match his brawny body.

"Wilfred!" said Omar. "Where you been, mi say where you been at? You were meant to be the one to collect Mucaro and the group from Annotto Bay!"

"Sorry," Wilfred replied dozily. "Mi was wild camping so that mi could forage in the forest this morning." He lifted the drawstring bag from his shoulder, wincing slightly as he did, and poured its contents onto the table. There was a batch of African dream herbs and bull's eye seeds that could be used for jewellery or medicines.

Omar shook his head. "Cho! Was your brother with you?"

"Mm, mi haven't seen Mikey since yesterday." Wilfred helped himself to some dried mango strips from Omar's table. "Thought he was with you, nuh?"

"You boys need to learn how to communicate. You're meant to be captains leading by example." Omar's annoyance was clearly contained in front of visitors, but his scowl revealed all. "Anyway, you can greet our guests now instead."

"Akwaaba. It's a pleasure to have you here," said Wilfred between loud chews. Omar shook his head again, at his wits' end.

Evie noticed that Wilfred seemed to have hurt his chest. That must be why he winced through his smiles at intervals.

"Sekesu is in the compound, Wilfred!" Marcia said.

"So mi hear! Mi should like to see the larimar at some point too. What a day!"

"Wilfred, yuh all right?" Marcia asked. "You're walking like you're constipated!"

"Oh, no." Wilfred laughed embarrassedly along with the others. "Just a little stumble in the darkness last night. Fell and hurt mi chest."

Omar grinned. "You are a clumsy guy, mi say you're awfully clumsy for an experienced mountain man."

"Why don't you let Clem see to it?" said Marcia.

Clementine eagerly stepped forward, rubbing her hands together with a green glow.

"No, no! It's all right, honestly. Don't waste your powers." Wilfred waved her off, causing Clementine to back up uncertainly. "Just a little herbal salve and I'll be right as rain. Nice to meet you Evie, Arthur."

So Clementine was a healer. Evie felt a little sorry for her as the girl retreated into herself again. She must have been excited to show what she could do.

"Well then," said Marcia, clapping her hands together. "Let's head next door!"

# Chapter Twenty-Two

# SANKOFA

## Evie

Large arched double doors to the Maroon Museum featured a decorative symbol of a mythical bird twisting its head back to grab an egg. The black painted image was so stark and so beautiful against the carved wooden doors that Evie stood rooted to the spot for a moment to appreciate it.

"You know this symbol?" Omar asked. Evie shook her head. "This is the Adinkra symbol for *Sankofa*, from the Twi language that our ancestors brought from Ghana. It means 'go back and get it'."

"It's about learning from the past to build a future," said Marcia. "We will not be held back by the past, but we will be sure to retrieve things of value from it."

She unlocked the doors and pushed on the handles that formed two halves of a heart. Holding it open for the guests with one hand, she flicked a switch on the inside with the other. The fluorescent lights above flickered to life with a strained hum revealing a library wall, a glass-cased scale model of Xaymaca and numerous ornaments and placards. The museum was humid so Omar switched on two standing electric fans at the wall.

"Come then." Marcia ushered Evie and Arthur over with a smile.

Arthur was the first to pounce up to her, and Evie followed. Marcia reached a shelf containing a row of tan, leather-bound books. She found the one she was after, took it down and brought it over to a desk where she placed it with a thud. Her deep brown eyes twinkled as she looked over to Evie. Then she wandered across to the glass case containing the Xaymaca model and pointed to the east.

"Nanny's amethyst, Quao's emerald and Sekesu's larimar were kept here in these mountains for years and years. We are the Windward Maroons of the east." She stepped a couple of paces to her right. "Cudjoe's coral stone was kept here in the west, protected by the Leeward Maroons. Nine years ago, Accompong Town, the home of the coral stone, was attacked by Blackheart Man. He captured the coral and…not one of the villagers survived."

"His plan was to attack the four host villages one by one, stealing the gemstones by stealth, leaving no witnesses," Omar chimed in. "But something musta gone wrong, mi say something went wrong. The shamans based in Accompong had left to do their duties, so weren't there at the time of the attack, and they managed to alert the other Maroon towns to what had happened. The shamans who first discovered the horrors of Accompong were Master Mucaro and his young apprentice."

"Mucaro?" Evie gasped.

"But wait," said Arthur. "Nine years ago? Cai would only have been a toddler then!"

Evie thought to herself for a moment before asking, "Was it Jujo?"

"Correct," said Marcia.

Arthur's cat pupils widened. "Mi laaaaawd!"

"We pieced together clues that Blackheart Man was behind the attack on Accompong. And after that time, we learned more about his operations. He would entice mages to join his cause. And despite everything that happened in Accompong, he recruited some Maroons. That was the birth of the Heartless. The most fearsome was a woman who seemed like a living demon. She became known as La Diablesse."

Evie frowned to herself. La Diablesse had given up her humanity to join Blackheart. Why?

"The Heartless tried to strike again, this time right here in Sekesu's Town." Marcia made her way back to the large desk and rifled through a leather-bound book. "But we'd already taken precautions. I tasked a squad of nine – five townsfolk and four shamans – with taking the larimar far away from here. Even I wouldn't know the location, so that if a diviner on the side of the Heartless captured me they'd learn nothing. All I knew was that the squad were to take a boat away from Xaymaca."

Marcia stopped on a page revealing an album of black-and-white photographs. "This album contains pictures of our settlement from the last decade," she said. "And here; this one was taken in 1950." Her finger landed on a photograph of a young man and woman in kente cloth. "This couple were among the nine who set off with the larimar. But they had a child with them – a daughter." She turned the page to reveal the couple with a baby between them. They weren't smiling for the photo, but they looked content. Their heads were raised, proud.

Evie's body shook involuntarily. As she looked over the photographs and saw the details of those faces – the woman with eyes far apart like her own; the rounded shape of the man's face, which she recognized instantly – she understood. She remembered.

Marcia smiled. "The resemblance is uncanny. Your parents were from Sekesu's Town. You are a child of these mountains. A descendant of freedom fighters and proud Africans."

Evie couldn't take her eyes off the page. Her thoughts were racing against a high tide, words snatched up and washed away like flotsam.

"Whoa, whoa, whhhooooa!" Arthur spun in circles chasing his tail. "You're a daughter of mages?! Well, this explains why your magic current is so strong."

Marcia removed the photograph of the couple and baby

from its plastic covering and passed it to Evie. "Welcome home, daughter of the Blue Mountains."

Evie took hold of the photograph with all the care of a mother holding a newborn. She had been stumbling in the dark, but now a spotlight guided her way. Now she knew for certain that she belonged. That she had been loved. But behind it all was the melancholy feeling that she'd never fully had the chance to love in return.

"What happened to them?" Evie asked. "My parents and the rest of the squad; what happened to their boat?"

Omar's body tightened. His mouth hung open for a moment before he spoke. "We can't say for sure as their spirits had departed this world before anyone arrived. We assume the four shamans with them guided them to the realm of the dead. It mighta been a storm that capsized the boat."

"When we couldn't find the larimar, we worried that the Heartless had attacked them. But it eventually became clear that they didn't have it either," said Marcia. "So all we know is that your parents musta placed the larimar on you as a desperate attempt to save you. Your mami was an enchanter, you see. So her powers woulda been amplified by the gem. They knew it was their only hope."

Marcia closed the book again and smiled sadly. "Your papa was a spirit waker, just like you. He musta called for our ancestor Sekesu's protection, and she really came through for you."

Evie wiped away tears, but there was joy, too, behind her

pain. She felt closer to her parents now. Her mother was an enchanter and her father a spirit waker. To understand these parts of their identity gave more shape to her memories of them. They were no longer a mystery.

Then came a fresh flood of warmth for Sekesu. Because not only had she saved her life then, she had been by Evie's side one way or another ever since.

"We defended Sekesu's Town and tried our best to fight the Heartless in the time that passed," said Omar. "But they struck again years later at Quao's Hall and stole the emerald. We became aware there was a traitor in our midst."

Marcia grunted at the memory. "That traitor turned out to be Mucaro's own apprentice. He'd somehow been swayed by Blackheart."

"Jujo!" Arthur shrilled. "Poor Mucaro...poor Cai! How him turn on his own people like that?"

The revelation rocked Evie. But it made sense now. This was why Mucaro was so hard on Cai. This must have been a constant weight on Cai's mind too. She remembered his tears as he lay on the bed at the safehouse.

"And that gave the Heartless two of the four gemstones they desire, to summon the Four Heroes and control their spirits – their magic," said Omar. "We've had to protect Nanny Town with our lives."

Evie was overcome by the urge to practise her magic, so that she could summon Queen Nanny with the amethyst just as soon as they reached Nanny Town.

"But that's enough history for now. I'm sure you have a lot to process, Evie," said Marcia. "Now that you've set foot in here, know that these resources are yours to explore for as long as you're under our protection. You can learn more about your magic and reconnect with Maroon culture."

Arthur's stomach growled so loudly that it made Clementine jump.

Marcia grinned. "Starting with a big Maroon breakfast!"


The "community yard" was more like a semi-covered auditorium. In fact, there was a stage at the rear with four banners hanging proudly overhead. They displayed the emblems of the four kinds of magic: a blue mahoe leaf for healers, a glinting eye for diviners, a dark quarter moon within the sun for enchanters, and a flame-like soul for spirit wakers. The stage was filled with drummers using their rhythms to talk to one another. The centre of the hall was open air, and sunlight streamed onto a lush lawn. Surrounding the lawn were multiple tables and stools that seated crowds of villagers. Everyone was transfixed by Sekesu, who was kindly greeting them.

Wilfred blew an abeng to welcome Evie and Arthur to the fold, and attention shifted to the ragtag pair.

"Sekesu!" Evie called, running for the spirit and embracing her as though she hadn't seen her in months. And even though they couldn't feel each other physically, she knew they were connected spiritually. Sekesu's warm energy flooded through her.

"How yuh doing, dearie?"

Evie caught sight of Mucaro and Cai at a table and she waved to them both. Soon she was seated with them and excitedly relaying everything she'd learned about her past and being a long-lost Maroon. She very much enjoyed the look of surprise on Cai's face as she did so.

Drinks were brought round on bamboo trays. Evie realized she was parched and eagerly sipped at the cloudy liquid. Her taste buds were awakened by the mild spice of fresh ginger combined with the sweet juice of june plums mixed with coconut water. She had never tasted anything so delicious in her life and told everyone who'd listen as much.

Then their meal was served in bowls fashioned from green coconut half-shells. Cai not-at-all subtly clutched at his bowl and dragged it as far away from Arthur as possible before dousing it with chillies. Evie thought he was ruining a perfect meal, and she wolfed down her ackee, rice and peas with curried pumpkin. Everything being served had been grown right there in the town. The Maroons – just as they had been in Sekesu's time – were completely self-sufficient.

Up on the stage, a line of children younger than Evie were taking their positions. They were dressed in costume: some wearing the traditional ambush camo and leaves of the Maroons, while others were dressed in the red coats of the British military. They acted out the great liberation, with Maroon warriors fighting off the British. More children joined the stage, representing escaped slaves who joined the Maroon communities and had their magic awakened. Four of the children were dressed as the Four Heroes, with Sekesu's young actress gaining massive cheers, as well as Sekesu's own unmistakable laughter rising above it all.

Cai shook his head or tutted every few minutes. "Why'd they start from the Maroon Wars and ignore that Taíno culture emerged on the island first? Way, way, way before the Spanish and the English came to colonize the islan—"

"Hush now!" Evie and Arthur scolded him in unison.

Sekesu appeared to be greatly enjoying the performance, and when the children danced she floated over to join in too. The revellers cheered and marvelled at the sight – so many generations apart. Other townsfolk joined in the dancing, and Evie's eyes widened as even timid Clementine was working up a sweat on the lawn.

"So what you doing sitting down over there?" Sekesu grinned at Evie.

Evie smiled back, not needing another invitation. She looked at Arthur apologetically.

"Don't worry 'bout me," he said, licking his lips hungrily. "Mmm, there's still platters out here to nyam up, completely untouched!"

Evie turned to a stoic Cai instead. "Come now, Cai!"

"No. Someone has to stay focused. What if we come under a surprise attack from th—"

"Cai, let joy happen, man! You ha'fi hold onto these moments when they come."

He seemed to consider this before begrudgingly getting to his feet. Evie flicked a satisfied smile.

She allowed herself to be free in the moment – in the movement. With the photograph Marcia had given her, she'd restored some precious memories of her parents. She could picture them both. Her joy was untouchable now.

What would her parents think of this? Their daughter returned. They were there, dancing with the ancestors. The magic was strong and so was the feeling of camaraderie. This place felt something like home. And, for certain, she would fight for it.

# Chapter Twenty-Three

# SPIRIT STATE

## Evie

A river flowed alongside Sekesu's Town, running all the way down from the Blue Mountains that towered behind. Evie walked barefoot to the riverbank, feeling the rich soil beneath her. Sekesu drifted serenely by her side, humming to herself.

"Well, that was such fun. What an incredible welcome for you."

"A-true," Sekesu said, grinning contentedly. "And you can dance, eh! Although now you look like you've been running against the wind. Keeheeheehee!"

Evie touched her hair self-consciously.

"Yuh oiled it this morning?" Sekesu asked, and Evie nodded. "Come then. Let me comb and style it for you."

Evie sat down on the ground, her curiosity piqued. Being pampered and groomed by a ghost wasn't on the list of things she'd thought would happen in her lifetime, but spindly cerasee vines crept up from the ground to act as Sekesu's surrogate hands. With this enchantment, she clutched Evie's comb, and deftly stroked at her hair, working from scalp to tip. It was an unspoken language of love. With the soothing sound of the river running by, it was bliss.

"Tell me more about Nanny," Evie asked after a moment. "What was she really like?"

Sekesu was quietly pensive for a while. Evie supposed there was so much to say that it was difficult to know where to begin. Sekesu must miss her sister dearly.

"Well, you know that Nanny was called the Mother of Magic and awakened the powers of those we freed from enslavement, and the Maroons who fought beside her. But what you don't know is that she came to Xaymaca for me. I was stolen from the Gold Coast, brought to 'Jamaica' as the British mispronounced it then, and sold into slavery."

The Gold Coast no longer existed by name. Five years earlier, it had become one of several territories to be thrust together as a new nation: Ghana. And Queen Nanny came all that way to rescue Sekesu?

"How?" Evie asked incredulously. "How did she manage that?"

"My abduction – the thought that we would be torn apart for ever – it awakened her powers. She was able to find my spirit, even an ocean away. She was willing to get herself captured by the slavers just for the slimmest chance to save me."

Evie could barely fathom such bravery. "How did she escape the slavers?"

"She awakened the magic of other enslaved men and women on the ship that took her. They were able to fight once they arrived on the island. Then they found the Windward Maroons of the east, and magic spread further among them. The magic of the ancestors brought from the Gold Coast to liberate the people on this island!"

Evie smiled just hearing the pride in Sekesu's voice. She felt safe in her hands, relaxed as though in a trance as the comb eased through her hair.

"Nanny led the raids on great houses and plantations to free many enslaved Africans. On one of these raids she found me. Found me when I'd lost all hope."

Sekesu tenderly drew the teeth of the comb through a particularly tough patch of hair.

"And she awakened the enchantress within me. Reawakened my spirit. From that point on I told myself that I'd devote my life to protecting my sister."

"Woah," said Evie, amazed. "That's incredible."

"Keeheehee! She was that," Sekesu agreed. "We had lost one life together – one of innocence. But we were both born anew in Xaymaca – in freeing the island from British chains."

"We absolutely have to bring Queen Nanny back," Evie said. "If I can summon her spirit with the amethyst stone, maybe she can wake the magic of the non-mage islanders who've lost their way all these years later. We can stop the Heartless for sure!"

Sekesu placed her arms over Evie's shoulders so that her warmth radiated. "Yes. I'm only sad that I won't see it," she said. "But I've already seen too much of this future world. I've had my time."

Evie didn't want this moment to be ruined by the lingering truth. She wanted it to last for ever.

"This feels so unfair. I'm just getting to know you, getting to understand my magic, and now mi ha'fi send you away."

"Mi know. But the longer mi stay, the harder the pull to remain in a world mi no longer belong in. Mi don't want to become...one o' dem things."

Evie closed her eyes to will away the image of Sekesu becoming a duppy. It was unbearable.

"We only met two days ago. I didn't expect it to hurt like this." Evie rubbed her eyes with the back of her hands. "Why does it feel like I've known you for ever?"

"Well, sistah, when the right spirits cross paths, you don't have to have known someone a long time to feel like you've known them a lifetime." She released the enchantment on the vines, put down her comb and stood, placing her spectral hands on Evie's shoulders once more. "Mi done. Take a look."

Evie got to her feet and moved closer to the water. A striated heron looking for its next meal beat its wings and flew downriver as she approached to catch her reflection. Evie beamed back at herself, her impish grin exposing the small gap between her teeth. Her hair was pinned back into a row of three Bantu knots. She looked older, more distinguished. Stronger!

"Mi love it, Sekesu!"

"Keeheeheehee." Sekesu chuckled. "Mi thought you would. Now that you look the part of a warrior, let's have you train like one!"

Evie nodded determinedly. She wanted to master her powers. La Diablesse, Blackheart Man, Jujo – she was going to beat them all to the amethyst in Nanny Town. "I'm ready."

"Good," said Sekesu, clearly pleased with Evie's vigour. "Now get into the water."

"Ehh?" Evie blinked at the spirit, thinking she must have misheard.

"Sit down in the river. The water's shallow, yuh know," Sekesu announced.

Perplexed, Evie obeyed, wading ankle deep before turning questioningly to Sekesu again.

"You heard me!" Sekesu folded her arms. "We'll be here for a while, so you'd better find a comfortable spot. Keeheeheehee!"

Evie sat with the water up to her waist, mildly irritated at Sekesu's amusement.

"We're going to stay here until you learn to project your spirit from your body at will."

This brought an excited smile back to Evie's face. The thought of leaving her body behind was both exhilarating and unnerving at the same time.

"Now remember what mi said about nature having much to

offer us. Close your eyes. Hear the bird calls. Smell the fruit in the trees. Feel the water on your skin. Feel the threads of everything and understand anything is within reach. Where yuh want your spirit to travel?"

Evie opened her eyes again, a moment of panic holding her back. "What if mi spirit leave and can't return?"

"Mm, it will feel strange being outside o' your body. Take it from someone who's dead! But use the river to guide you back downstream to your body if you lose your way."

Minutes seemed to have passed without any progress. Evie felt restless.

"You ha'fi see yourself as the spirit, separate from your body," said Sekesu. "Think of it as a container, just a vessel that you need to step out of."

Evie brought her focus back, tried to think of herself as a butterfly escaping a cocoon.

"Step out, Evie."

This time it happened. She went from the darkness into infinite light.

"Lawd have mercy, I'm doing it!"

"Just stay in the moment." Sekesu's voice funnelled through to Evie as though from another realm.

Evie's spirit was above the water, drifting as though she were an early-morning mist. She started to turn to see the distance she'd travelled.

"Don't look back at your body yet, tempting as it is. You'll lose focus and might feel anxious," Sekesu cautioned.

"Well now that you've said that, all mi want to do is look back!" Evie called, still drifting.

"Mi not a spirit waker so it's all you from here. You ha'fi learn how to control it."

To her own eyes, her spirit looked no different to her body. Evie focused on that instead of the river, moving an arm and seeing the world around her seem to bend with it. Then a leg, and the water underfoot rippled. She was viewing the physical world through a haze and becoming aware that her existence was between two worlds. She could move and shape the spirit threads to affect both.

Then an anxious feeling came over her. Her proximity to the spirit world suddenly felt overwhelming. She followed the river's flow, suddenly longing to get back to her body. Her eyes jolted open as she returned to it. For a moment her mind was active but her body wouldn't respond, like waking with sleep paralysis. She cried out, finally managing to take back control. Sekesu watched her, a relieved half smile on her face.

"Take a moment, then do it again."

# Chapter Twenty-Four

# UNDONE

## Evie

A few repetitions and one soggy lower half later, Sekesu called time.

"Not too bad," she said as Evie stepped back onto the riverbank.

Her legs felt heavy as though she'd woken up from a deep sleep. The experience of projection was, indeed, dreamlike.

Across the river, shrubs rustled and caught Evie's attention. A broad figure emerged and then waved awkwardly in greeting.

"Evie, Sekesu. It's good to see you again," said Wilfred.

"Hello, Wilfred. Where yuh coming from?" Evie asked.

"Our cemetery is just over there." Wilfred pointed vaguely. "Every week mi go and speak with my grandparents."

Evie gasped. "Wait, you're a spirit waker too?"

Wilfred nodded. "Me and my twin brother, Mikey. The village got lucky that year!"

He laughed heartily at his own joke, but Evie's mind was racing too fast to acknowledge it.

"Wilfred," Evie began. "Would you...? Mi want to be able to do that too. Could you show me?"

Wilfred looked momentarily taken aback but gently smiled. "Well, mi have a lot of demands on my time today. Mi being pulled left, right and centre to make sure the town's prepared against an attack from the Heartless. But tomorrow I'd be happy to show you something."

Evie was watching him with her spirit sight, and she could see that he was lying. She tried not to show her immediate disappointment. "I'd be grateful," she said anyway, knowing full well "tomorrow" wouldn't come.

Wilfred nodded and continued gingerly on his way, holding his chest. Evie wondered why he'd refused to have Clementine take a look if it was giving him so much trouble.

"Evie."

Sekesu's voice pulled her out of her thoughts.

"We should go back now. It's time." Sekesu smiled without showing teeth. The early evening sun was so low and bright Evie had to squint. When night fell it would be easiest to reach the realm of the dead, to send Sekesu back. There was a quiet dignity – a resolve to Sekesu's spirit. She was ready, but Evie was less sure that *she* was.

\*    \*    \*

As night fell, the residents of Sekesu's Town made their way back to the community yard. In stark contrast to the jubilant, lively scenes from the morning, the night carried a sombre air. Instead of the pounding drums, Maroon women raised their voices in chorus. Instead of guests at the tables, a crowd gathered round the open patch of moonlit lawn where they would say goodbye to their ancestor – their hero – as she returned to the spirit world.

Evie held her breath as she sipped at a cup of cerasee tea, wishing that she could hurry up and acquire this "acquired taste". She watched, perching on the edge of the stage as Chief Marcia embraced Sekesu's spirit. Mucaro and Cai came forward then, and placed their hands over their hearts. Their private words to Sekesu were impossible to hear over the song, but their body language suggested the deepest respect and gratitude.

Arthur padded up to her next, and he must have said something amusing because Sekesu's birdlike laughter cut through the voices of the singers. Then she bent down to him and whispered something. He doffed his hat and padded away again.

Then Marcia approached Evie with slow steps and a wistful smile. In her hand was the larimar. Marcia reached out and nodded. Evie was being given a chance to say goodbye to the larimar, which would remain in Sekesu's Town, as well as to the hero whose magic it contained. "You ready, Evie?"

Evie reached for the pendant, feeling the familiar weight and smooth texture in her hand. It was a matter of paces from the stage to the lawn where Sekesu hovered, but every step felt heavy. She was face to face with Sekesu. This really was it.

"See you again, sistah." Sekesu smiled.

Evie's shoulders shook, and the vision of the spirit in front of her blurred through her tears. Sadness left an ache in her chest because she had to be the one to break this incredible link and send the spirit home.

"Mi know you feel the connection between us stronger," said Sekesu. "You can feel the thread that binds me here. But you ha'fi let it go."

Evie returned the spirit's smile through her tears. "Thank you for everything, Sekesu."

The two of them held each other closely and the chorus died down, leaving instead the raucous singing of tree frogs and crickets.

"Come now," Sekesu said softly. "I'll be with you all the way."

Evie slowed her breath, refocused, and saw beyond the physical world. She could see the spirit thread – from the larimar itself where Sekesu's magic resided, right through the worlds, to where Sekesu had been summoned from. Evie understood that Sekesu was only here because *she* maintained the thread that bound her. Her spirit had called out to the hero, and now her spirit had to let the hero return.

"Dispel."

The larimar glowed an ocean blue in Evie's hands as Sekesu's magic reacted to her own. Sekesu smiled again as she faded from the physical world – the summoning undone.

# Chapter Twenty-Five

# THE LIBRARY

## Evie

Evie lay awake for a while that night, thinking about their dangerous journey onwards to Nanny Town. She, Arthur and Clementine had been chaperoned back to Chief Marcia's house by several of her best Maroon warriors. And there was a heavier presence of warriors watching the roads, and lurking in the bush, awaiting any attack from the Heartless.

As sleep refused to come, Evie drew out the photograph of her parents and her infant self from underneath her pillow, angling it to catch the light of the lamp outside their window. She had so much to say to them now, it only fuelled her fire. She wanted to master her magic – to speak with them. But there was so much more at stake. First she needed to get to the amethyst, summon Nanny and defeat Blackheart Man, La Diablesse and their legion of duppies. It felt daunting now, without Sekesu. Evie wished she had as much faith in herself as the earth enchanter had.

She must have eventually dropped off to sleep again because soon Clementine was knocking for her and Arthur. But the anxious feeling in the pit of her stomach remained.

Guarded by warriors once more, the trio apprehensively walked back to the centre of the town and into the community yard. The sweet smell of plantain frying in the kitchen was more than welcome. Cai was sitting patiently at a table adorned with fresh fruits – sweet guinep, green coconuts and pineapples. He nodded reservedly as they joined him.

"How's the arm?" Evie asked.

"Almost good as new," said Cai, rotating his wrist and conjuring a flame in his palm to punctuate the fact.

"Healers are pretty amazing, hm?" Evie glanced at Clementine, and she bashfully returned her smile.

"Speaking of healers, where's Mucaro?" Arthur asked.

"Making a phone call to Nanny Town," Cai replied. "Many of our shaman comrades have already gone ahead to protect the amethyst. The sooner we get there, the sooner Evie can try and summon Nanny. Then we can fight."

Evie noted Cai's doubt in her abilities, having used the word "try". It unnerved her, even if she, too, was uncertain.

"After breakfast, o' course," said Arthur drily.

Cai shook his head and actually slipped a grin. "Yes, after breakfast, yuh craven cat. The mountain hike will be about twelve hours after all."

"How many hours?!" Arthur exclaimed. "I'm hitching a lift on one o' you."

"Um…Evie?"

All heads swung in Clementine's direction and her voice quietened further.

"I'd like to show you some things in the museum's library. To help you understand spirit waker magic."

Evie smiled broadly, immediately feeling a lift in her mood. "Mi appreciate you, Clem," she said, getting up from the bench. She shot a glance at Arthur, who was watching them curiously. "Don't nyam all the plantain, Arthur."

"Mi promise nothing," he replied with a swish of the tail.

Evie ran her hands over the beautiful Sankofa symbol on the double doors of the museum, before Clementine pushed them open.

"It's a whole heap o' weight on your shoulders, so mi want to help you any way mi can," said Clementine, rifling through shelves and drawing out books.

"Thank you. That's so thoughtful," Evie replied. She watched how Clementine's eyes lit up, magnified under her large glasses. Clearly books were something she was passionate about.

Clementine placed a stack of books on the table before rushing back to get more: *Spirit Magic*, *Greatest Spirit Wakers in History*, *Understanding the Spirit World and other Impossible*

*Feats…* Evie leafed through the contents, before settling on the pages she thought would be most helpful.

*At the time of writing, spirit wakers make up around four per cent of the mage population in Xaymaca.*

Evie was in awe. She knew her magic was rare but not that rare. Enchanters were the largest percentage, followed by healers, with diviners the second least common.

*Known abilities: acting as a medium to the spirit world, spirit projection (also known as spirit state), spirit summoning, spirit reading (also known as spirit sight). There have been accounts of spirit reincarnation (see also rebirth), but legitimacy is near impossible to prove.*

Spirit wakers were powerful mages, but as well as the strengths, Evie wanted to learn the weaknesses. She had to, if they were to gain an advantage over Blackheart Man and his duppies. Evie moved from text to text, scouring the pages for insight. She stopped when she got to one small hardback titled *Obeah: A Brief Introduction to Ancestral Magic*. But as her eyes landed on the author's name, her breath snatched and a feeling of pure dread clutched at her. She dropped the book with a thunk and stepped back.

"What is it?" asked Clementine. "Evie, what's wrong?"

But Evie's heart was racing so fast that it seemed to be taking all of her focus just to try to slow it down. "It's her," she said eventually.

"Who?"

"La Diablesse." Evie picked up the book again and leafed

through the pages to be sure that her eyes weren't playing tricks. *Lana Walters*. There was no mistaking it. "That's her real name."

The blood drained from Clementine's face. "I…I've read this many times and…"

"It's okay, Clem, it's okay. Mi think that… Mi think that something musta happened to her. To turn her into the devil we know." A morbid curiosity took the place of Evie's fear and she scanned through page after page. "Perhaps there could be clues in here about why La Diablesse changed, and how we can beat her."

"Mind if mi help out?"

The sudden voice shattered the museum's quiet and nearly made Evie drop the book again. "Cai…"

"Mi was supposed to tell you to come and eat before we set off. But it sounds like you've found something useful here." The young shaman reached out for the book and studied it, brows meeting in a frown.

"Mi think Lana Walters came to Obeah late in her life," said Evie. "The way this is written, it's as though she's on the outside looking in…"

"She was," said Cai, delving through the text. "She stayed with the Accompong Maroons as a scholar. She learned so much from us, only to use it all against us."

More pieces of a puzzle were slotting into place for Evie. Back in Ochi, Mr Bennett had warned them all how formidable Blackheart Man was.

*He'll make it so you're happy to let darkness in.*

Lana Walters had lost a daughter…

"Blackheart Man awakened her ancestral magic, didn't he?" Evie asked.

Cai nodded, passing the hardback book back to her.

"Mi don't think this was solely academic research," she said. "La Diablesse was searching for a spirit waker for personal reasons. That's how Blackheart Man was able to snare her."

"She…wanted to commune with lost ones?" asked Cai awkwardly. Evie realized that it was her own desire to commune with her parents' spirits that had made Cai uncomfortable.

She shook her head and returned to the pile of books, opening *Understanding the Spirit World and other Impossible Feats.* "Not just to commune," she said, pointing out a passage she'd read earlier. "Back in Ochi she talked about researching whether spiritual energy could become a physical bridge between worlds. Mi think she was exploring a way for lost ones to be *reborn.*"

Cai's eyes widened. "Blowing a hole through to the spirit world is a very twisted way of achieving that." Disgust laced his every word. "Blackheart sold her a vision, but the reality is a fate worse than death."

The urgent drone of an abeng suddenly pierced through the air. This was a very different sound from the warm, welcoming tones of the previous day.

Fear dripping from every pore, Evie dared to ask, "Clem, is it an attack? Is it the Heartless?"

When she turned to Evie, Clementine's face was a mask of pure dread. She ran from the museum, leaving both Evie and Cai to call after her.

Out in the morning light once again, Evie followed the wails of those who'd been drawn to the horn. She stifled a cry, placing a hand over her mouth. The door to the chief's office was wide open and on the floor, lying in blood, was Omar's body. Marcia knelt beside him.

Mucaro thundered towards the group, his expression grave. "It's the larimar," he said in a panic. "It's been stolen."

# Chapter Twenty-Six

# BETRAYAL

## Evie

"Wh-what?!" Evie stuttered. It felt like Blackheart Man had snatched her spirit clean away from her body.

"How? From right under our noses?!" Cai exclaimed.

Mucaro looked incensed. His eyes darted to the chief's office like the needle of a compass.

Clementine was shaking, her eyes never leaving the open door. "Is Omar… Is he…?"

"Not if we have anything to say about it, Clementine. Come on." Mucaro marched over, making a pathway through the stunned crowd that had gathered, as the abeng still blasted.

Chief Marcia cradled Omar's limp body. He'd taken a blow to the head and Evie grimaced at the sight of all the blood covering his face. Marcia glanced up in desperation as the group entered the room.

"He still has a pulse. Come, Clem!" she urged her daughter, and Clementine got to work on healing Omar immediately. Marcia's face bore the weight of it all.

"Mi think we ha'fi accept the probability," she said sourly, "that we have traitors in our midst."

"Without a doubt," Cai agreed.

"Where are the other captains?" a Maroon with tied-back locs asked.

"We haven't seen Mikey in two days," Marcia answered. "And just like yesterday morning, Wilfred is nowhere to be seen."

"Do you think…?"

"Whoever did this," said Marcia, "they've taken the larimar, left our strongest captain on the brink of death and have a head start on us."

"We'll track them!" declared another Maroon, her aura glowing the red of a diviner.

"Wi… Wil…"

Every soul in the room silenced, as in front of them a barely conscious Omar tried to speak, his voice a whisper.

"Omar! Omar, what is it?" Marcia asked. "Who did this to you?"

"Wil…fred…"

Marcia's deep brown eyes hardened, taking in the full extent of her captain's betrayal. Her fists clenched until they shook. The Maroon with locs banged his own fist against a wall and cursed.

"We'll send out a team of a dozen to hunt him," said Marcia. "Wilfred has the larimar and he might not be alone – we'll take no chances. Robin," she turned to the man with the locs, "you'll lead one half of the squad. And Joy," she turned to the diviner, "you'll lead the other six."

"Take us with you!"

Everyone stared in shock as Evie spoke.

"Mi want to help track Wilfred down. Mi can't let him get away with taking the larimar and turning his back on you all."

"You have no experience fighting in the bush – in the mountains. It's far too dangerous," Mucaro cut in.

"But you *do*," said Evie. "And mi trust you." She locked eyes with Cai. "I trust both of you with my life."

Cai's features softened. What he was thinking, Evie could only guess. But her words had taken him by surprise.

"Mi can help track enemies with my spirit sight," Evie insisted. "I'm the *only* one here who can."

"We need to get you to Nanny Town. That's the priority," said Mucaro. "Because the Heartless could soon have three gemstones. We absolutely can't let them get the fourth."

"Then Robin's team will get you there safely," Marcia followed up. "Joy's squad will focus on tracking Wilfred down."

Evie accepted the decision of the chief and nodded her agreement. Whether she could have been helpful in the hunt or not, if she was captured their plan to defeat Blackheart Man would fall to pieces.

"Everyone get into camouflage and head out," Marcia

commanded. "Wilfred may be carrying an injury, but he knows the mountain trails like he knows his own face. Mi daren't think about who he's meeting out there. There's no time to lose, but be careful."

Galvanized, they poured out of Marcia's office, every step purposeful. But Evie came to an abrupt halt when Arthur darted in front of her. His slender body trembled.

"Evie, if we carry on there really will be no turning back," he said. "I'm a deadweight in this body. Mi can't do nothin' to help against Blackheart Man. Mi lawd, even in my own body mi nah have magic!"

Evie tried not to panic. She needed him. "What if there's an opportunity to steal the larimar back again? You're no deadweight, brudda."

"You're living in a fantasy," Arthur argued. "You're all caught up in Obeah, so you can't see we're in over our heads!"

Anger took a hold, because what Arthur was saying might have been true, but Evie didn't want to hear it with so much at stake. "I summoned Sekesu – I can do this. I can summon Nanny too. We need her to win!"

"Evie, Omar was almost killed for this. I just want my friend back and my body back," said Arthur, eyes wide and imploring. "Let's go back to Ochi. Don't do this."

Evie was torn. She didn't want to abandon her friend. But she couldn't abandon the Maroons either. Especially not now.

"This is where I'm from. Mi want to help these people. Mi don't want the Heartless to win!"

"Help *me*, Evie. Mi don't want to die like this – in the body of your hotel cat!"

"Hey." Cai raised his palms, searching for calm. "If we don't get Evie to Nanny Town before the Heartless, and they somehow manage to get hold of the amethyst stone, then you won't have a body. You won't even have a world!"

"Could you, for once, butt out, Cai!" Arthur fumed.

"Arthur, come now, this isn't helping nothin'!" Evie said, stepping between the pair. "Mi know, Arthur. You never asked for any o' this. You just want to leave. Mi heard what you said to Mucaro that night at the safehouse."

"I…" Arthur's large cat eyes blinked, then he lowered his head so that his hat covered them, avoiding her gaze. "Mi just want to go back to Ochi, where my body is."

Evie crouched down to be closer to him. "We don't have the freedom now to do what we want to, Arthur—"

"It's easy for you to say. You're happy *here*. You belong *somewhere*." He dropped his head again and wiped his eyes with the back of a paw.

Evie reached out instinctively to hold him, but hesitated. Arthur had no family waiting for him, and he no longer had a home at The Mangrove either. It must have felt like she was slipping away from him too. She could feel the thread of their friendship unravelling. What could she say, or do, to hold it together?

"If it makes you feel any better, I spend my days training to take dead people – mostly kicking and screaming – to a place they might not be ready to go," Cai offered. "So mi know a thing or two about sacrifice. And right now, it's not a question of what the world can give to us. It's about what we can give to the world."

Evie half expected Arthur to react angrily again. But he was silent this time. Cai crouched to a squat – the three of them sharing a pensive silence for a moment.

"Mi know from…experience," Cai continued, "that you have plenty to offer."

"You need to get over the chicken wings, man," Arthur murmured.

"Mi nah talking about that!" said Cai, annoyed. "Mi talking about the safehouse. If it weren't for you sneaking through with the fire, well…we'd all be destined for duppies."

Evie nodded vigorously. She could feel the energy changing. "You're a thief, Arthur. A master thief," she said, shuffling her body closer to him. "And I'll never make you deny who you are again."

Arthur's tail batted the ground once. "You trying to sweet-talk me, Evie Bell?"

"Is it working or nuh?"

Arthur let out a dry laugh. "Cho…"

"Come on, Arthur. Mi need you with me," she said, one hand over his paw. "If mi ha'fi go to hell and back, then there's no one I'd rather be with."

Arthur sighed so deeply it sounded like a hiss. "Body back and duppy destruction, or stuck as a cat and save the world?"

He kissed his teeth for good measure. "All right," he said. "Into the depths of hell we go. Quick, before mi change my mind."

Arthur let out a yelp as Evie smooshed him into a hug. A moment later, his furry body relaxed, and he nuzzled back into her.

# Chapter Twenty-Seven

# THE BLUE MOUNTAINS

## Cai

Smeared with mud and stripped back to a sleeveless khaki vest, Cai waited at the edge of the river with Mucaro and five of the six Maroons from Robin's squad. Across the river was the start of the mountain trail they'd follow to reach Nanny Town and the amethyst stone. Joy and her squad had already crossed and gone ahead in pursuit of Wilfred. Robin's team waited for their leader, Evie and the cat in the porkpie hat to join them.

Ankle deep, Cai stared out at the flowing river. He replayed Evie's words in his head. *I trust you with my life.* For so long, Cai had been marked as a future leader, but this was the first time someone had made him feel like one. He felt...happiness? What was it that Master Mucaro had said? *People reveal their true selves in time...* Cai had put his faith in Evie and Arthur as comrades too. That was why he'd known he had to intervene to keep the pair together. Without Arthur, Evie's focus would have been shattered, and they needed her at her best to summon Nanny with the amethyst.

"They're here," one of the Maroons called out.

Cai turned back to the riverbank to see Robin stripped to the waist and smeared in mud for camouflage. An abeng and a regular akrafena were holstered at his hip. Arthur padded along at his heels. And following behind was Evie – also painted in mud. She looked striking, with her hair in the Bantu knots that Sekesu had made, and she wore a sleeveless khaki top similar to his with black shorts. She looked...like a Maroon warrior. The squad members, approving, greeted her as their own. Evie locked eyes with Cai. She looked more serious now than he'd seen her before. He gave her a determined thumbs up, and she nodded back with the shadow of a smile on her lips.

"Let's cross," said Robin. "No time for delays."

The river water at their point of crossing was shallow enough with the right steps, but it still lapped up to the adults' thighs and Cai's waist. He heard a struggle behind him and caught Evie fighting not to be washed away by the current.

"Fix up and pay attention to where you're stepping!" Arthur shrieked from up on her shoulders.

"I'm trying!"

"Well try harder. Mi nah know how many lives mi have left at this point!"

"Step sideways, instead of forwards. Face the current like

this," Cai called. He stopped to show Evie how he wasn't being pushed by the rapidly flowing water, and she followed his example. "There you go."

They continued to cross together, Evie growing in confidence with each step.

"Looks like you saved my life already," she joked.

Cai's face felt like it was burning, and not just because of the blazing sun above them. He looked every way but at Evie. "Well, don't thank me yet," he muttered awkwardly, containing a smile.

Once the squad had crossed, Robin led them up a trail into the dense forest. They travelled barefoot and in silence, so as not to warn enemies of their movements. The lush trees provided temporary shelter from the sun, and the sound of a spring and placid waterfalls, leading down to the river below, soundtracked their steps.

Cai kept Evie and Arthur in front of him, flanking protectively at the rear alongside Mucaro. Everyone was silent, knowing that the forest was as much a place for the enemy to hide in as it was for them. But Cai sensed a mountain of tension in Evie and Arthur's quiet steps. He understood how frightening this quest was for them, and that they would need his reassurance. Not as a leader, but as a friend. He'd never had friends before, what with his dedication to training. Unless you counted...Jujo. His hand reached for the feather necklace over his collarbone. He wouldn't let anyone down like his brother had.

"Don't worry," Cai whispered. "We'll look out for one another, and we'll make it. You'll see."

The day wore on, and although the air became slightly cooler the higher up the mountain they climbed, the path became more arduous. The Maroons had to use their akrafenas to chop through some of the bush. But the hacking stopped when one of the squad up ahead held out a palm, signalling for the others to halt. He'd found something on the ground and beckoned the others closer.

"Blood," he said. "A trail of it leads this way."

"Wilfred was injured, nuh?" said another.

Cai studied the scene with a frown. Something wasn't right. "This is animal blood not human," he said. "There are smaller tracks which stop back here. Something was shot with an arrow, maybe. And these footprints alongside the blood drops are so obvious, it's like someone wants us to follow them."

"Well done, Cai," said Mucaro. "It must be a trap or deflection."

"Which means the real path Wilfred followed is somewhere close," Robin concluded. "We'll take the higher ground to be safe, in case Joy's squad haven't already captured him. Keep your eyes peeled. We don't know who's waiting out here."

"Mi see someone's spirit!" Evie whispered harshly. Her irises had a hint of violet to them. "They're anxious."

Robin turned towards her, eyes wide and urgent.

"Where?"

"They're further along this path. I think they're hiding."

Robin signalled for silence and pointed his squad in separate directions. They melted into the bushes and trees so that if Cai so much as blinked he might lose them altogether.

Mucaro nodded at Cai and they guarded Evie – Mucaro covering the rear and Cai the front.

After a moment they came to a large tree and, sure enough, Wilfred's bulky frame was crouched in a hollow at the bottom.

"Wilfred!" Robin called out. Wilfred shot to his feet as if to run, but glancing left and right he realized he was surrounded. "Where's the larimar?" Robin demanded.

"Just stay back!" Wilfred barked. "Leave this alone, you hear? You've already lost."

One of the Maroons blew his abeng, and Wilfred cursed. It would be heard within a two-mile radius. It was a signal to Joy's team to find them.

"Hand over the larimar right now and don't resist us!" Robin pressed him. "It doesn't have to be this way."

Wilfred scoffed and smiled unnervingly. "Yuh fools! Which other way could it be?"

Before their eyes, Wilfred's smile grew wider and wider still, until he was baring ferocious fangs. Cai stared in horror as the captain's muscular body grew even thicker and his skin rippled. Fur sprouted from his torso, and his shirt was shredded to pieces.

"It can't be…" Mucaro muttered.

But there was no room for disbelief, because a transformed lagahoo was standing right before them. There was a scabby gash across Wilfred's chest from where Mucaro had cut him down at the safehouse days earlier.

Wilfred spread his arms, thrust his powerful head backwards and let out a blood-curdling howl. A moment later there was a distant howl in response, coming from directly behind them.

# Chapter Twenty-Eight

# AMBUSH

## Cai

The revelation of one lagahoo was terrifying enough without there being a second lurking out in the forest too. And the distraction proved disastrous. When Cai turned his attention back to Wilfred, it was already too late for one of the squad members. With both size and speed, Wilfred clawed through an off-guard enchanter who was in his path. The enchanter barely uttered a moan as his body landed in a lifeless heap.

"Delroy!" a squad member yelled for their fallen friend.

Despite his chest wound, Wilfred tore off at pace, avoiding Robin's attempt to bind him with the enchanted roots of the trees he leaped over.

"Two of them together will be trouble. Quick, we can't let him reach his comrade!" a squad member yelled.

"Don't be reckless." Robin tried to urge calm. "There could

be traps. We'll split up." He pointed to two of his remaining four team members. "You go on ahead to Nanny Town with Mucaro, Cai, Evie and Arthur. Evie, use your spirit sight to avoid anyone you sense outside of this group. *Anyone*, you understand?"

"What about you, Robin?" Mucaro asked. He'd hurried over to Delroy's body to check for any signs of life, but Cai could tell from the way his shoulders sagged that there was no hope of saving him.

Robin's expression darkened. He was stowing his grief away to focus on the deadly matter at hand. He gestured to the remaining two squad members. "We're going after the lagahoos. Joy's squad might need the help." With that he blew his abeng again. "We'll get the larimar back. You just get to the amethyst. Go safely!"


Gone was the caution with which the group had moved through the forest before. It was replaced by an urgency to simply make it through alive. Cai had one hand on the grip of his akrafena. The two Maroons led a route away from the common mountain trail. They soon reached an incline where the path had been weathered away by earthquakes past, making it treacherous to climb. Cai jumped up and held out his hand to Evie, pulling her up with him. Mucaro, Arthur and the two Maroons leaped up after them and did their best to forge a safe path along the remnants of the trail.

"Stop!" Evie said, as though the breath was being stolen from her lungs.

Cai heard but the others didn't seem to.

"Master!" Cai didn't want to raise his voice but was left with no choice. He turned back to Evie, noticing once again the purple hue of her irises.

"Mi felt this before," Evie said. "He's here, right here with us."

"Who?" Cai asked.

Evie's eyes were apologetic. "Jujo."

Cai tensed up. Was he going to have to face his brother right here and now?

"Not him again!" Arthur whimpered.

One of the Maroons cursed. "We know this forest well, but against a diviner? We won't be able to take him by surprise because he's already predicted our moves!"

"We can't lose confidence. We don't know what he sees, but we know our capabilities. Let's press ahead," said Mucaro.

The Maroon duo nodded and moved on swiftly. Cai hoped that someday he could be half the natural leader Mucaro was.

Cautiously, they carried on until they reached a crescent. Cai knew that if he was going to ambush a foe, the high ground and a blind crescent would be an ideal place to do so. The two Maroons split and sneaked into the thickets to stay hidden while Cai waited with Mucaro, Evie and Arthur, who was pressed against Evie's leg. After a moment, one of the Maroons appeared above them. He gave a thumbs up.

"All clea—"

Cai gasped as the Maroon disappeared into the ground. A pitfall. Then a shriek rang out, making his arm hairs stand on end, before it broke off abruptly. They had lost the protection of the second Maroon too. Cai and Mucaro edged towards Evie. Up at the top of the crescent, where the trap had been sprung, Jujo emerged. He was stripped to the waist and smeared in dirt. He sheathed his akrafena and looked down on them all.

"Jujo!" Mucaro called, but the diviner held up his palm for silence.

"No more lectures, Mucaro. I've already had to unlearn everything you taught me."

Mucaro hissed air through his teeth. Former master and former pupil locked eyes as rams lock horns. Cai's fear mounted at the thought of losing either of them. But could a fight be avoided when Jujo had just killed two Maroons without hesitation?

"The lagahoos!" Evie was looking back down the trail, her eyes gleaming wild violet. "I can sense their spirits. If they're here, then what happened to…? What happened to Robin's…?"

Cai's heart sank. Robin's squad were defeated? This was bad. "No, there must be someone out there," he reasoned. "Joy's squad might have—"

A thunk of something landing and sliding down the trail stopped Cai mid-sentence. It was an abeng. The horn that had belonged to Joy. Cai looked back up the path at his brother, who shook his head pityingly. Then Cai knew the situation was dire.

"Is this what it's come to, Jujo?" Mucaro sounded pained. "The casual murder of our Maroon comrades? For *that* man?"

"You don't know Blackheart," said Jujo defensively. "To think I wasted so much time living the way of the shamans. Blackheart is the truth while you all live in your lies. I saw everything."

"You saw whatever he wanted you to!" Mucaro snapped. "He's a master at bending desires to fit his needs. He's using you for your abilities, Jujo."

"Don't yuh dare patronize me." Jujo scowled. "You're the ones obsessed with control."

"We are duty bound, Jujo. Like our ancestors before us—"

"And that's the first lie you tell yourselves. Just because it's been one way doesn't mean it should stay that way for ever," Jujo argued. A large vein throbbed at his temple. "For decades, you put the fear of God into your apprentices. You stole my childhood and you've stolen his too." He jabbed a finger at Cai, whose heart raced at the wild look in his older brother's eyes. "*And* that's not even mentioning how we treat the spirits of the dead. Acting like boogeymen when they're just trying to understand their world beyond ours. Where's the compassion, Mucaro? Tell me!"

Cai understood his brother's rage. It was hard, living up to the expectations of the Society of Shamans. Strict traditions going back hundreds of years to the early settlers. Living simply to ferry the dead. He'd been fighting duppies when other children hadn't even learned to tie their shoelaces. And Cai recalled Evie's shock when they'd stopped days earlier to send the lost spirit to the realm of the dead. He was seeing, now, how shamans appeared to those outside of their closely-knit community.

They brought fear.

For the first time as an apprentice shaman, Cai felt... remorse.

He looked to Mucaro desperately. His master was silent but radiating fury.

"Someone has to protect this world from duppies." Mucaro's voice was quieter now, resolved. "The threat is real for every spirit we ha'fi send to the realm of the dead. Someone has to stop the dead from staying in our world and becoming corrupted. That is our duty, as well you know."

"What I know is that by tearing down the wall between realms, the Heartless will usher in a new world." Jujo held his head high. "You think that the shamans protect this world – that you're somehow great defenders of freedom. No, you're all standing in the way of freedom. You're not the shepherds, you're the wolves!"

There was a whooshing sound through the trees and Wilfred, in his lagahoo form, landed beside Jujo. He carried the pendant, holding the shimmering larimar in his clawed grip, and handed it to Jujo. The former shaman placed it around his own neck, and Cai heard Evie utter a strangled cry.

"Why, Wilfred?" Evie uttered, her voice paper thin.

"Because my grandparents and their parents can't believe

what Xaymaca has become. They devoted their lives to magic, and now it's falling by the wayside on our watch," said Wilfred defiantly. "What was the point in using ancestral magic to free ourselves from slavery only for magic to be rejected by the masses today? The ancestors will return and show us the way again, thanks to Blackheart. It's time to start over."

A scraping, clawing sound came from behind them, and the second lagahoo appeared at the bottom of the trail. Cai stared aghast at the wounded wolf-man. His body was covered in patches of red-pink skin and charred brown fur. The lagahoo's face was scorched on one side so only one eye appeared to be fully functioning. Cai flinched. The lagahoo he thought he'd taken care of in his fire trap at the safehouse was still very much alive, and glaring at him as though he were his next meal.

Jujo leaned in to Wilfred, tapping at the larimar. "I'm taking this to Blackheart. Get rid of Mucaro and the cat. Then bring the shaman boy and the girl with you." He turned and started back over the crescent.

"Running away again, Jujo?" Mucaro called. Cai stared at his master. How would taunting Jujo help get the upper hand? Then he noticed that Jujo had stopped in his tracks. Cai understood Mucaro's thinking. He believed Jujo's ego was a weakness.

"See, you think you know me, Mucaro. But you don't," Jujo replied, icily calm. "You can't goad me. I'll let my friends take care of you. See you in the new world."

And with that, he disappeared.

"Brother!" called the seared lagahoo, his face a snarling mask of rage. "Mi think we'll tell Blackheart there was a little accident and sadly the fire enchanter boy didn't make it back with us."

Cai's heart pounded so hard he could almost taste the blood.

"No problem, Mikey," Wilfred replied, flashing his fangs. "He's all yours. Mi have a bone to pick with the man who slashed up mi chest, anyhow."

Mucaro drew his akrafena and spoke in hushed tones.

"Cai. Take Evie and Arthur, and get to Nanny Town as fast as you can."

"Master, no!" Cai protested.

"Don't question the order. There's no time!" Mucaro reached into his inside pockets and drew out a packet of white starch – arrowroot. Cai gasped. The root would double his strength, but would quickly take its toll. Once the effects wore off, he'd be near incapacitated from the exertion. Mucaro was willing to go that far… No, he had no choice *but* to go that far.

"Listen, Cai. You have to bring your brother to the light. Only you can help him atone and make this right. It has to be you. You're ready, Cai." Mucaro quickly devoured the root and his body emitted a verdant aura. "Protect Evie. Secure Nanny's amethyst. If we can't bring back Nanny to stop the Heartless, everything is lost."

"But…mi can't just leave you to fight them alone, master."

"Cairi!" Mucaro bellowed. "After everything we've been through, do you still doubt me?"

Pain fell in waves. He wanted to stay – to fight. To be by his master's side as Mucaro had been by his. "N-no, master, but—"

"I won't lose," Mucaro insisted. "I'll catch up to you as soon as I'm able. Now go!"

Cai backed away as the lagahoos charged. True to his word, Mikey tore up the pathway – claws brandished for Cai's neck. But Mucaro slipped past with incredible speed to intercept the deadly blow. Fuelled by the power of the arrowroot, Mucaro struck first with force – uppercutting the wolf-man and taking him off his feet.

Cai grabbed Evie's arm with one hand and cast an enormous fire wall with the other, to block Wilfred's pursuit and create a veil of escape for Evie, Arthur and himself. They fled deep into the forest, the sound of Mucaro's ferocious battle with the lagahoos echoing back to them from the trees.

## Evie

Following Cai and Arthur's desperate lead, Evie ran. Fear of the lagahoos gave them all wings. Tears pricked at her eyes as her spirit sight returned to normal sight. She had seen into Mucaro's soul. And when he had said that he'd catch up to them, he'd known it was a promise he could never keep.

# Chapter Twenty-Nine

# BLACKHEART'S SHROUD

## Evie

They stopped running only once exhaustion had overtaken the power of adrenaline. Everything ached – feet, arms, chest… spirit. Evie hadn't said much to either of the boys, and vice-versa. But she'd needed to stop, feeling a shell of her usual self. Arthur – in cat form – was naturally quicker than both humans, but better in bursts than long distances, and had been reliant on Cai to lead the way.

They found shelter by a set of gushing waterfalls. The mountain water was fresh and inviting – the first taste was the sweetest in the world to parched lips. Evie dipped into a large, bubbling pool, longing to be cooled and soothed before setting another foot along the trail.

Showing a little more restraint, Cai splashed water over his face alongside Arthur, who'd developed a fear of water beyond dipping his tongue in to cool down. Cai found a space for them by the waterfalls, as hidden as possible from the view of the surrounding paths. Realizing she was more exposed, Evie reluctantly left the frothing waterhole and joined her friends to sit and rest.

Cai reached into his duffel bag and handed a saltfish patty to Arthur, and a sandwich of sweet coco bread with a vegetable patty jammed between to Evie. While many considered this a pauper's meal, to Evie right there and then it was a feast fit for a queen. She guzzled the pastry, barely pausing for breath, and Cai must have been tired because he didn't cast a withering look her way as she did so.

Above the canopy of trees and cascading falls, the Blue Mountain peak loomed over them.

"We'll follow the Stony River," said Cai. "It'll lead to the town. The mountain peak is to the west, which means we need to keep forging a path eastward along the river."

"So we're close?" Arthur asked.

"Still a way to go yet."

And then the silence returned.

Evie could sense that Cai was overwhelmed by thoughts and feelings.

"Cai," she began. "I'm so sorry about your brother. Chief Marcia told us about…about what happened at Quao's Hall. Jujo turned his back on the shaman and Maroon communities. He helped Blackheart to steal Quao's emerald. This is so hard on you."

Cai glanced at her. He swallowed his coco bread then turned away again with a deep breath.

"That night, at the safehouse… You were upset. You must miss him."

Arthur looked from Evie to Cai quizzically, but stayed silent.

"I do. But it's not just that," said Cai. "Jujo broke our parents' hearts; broke Master Mucaro's heart. I've had to grow up with it all hanging over us like a bad fog."

Evie nodded, wanting him to have the space to continue talking.

"The way of the shamans isn't easy – growing up becoming numb to death, because we ha'fi deal with it every day. And with Jujo, he was marked as a future chief with all the talent he had. But Mucaro said the praise he was given went to his head. He was a gifted diviner so questioned the decisions of those above him. He often saw things his own way and believed in himself over his seniors…even his own master."

Cai stopped. He wrapped the cloth back over his nearly finished sandwich – appetite gone. Arthur sniffed at it, pupils widening before gaining some self-control.

"Blackheart Man would have seen into Jujo's spirit. Must have known exactly what to say to make him feel valued and special. But whatever hold Blackheart has over my brother, I know that Jujo's always cared for me." Cai brandished his necklace with the small feather. "This is the only thing I have left of him…until I can bring him back. I can help him see straight. It won't be easy at first, but if he helps us defeat

Blackheart he can go some way to redeeming himself. Then maybe...maybe we can make our family whole again."

Evie was crushed. No one should have to carry that much pressure.

"It hurts, doesn't it?" Arthur's voice was small. "When all you've known and loved is taken away, and it's completely outta your control." He sat back on his hind legs. "Mi understand you now, Cai. And even after everything, you're still willing to put your life on the line for others."

Evie placed a comforting hand over Cai's. "It's been a long time since I had a real family like yours. But I understand wanting to feel whole again." Cai met her gaze and she glimpsed something like acceptance in his watery eyes. She placed her other hand over Arthur's paws. "Although, perhaps family doesn't ha'fi mean being related by blood. Perhaps it's bringing joy to each other's worlds and standing by each other no matter what we face. I'll never abandon you, Arthur."

It looked as though it was taking everything in Arthur's tiny body not to cry. But there was a twinkle in his glistening eyes.

"We'll put an end to the Heartless. Together."


The trio set off again, along the river. Fretful minutes became tense hours, and evening drew in, gradually robbing them of light under the cover of trees. Evie's body ached beyond any tiredness she'd felt before. If the Heartless were to attack, she wouldn't have anything left to defend herself.

They soon heard rushing water ahead. Looking at each other with hope, they picked up the pace as much as their bodies would allow. They came to another waterfall – this one several times larger than before.

"This is it," said Cai, signalling for them to stop before they left the safety of the leafy thicket. Beneath the falls they'd be fully exposed in a large, open pool. "It worried me that only Jujo came for us earlier and not La Diablesse or Blackheart. The last thing we need is to face an ambush. Let's sit tight for a minute and observe."

An abeng sounded, low and long, causing Evie to flinch. She tried to locate the source of the sound and saw a man at the very top of the falls.

"A Maroon!" said Cai, relieved. He stepped out towards the pool, hands to the sky, and called up to the man.

"Hello! We've come from Sekesu's Town as friends of Chief Marcia. Please show us how to enter. We ha'fi speak with your chief right away!"

The Maroon watched the pair from above before pulling back from view. Cai's arms lowered and he stared up in confusion. But then the water of the falls in front of them slowly split apart and the rock face behind it opened up – a secret doorway! Evie gawked. There were no words to describe such a marvel. The pool in front of them parted down the centre, forging a tunnel directly to the opening in the rockface. The Maroon they'd seen above must be a powerful water enchanter.

"Let's go," said Cai with renewed energy.

He stormed through the shallow water and Evie trekked after him with Arthur digging his tiny claws into her shoulders. Evie marvelled at the makeshift tunnel. The split walls of water sprayed apart like fountains towering above her. Soon she was underneath the separated falls. The spray met her skin, and sunlight through the water drops caused a rainbow effect in the air. Evie found another gear, eager to discover what lay beyond.

On the other side of the falls, the cavern continued downwards in a tunnel of stone and dry earth. There were plants, moving vines and creepers all across the ceiling and walls.

"This is just like the mangrove!" said Arthur, springing back down to the ground. "Must be an earth enchanter here too."

The tunnel came to an end, but a large shaft of light poured from an opening above. A towering wooden structure stretched upwards and after a moment Evie realized that it was a lift.

The base was constructed from several logs with enough space for a dozen or so people. There was a pulley system that made use of rope and mountain stone to raise the platform or lower it. Cai glanced at Evie and Arthur with a weary smile.

"We made it," he said. "Now let's find the chief and get you to the amethyst."

They stepped onto the platform, Cai pulling at a lever that set the pulley off, lowering the stone weight and sending the platform shooting upwards. The acceleration caught Evie off guard and she steadied herself. As they ascended, a mechanical low humming grew ever louder. Then the platform slowed and emerged into daylight.

The trio found themselves on a raised platform sculpted from stone, and beyond it was Nanny Town itself with its colour-washed buildings and a large clock tower overhead.

But there was no time to take in the scenery.

Evie startled at the uncanny welcoming party in front of her. Rows and rows of men and women stood to attention like an army. They were living statues – not one of them turned their heads in acknowledgment of Evie and Cai's presence. Evie knew immediately that something was wrong, and her relief at making it to Nanny Town ebbed away, leaving only fear.

Lit by tall bamboo torches with flames flickering in the dying light of day, a makeshift walkway was cleared through the centre of the group – the two sides facing each other across it. There were the Maroons of Nanny Town; there were shamans adorned in the same style of off-white robes and loose black trousers as Mucaro and Cai. But most shocking of all was that Evie recognized several of the mages who stood there: an elderly healer with a calabash tied to her hip, a top-hat-wearing enchanter…

They had been at the Myal nights before.

Arthur hissed, his back arched at the ominous threat. The remaining strength left Evie's legs and she fell against Cai, whose shaking arms held her up. The sun was setting beyond the mountains surrounding the town and shadows were cast across the stone-slabbed ground.

It was from those shadows that La Diablesse emerged, her wide-brimmed hat shrouding her face.

"No," Cai whispered, and Evie felt the air leave his chest. Her heart sank further when she saw Jujo, still in his camouflage, approaching them down the walkway.

They had no backup – the Maroons who'd left Sekesu's Town with them were likely all defeated. Evie turned desperately to Cai for a plan, but his fighting spirit seemed to have been sapped. They were exhausted; they were outnumbered; they were afraid.

"Evelyn Bell, and Jujo's younger brother, I presume." A deep voice reverberated from somewhere above them.

Atop the whitewashed bell tower stood a man dressed in a black cloak. His face was hidden by a horrifying ram's skull mask – the horns curved threateningly at the sides.

"Akwaaba," he said, with the hint of a smile in his voice – his mocking tone completely twisting the words of welcome.

It was him. The source of this cycle of pain.

Blackheart Man pulled the rope in his hand and rang the bell. Each row of living statues turned their heads sharply towards Evie, Cai and Arthur. Pinprick pupils were all but lost to the whites of their eyes, every one of them possessed by Blackheart's duppies.

Blackheart Man brandished all four gemstones – the coral, the emerald, the larimar and the amethyst – in his hands as the bell's chime reverberated across the town.

"You're just in time for the great summoning."

# Chapter Thirty

# NANNY TOWN

## Evie

"We'll summon this island's legendary heroes right here, in the first Maroon settlement, Nanny Town. There couldn't be a more fitting place."

Evie could barely stand to listen – could not believe that they had failed in stopping the Heartless. She felt nauseous.

"With the power of their combined magic, we'll bridge this world to the spirit world. Cudjoe, Quao, Queen Nanny…" Blackheart Man laughed – a low rattle underneath the mask. "Mi regret that mi never did meet Sekesu when *you* summoned her, Evelyn. So, how 'bout an encore?"

"No!" Evie yelled.

"Actually, yes," said Blackheart Man. "And you may have noticed that as well as La Diablesse and Jujo by my side, mi have the most powerful mages in Xaymaca at my disposal."

The army of possessed turned on their heels, now facing Evie, Arthur and Cai head on. They were like puppets with Blackheart Man pulling the invisible strings.

"I'm going to retrieve the Four Heroes right now. I would like for you all to witness the birth of the new world. However, if you try and oppose me, I'll do much worse than have you possessed." Blackheart sat cross-legged, and his head lolled as he projected his spirit from his body to follow the magic threads of the Four Heroes.

"Jujo!" Cai yelled. "How could you watch him do this to our shaman comrades?"

"This goes deeper than blood!" Jujo snapped. "Just because a village raises you, doesn't mean it should control you. If that village stands in the way of what's just and right, then that village deserves to burn."

Cai lowered his head and covered his face with his hands. "Evie," he whispered. "Don't turn this way, look straight ahead."

Evie did so and listened.

"You ha'fi stop Blackheart from completing the summoning. Dispel it, just like you did with Sekesu last night."

Evie sighed. She had nothing left with which to fight. Cai fell to his knees, it would look to the Heartless as though he were accepting defeat, but in reality he was keeping his face covered to speak to Evie in secret.

"The food we ate back at the waterfall, there were cerasee leaves sprinkled into your coco bread, and chillies in mine.

That should give us something! You focus on Blackheart, and I'll…I'll do what I can to stop the others."

Evie looked up at the looming tower – at the powerful spirit waker she'd need to contend with. The gems in Blackheart's hands illuminated his terrifying mask, but his body was completely still, lightly sparking violet. Evie would confronting him outside of their physical world. Alone.

Arthur nipped at her hand, and the shock brought Evie back from the eye of her anxious storm.

"Don't forget, you're a daughter of these mountains," he said. "You can do it. Take care of his spirit and I'll climb the tower and steal the gemstones back! It has to be now while his body is vacant."

"Arthur…" Evie hesitated.

"Don't worry about me," Arthur insisted. His shining eyes were determined. "It'll be child's play."

Evie returned his stare. She had to believe in her friends. In herself. What would Ms Bell say if she were here? Her headstrong mama would probably tell her to fix up and focus. And Sekesu – her parting words came to mind:

*I'll be with you all the way.*

She clenched her fists, the power of love proving stronger than her fear. She needed to focus.

Evie sat back on her heels and her spirit stepped out beyond her body, into infinite light.

\*   \*   \*

She found Blackheart's thread within seconds. The energy his spirit emitted was pure malice and cold ambition. His back was to her, arms spread and reaching out to the world beyond. He acknowledged Evie's spirit with utter disbelief when she appeared beside him, palms out and pushing back.

"You!" From beneath the ram's mask, Blackheart's eyes darted around in surprise. He'd clearly had no idea that Evie could use spirit state too and hadn't been expecting her to challenge him head on. In a physical battle Evie wouldn't have stood a chance, but with her spirit she'd give everything she had.

Blackheart was connected to hundreds of spirit threads. His incredible powers were vast, but this surely meant that he had his hands full? There were thick, silvery threads for all the duppies he'd summoned from the spirit world, and the live hosts that those duppies controlled. And there were also four colourful threads – red, green, blue, purple – from the gemstones. It was those that Evie needed to seize, before a link to the spirit world could be forged, and the Four Heroes were summoned.

With a fierce cry she took hold of the four threads, willing her own energy to break Blackheart's connection. But then came the strangest sensation.

Her spirit was glowing purple, and it felt as though her energy had trebled. Blackheart Man was awestruck.

"How can this be?"

Evie realized then that the magic of the amethyst – Queen

Nanny's magic – was flooding through her. She had to summon her! The thread to the amethyst was connected to her spirit now, but try as she might, she couldn't find a path to the spirit world.

Blackheart's magic visibly dimmed in contrast to her own – his purple aura waning. Evie cussed as she struggled to locate Nanny's spirit thread in the realm of the dead. Right now, with Blackheart weakened, she needed to strike. But if she couldn't summon the spirit of Nanny herself, she could at least dent his magic using Nanny's amethyst power. The spirit threads surrounding Blackheart Man snaked around him. He tried to clutch back at the four gemstone threads with one hand, and a colossal tug of war began.

Evie could feel Blackheart's power surging again. The element of surprise was gone, and he wasn't taking her lightly. The colourful gemstone threads strengthened in his grip with every passing second. Blackheart's eyes narrowed beneath the horrifying mask, as if sensing the turning of the tide and silently berating her for daring to challenge him.

Evie was shaking with the strain of holding off the powerful mage. She made a desperate plea to the spirit world, focusing her thoughts on the blue thread. In response, the larimar glowed brightly alongside the amethyst. This had to do it! Evie felt the power building and let her spirit energy bloom.

In a burst of blinding light, Blackheart's connection to the gemstone threads shattered.

"No!" he wailed as the colours faded into the white light.

He glared at Evie before turning his attention back to the physical world.

Evie followed his gaze. Cai was below, kneeling protectively beside her vacant body. A surge of panic hit her, but she couldn't go back to her body. It wasn't over yet.

Blackheart used the distraction to attack her with a burst of his own spirit energy, and her panic spiralled as she was blown back.

"Mi did warn you not to oppose me!" He'd regained his composure, and the silvery threads controlling the summoned duppies became more rigid. Following a flex of his fingers, Evie could see two of the possessed shamans under his control twitching in the physical world beyond. Her friends were in grave danger. She had to find a way to stop Blackheart Man.

# Chapter Thirty-One

# CAI'S LAMENT

## Cai

Cai side-glanced at Evie's kneeling body and saw that she'd projected. They might have a bit of time before Jujo or La Diablesse noticed, given the distance between them. Blackheart Man was in the same spirit state. That meant that his attention would be divided – it'd be more difficult for him to control the possessed mages *and* complete the summoning. At least, Cai hoped so.

Arthur had slunk away, thankfully without being seen. Cai knew that he and Evie had to buy Arthur enough time to make it to the gemstones undetected.

Suddenly, two possessed shamans broke free from their line and charged towards him and Evie.

His fight started now.

"It's the girl! She's attacking Blackheart in another plane!"

La Diablesse yelled at Jujo, realizing that Blackheart must be under threat to have made this move.

Cai swiftly channelled the live flames from the rows of bamboo torches. He fashioned a protective fire cage that surrounded him and Evie, and blocked off the attacking shamans.

"Cairiiiii!" Jujo roared, joining the possessed shamans in attack.

More possessed Maroons broke free from their lines and attacked Cai. A water enchanter among them called up a great wave from the waterfall below and brought it crashing down on top of them. But Cai only strengthened the cage, the flames turning blue, and the water turning to steam – causing the attackers to step back or else be burned. *Protect Evie,* his master had said. He wouldn't let Mucaro down.

As his arms shook from the strain of holding the cage, a light bloomed beside him. Evie was radiant in a white and violet light. The light exploded in a flash of purple, not only breaking the cage but knocking down the attacking possessed fighters. Cai collapsed, exhausted, and watched in awe as the wave of spirit energy flooded through the rows of possessed mages, who fell like dominoes to the ground.

The raw energy struck the tower on which Blackheart Man stood with so much force that the bell chimed, breaking free of its fixings. It crashed onto the balcony and brought it crumbling down to the ground in a cloud of dust and debris, taking Blackheart with it.

"What in the…?" Cai gasped. He looked back at Evie, who remained in her spirit state, eyes closed and a slight furrow on her brow. What kind of power was this, that a battle taking place on a spiritual plane could be felt in this world?

As the echoes of the bronze bell rang out and masonry collapsed, duppies joined in the hellish noise – shrieking as they were exorcized from the bodies they'd possessed. They dissolved from view, returning to the spirit world.

Murmurs from the Maroons, shamans and mages strewn on the ground became confused cries as they regained control of clouded minds. Jujo and La Diablesse looked just as overawed as Cai felt. How had Evie done this?

A loud crash brought Cai's attention back to the wreckage of the bell tower. His first thought was for Arthur's safety. He managed to turn his head and prop himself up on an elbow, his fear mounting again as Blackheart Man emerged from the wreckage. His mask was cracked on one side, a curved horn now missing and a furious eye glaring over in his direction.

"It's impossible!" Blackheart uttered to himself. He gazed over the men and women he'd once controlled. "Evelyn…" he said resolutely. "You are the key!"

Unlike Blackheart, Evie was unconscious. Her body had slumped to the ground so that Cai wasn't sure whether her spirit had returned or not.

"Evie! Hey!" He shook her shoulders, to no avail. In sheer panic, Cai looked to the shamans in the crowd and yelled.

"Help! Help us! I am Cai of the Leeward Shamans. Friends, please help u—"

The air was knocked out of Cai, immense pressure landing on his back and pinning his body to the ground. He tried to turn his head to see what had caused it. He heard snarling and something sharp dug into his back, causing him to cry out. Claws?

"This...this is too perfect," a familiar voice snarled. Then something landed on the ground by Cai's face with a rattle. "The fate of the master becomes the fate of the student." The lagahoo growled with laughter, and his brother lagahoo howled with him.

It felt as though Cai was falling into some deep and terrible abyss. His eyes widened, flooding with tears.

He was staring at Mucaro's neck beads.

The howl that escaped Cai's throat could have been heard in the spirit world. And as the fire-scorched lagahoo struck him again and again, the pain didn't matter to Cai. It was as though he were elsewhere.

"That's enough!" he heard a voice say. Jujo's voice? "He can't even defend himself."

Cai lay on the ground as an argument ensued, utterly defeated. Soul-tired.

"We're leaving, now!" came the rattle of the voice under the ram's skull mask. "Mi need to recover. La Diablesse – keep the mages restrained in shadow until we're away. We can't fight them all. Jujo, I'll take this boy. You get the girl; we *need* her. She's the one to destroy the barrier."

There were footsteps drawing nearer, before Cai felt his battered body being lifted from the ground. His vision was a kaleidoscope, but the shifting colours were growing darker and darker.

# Chapter Thirty-Two

# DEEPER THAN BLOOD

## Cai

When Cai came round, he felt the heat of the morning sun on his face and tried shielding his eyes with his arm. It was then he realized, with a stab of fear, that he was chained – metal cuffs round his wrists and arms over his head. As he struggled, he winced from a pain in his ribs. He found that his feet were chained, too, and the clash with the Heartless came rushing back to him. The lagahoos. Mucaro's beads. He wept for his master, knowing that he had abandoned him to a dreadful fate.

But after a moment, his thoughts turned to his friends. Evie, where was she? And had Arthur survived the collapsed clock tower?

Eyes having adjusted to the light, he checked his surroundings. He was in the ruins of a small old building. The roof was long gone, and parts of the whitewashed walls on all sides had crumbled away too, meaning he could see out to the surrounding land. The overgrown lawn around him suggested he was on an estate somewhere. The sky had a reddish hue and Cai saw, as well as felt, the rift where the Heartless were tearing through the fabric of the worlds. It was almost as though he could taste death in the air. Despite Evie sending the duppies back to the spirit world, and stopping Blackheart Man from summoning the Four Heroes there and then, he was obviously determined to finish what he'd started. Cai's dread mounted and he struggled again to break his chains, groaning as the metal bit into his skin.

He stopped as he heard footsteps approaching. Cai steeled himself for further punishment, his head still throbbing from where the lagahoo had clobbered him. His heart pounded faster as Jujo stepped through a gaping chasm in the wall.

Jujo stood regarding Cai in silence for a moment. Without a word, the brothers were able to share their feelings: Cai's disappointed glower and Jujo's judgemental stare.

Jujo was the first to break the deadlock. "Mi really didn't want it to come to this." He walked towards the far wall where Cai was chained, and sat down beside him. He held a cup up for Cai to sip, but he turned his head away. "Don't be a child. Drink the water."

Cai begrudgingly sipped from the cup without making eye contact. When he'd finished, Jujo took the cup away and pressed his head back against the dilapidated wall. The rift in the sky punctured the horizon like a rotting peach: Blackheart's gateway to the world of the dead. And it looked as though it was slowly expanding. After everything he'd been through, Cai was helpless to do anything but watch.

"Mi put you here so you can watch the show for yourself. With the heroes of Xaymaca under our control, it won't be long before it's done and the world changes for ever."

Cai shut his eyes tightly. He could hear pride in Jujo's voice. He had always been too proud. That had been his failing.

"Change it to what?" Cai said. "A lifeless place overrun with duppies? You can still stop this."

Jujo placed the cup down hard on the cracked tiled floor. He exhaled. "Why would I do that?"

"Because you care about people," Cai answered. He searched Jujo's eyes for the brother he knew. "You saved me from the lagahoos last night when you didn't have to. I remember. Mi nah believe the Heartless have stripped your conscience away. Not the brother I know."

"You haven't seen what I have. And not just my visions, either. You don't understand how this world can really be."

"Then talk to me!" Cai said. "Help me understand."

"Xaymaca has suffered enough through the years, brother. The world has suffered and continues to." Jujo reached out for the sky – out to the rift. "You think there won't be more wars? More conquerors and conquered people? When we're finished, there will be no death – not any more. There will be no suffering, no more killing each other for material things. There will only be a pure, spiritual state of existence. That's the world that Blackheart showed me. That's the world we'll create!"

Cai shook his head in disbelief. "You're causing suffering right now. For the living. What about our master, Jujo? *He* suffered. He's dead!"

Jujo got to his feet angrily. He leaned against a decaying wall, his body etched with distress, bowing like a tree in a storm. The light of the sun caught the broken wall, casting dark shadows across his face. "It won't matter once we open up the realms. Death won't be finite."

"We're shamans – that's who we are," Cai argued. "We're supposed to maintain the balance of the worlds, like every generation before us. Death is a part of life! People deserve to live it to the fullest!"

"And tradition is the enemy of progress!" Jujo seethed. "You're too naive, Cai. The shamans aren't great protectors of life and guardians of the dead. What about your life, and every other apprentice forced to live this way? The shamans are too wrapped up in the ways of old. They make you give so much of yourself!" He stopped, breathing deeply to calm himself down. "You need to see through this and unlearn everything Mucaro has beaten into you."

Cai's head dropped. Tears came as he realized with certainty that there was no changing Jujo's mind. Blackheart Man had won. "Please, brother. How can you think that this is freedom? Snatching away life. Snatching away *hope*." He shook the chains holding him in anguish. "How can mi bring you home like this?"

Jujo's head jerked upwards, his startled face gazing back at his younger brother. "Bring me—? Cai. You don't... Do you actually believe you were sent here to take me back to the fold?"

Through a mist of tears, Cai stared at his brother. The question confused him because of course he did. Bringing Jujo home was his sole task.

"You think they'll just welcome me back with open arms?"

Cai tried to answer while his head spun. "You...you'll have to atone for your crimes, of course. But—"

"Atone with *death*, Cai!" Jujo's voice cracked. "How do you not see?"

Cai felt like he'd left his body and was lost in some hellish spirit state. He couldn't seem to inhale enough air. "No... Mucaro said... He told me only I could help you atone and..." Cai thought hard about the words his master had spoken when he last saw him.

*Only you can bring your brother to the light...*

Cai stared at his brother, horrified. Mucaro didn't mean to help Jujo see sense, but to take his spirit to the light that broke above the sea of spirits. The realm of the dead.

*It has to be you...*

Jujo nodded gravely, seeing that Cai had accepted the truth. "The markings on you arms aren't active. You aren't connected to the spirit world yet. Mucaro didn't send you to bring me home. Mucaro sent you to kill me and take me to the spirit world as your first. To finally become a true shaman."

Tears came swift and sudden, and Cai felt lost and untethered. As much as he wanted it to be a lie, he knew in his heart that Jujo was right.

Rather than satisfied, Jujo looked pitying. "Now that you see the truth, you can decide your own path," he said as he walked away. "Because mi tell you now, brother. Killing me is the only way you could stop me."

# Chapter Thirty-Three

# VISIONS OF THE PAST

## Evie

Evie felt as though she were still out of her body, seeing the world with her spirit. But in this field of blinding white, she realized she was no longer in control. There were no spirit threads to be seen, and this wasn't her spirit projected.

Blackheart Man was gone, and she had no way of telling whether she'd been able to stop his attack on her friends. The last thing she remembered was using spirit sight to reach Blackheart's duppies and trying to sever their threads of connection, just as she'd done with the Four Heroes. But with the amethyst stone nearby, the power of her spirit energy was so great that she'd blacked out.

*Am I…dead?* The thought crossed her mind as she stared into the emptiness. Then mists of red bled into the white, in every direction. She turned again, and flinched at another presence. Staring back at her was a young woman in a blue headwrap and matching kente dress. She looked unsure of herself, cradling her arms as though there were a cold wind nipping at them. It took a moment for Evie to realize who this woman was, taking in the flawless umber skin and sharp, dark eyes that looked deep into her spirit.

"Lana..." Evie said in astonishment. "How are you doing this? You look so much..."

"Younger, yes," Lana Walters answered. "This is Jujo's doing, with the coral stone enhancing his diviner magic."

Lana dropped her arms to her sides and straightened, more like the distinguished woman Evie had first met at Myal. She stepped closer to Evie.

"With the coral, Jujo can access anyone's memories. In this dreamscape, I'll share with you my own."

Evie stared up at her, confused and curious all at once. "Why?"

"Because..." Lana replied, "I want you to truly understand."

The mists of red became a thicker smoke, and from the smoke images gradually formed. Evie watched in awe as this younger version of Lana was joined by two people: a moustached young man of a similar age and a child, barely knee high. A girl.

"Long before I was given the name 'La Diablesse', I was a scholar, a loving mother and wife. I married my childhood sweetheart, Harvey. He was an academic, just like I was. We had a wonderful life over in Spanish Town, and that life only became sweeter in 1948 when we had a daughter, Rosetta. We called her Rose for short."

The smoke-scene shifted like a diorama. Lana cradled her child, embraced by Harvey. They looked contented.

"For three years, I was the happiest I had ever been. Life had opened up for us. I received more recognition for my research. I travelled to improve my scholarly understanding of ancestral magic."

"Mi found your book in Sekesu's Town," Evie admitted.

"Yes. Another life." Lana smiled sadly. "In July of 1951, I travelled to Accompong Town to live among the Leeward Maroons for a month. I had no magic of my own when I arrived. It was pure fascination and hunger for knowledge that drove me. But a spirit waker found me. He never appeared to me as a person, only in the form of a jancrow. He told me that he saw magic in me, and that it would surely awaken there in Accompong."

The smoke showed the beautiful town with the large Kindah Tree at its centre. Then the image clouded over as a furious wind shook the tree and blew smoky debris past Evie's face.

"In August, a ferocious storm hit the island – Hurricane Charlie. It destroyed townships, crops, livelihoods. It set Xaymaca back generations. Spanish Town was among the worst affected places. But I was in Accompong…"

Lana's body tensed. Her eyes gazed in horror at the memory replaying before her.

"Phone lines were disconnected. Roads and whole areas were flooded. I had no way of contacting my family. It was weeks before I could get home. And when I did… I'd never even had the chance to say goodbye."

With a deep sigh, Lana manoeuvred the smoke and a broken-looking version of her appeared – isolated and lost in her grief. Evie's eyes widened with realization. This was what Lana had lost. Everything.

"When my husband and child died, a part of me died with them. My present and future were shattered in more ways than one, and I didn't care to rebuild. I stayed in a dark, dark place. But it was during that time, too, that my magic awakened."

Lana's body became entrenched in shadows. But rather than welcoming her magic, the young woman seemed afraid of her abilities.

"My grief and my fear threatened to destroy me. I realized there was no life for me in Spanish Town. How could I try and start again there, where the life I knew had ended? I returned to Accompong Town – to find the spirit waker and understand my powers."

"The community was even more supportive to me as a mage than they were to me as a researcher. I began to understand what I could do with my shadow. I began to find a way to heal the broken pieces of me."

Evie watched the young woman in the blue headwrap play with her shadow on the Kindah Tree.

"But no one seemed to know who the mysterious spirit waker I'd first met was. In fact, they were alarmed that an unknown spirit waker had walked among them. One night he finally found me again, speaking to me through a jancrow from the branches of the Kindah Tree."

Evie bristled, knowing full well the feeling of being watched by those birds.

"With all of the research I'd done, I had never heard of, nor come across, anyone who could project their spirit into another living thing. Even the spirit wakers with lagahoo abilities channelled animal spirits into their *own* bodies. This spirit waker reintroduced himself as Lester Heartman. He never revealed his true self to me, but he helped me in ways no other Maroons would to master my abilities.

The red smoke showed Lana alone in her room while items of clothing became animated, taking on a life of their own. With her own shadow, and the shadows of the clothing, Lana floated a trilby hat, jacket and trousers that must have belonged to Harvey. Then there was a dress and a bonnet that had belonged to Rose. The items moved around Lana, just like humans. They sat beside her on the bed as though occupied by invisible bodies. The arms wrapped around her as if in a hug. Evie felt an ache in the pit of her stomach; a pang of longing for her own parents. She understood this pain. She understood this profound loneliness.

"The jancrow said I could always find him in the forest north of the Kindah Tree, in Cockpit Country. He told me how unique I was, and as well as showing me how to make my magic stronger, he helped me to understand the connections between Obeah and the ancestors of the spirit world. I asked him to help me commune with Harvey and Rose, and he was able to grant me this joy."

Evie watched in astonishment as the jancrow sat in a spirit state on Lana's shoulder – the bridge that allowed the spirits of her husband and child to appear before her.

"I would return to the forest each day to be with them. Until the day that the jancrow refused…"

The smoke showed a desperate Lana calling out to the jancrow, who remained in the high branches.

"He told me there was a way to do more than just speak to my family in the spirit world. He told me there was a way to destroy the barrier between us entirely – to bring my family back." Lana swallowed, her brow furrowed as the smoke shifted again to the township. "But that involved harnessing the magic of the heroes of Xaymaca – stealing the gems that were held sacred to the Maroon communities. How could I betray the people who'd taken me in at a time of great despair?"

The jancrow appeared again in the smoke, pecking at the windowpane of a dark room as Lana sat worriedly on the other side.

"He came to *me* then, for weeks on end, to remind me what I could have. What I could hold…"

Evie's eyes never left the scene. She was feeling everything with Lana – every horror, every fear, every longing to have her family back.

"Until one day I couldn't bear it any more. I had to see them again. I had to try to bring them back whatever the cost."

Evie saw the celebrations by the Kindah Tree, Lana's shadow reaching out to entrap the townsfolk and the jancrow swooping down to take the coral stone. The beginning. The red smoke faded away leaving endless white – Lana, Evie and a chasm of pain between them.

"I understood then who Lester Heartman really was. And from that day I did whatever I had to do, and became whatever I needed to be, to make sure Blackheart Man's plan could be fulfilled. To bring back those I'd lost – for ever."

Lana stared into Evie's eyes, searching for a sign, an understanding. The promise that Blackheart Man had given to her, she was now extending to Evie.

"We gained supporters to our cause. We became know as the Heartless, and I became feared as 'La Diablesse'. So be it."

Lana extended her hand out to Evie. "Will you join us, Evie? To be with your family again, will you do what needs to be done?"

# Chapter Thirty-Four

# GHOSTS OF XAYMACA

## Evie

Evie lurched upright with a startled cry. A surge of adrenaline quickly cleared her blurry vision. She was lying on a four-poster bed and covered with a woollen blanket. Where were the Heartless? More to the point, where was she? Evie tried to pull off the blanket only to discover that her hands were bound together with rope. Panic swirled like a typhoon. Her sudden movement gave rise to a dull pain in her head.

A grandfather clock tocked loudly in the corner. The high-ceilinged room was scarcely furnished, old and musty. Cobwebs hung in the corners, and from bedpost to drawer. It might have been a grand place once, but not now.

Evie turned to find herself looking straight at a terrifying ram's skull mask and scurried backwards in surprise. The long-horned mask that belonged to Blackheart Man was broken –

a chunk missing from one side. A single eyehole stared back at her emptily from a bedside table. But the man himself was nowhere to be seen. An intentional game of intimidation. A message.

Evie quickly swung her feet to the floor and the wooden boards creaked in protest as she put weight on them. She was scared to stillness again, listening hard. She heard slow footsteps creaking on floorboards below, soon growing louder – someone was climbing a staircase towards her.

Evie bolted for the door and clumsily tried to turn the handle, but it was locked from the outside. The slow footsteps were just beyond the door, and Evie backed away. Then a key turned in the lock and the door was cautiously opened.

Evie tried and failed to look less afraid than she really felt. Fear turned to shock on recognizing the man staring back at her from the doorway. Her mouth dropped open, and she struggled to speak.

"You!" she gasped. "From the Myal."

The elderly spirit waker with the gentle eyes – the man who'd told Evie that her parents' spirits didn't want to communicate – was standing in front of her.

"Evelyn," he said cordially. "We regretfully got off on the wrong foot, mm? Let me properly introduce myself. I am Lester Heartman."

Evie didn't realize she was stepping backwards until her legs touched the mahogany bed frame. This was Blackheart Man, unmasked.

"I've learned a great deal about you during our brief encounters." Blackheart Man strolled into the room, hands clasped behind his back. "Mm, and I'm sure you've heard plenty about me." He raised his eyebrows with the look of a boy who'd been up to mischief, rather than a maniac threatening to destroy the living world. "But mi hope you'll allow me the chance to tell you everything, in my own words."

Evie glowered at the man, wanting to break out of the ropes binding her hands and go for him. "Where are my friends?" she demanded. "What have you done with them?"

A confused frown cast over Blackheart Man's face. "Friends?" he asked. "The boy is safe, for now." Then he raised his chin, a look of realization in his eyes. "Shaman Mucaro, however... Well, I'm afraid he's dead."

Evie tensed. Her fears about Mucaro were confirmed. But Blackheart Man didn't know about Arthur! Perhaps he'd escaped Nanny Town. She hoped he was safe. And Cai was alive, but she didn't like the sound of "for now". "I want to see Cai."

"Time soon come. We have a lot of important ground to cover first." Blackheart Man turned and propped the door open. "Come now. We would like you to feel at home. I'll untie you once we're seated at the table. Just a precautionary measure – you understand." The elderly man disappeared, and Evie had little choice but to follow until she came up with a plan.

The hallway was long and just as neglected as the room she'd been locked in.

"This is an old plantation house," said Blackheart. "Not many of these still exist. Most were destroyed during the uprising against the British. A handful survived, but after some time it was felt to be in poor taste to keep the spectres of our enslavement standing. They were burned down, too, before the nineteenth century. However, this one was left to ruin for reasons unknown."

Blackheart stopped at the bottom of the curved staircase as though lost in a memory. "Some say the place is haunted by duppies of the past. I used to think so too, once upon a time. But live long enough and you come to understand that it's people who are haunted, not places." His eyes became distant and glassy before he gathered himself and motioned for Evie to follow.

Soon they were in a large dining room with a crystal chandelier above them. The long mahogany table seemed to be the one thing in the house that had been looked after. Blackheart pulled out a chair for Evie, his small eyes blinking into hers. With distrust she sat down. Blackheart took hold of the ropes binding her hands and sliced through them – a hidden blade retreating back up his sleeve. Evie froze, watching the pieces fall to the floor, barely processing the speed of Blackheart Man's movement. The spirit waker poured her a glass of dark red sorrel before pacing to the head of the table and taking his seat. His narrowed eyes never left Evie's. The act of releasing her was also a coded message – a threat of just how dangerous he could be if she stepped out of line.

Blackheart picked up a small bell on the table and rang it. Evie watched with equal fear and fury as Wilfred, the treacherous Maroon captain, walked in, carrying a tray of dishes. Blackheart looked satisfied with the meal placed before them – red bean stew, callaloo and peppers, rice, roasted jackfruit – but Evie glared at Wilfred as he laid out the dishes. He stared defiantly back with no hint of regret or remorse for betraying Sekesu's Town.

Evie took a long sip from her glass of sorrel and angrily sprayed it in his face. Dishes clattered as Wilfred slammed an angry fist on the table.

"Yuh little swine!" he fumed.

"Wilfred…" Blackheart Man warned, leaning forward to grab one of the dishes. "She is an important guest."

Wilfred glowered, breaking Evie's gaze only to disappear back through the doors.

"Thank you, Wilfred," Blackheart called, picking up his cutlery. "Always such a faithful friend."

Evie bristled while he took a spoonful of callaloo and another of red bean stew and spread both over his plate.

"What's on your mind right now, Evie? What would you like to know?"

Evie held his stare then looked away. Blackheart's pleasantness was disconcerting. She thought about La Diablesse's story, about how Blackheart Man helped her commune with her lost family. "At the Myal you told me my parents' spirits didn't want to talk back. Was that the truth?"

Blackheart took a couple of mouthfuls of food, then he peered up at her. "No."

Evie felt anger mounting, like steam in a boiling kettle.

"Instead of channelling the spirits of your parents, I combined Sekesu's magic from the larimar with my own, and summoned the most powerful duppies from the spirit world. It helped our cause doubly to have so many talented mages present at the carnival. Jujo only had to use his diviner powers to learn what it was that they desired most – what their weaknesses were. Then they were susceptible to me; powerful host bodies for the duppies to take over and strengthen our numbers."

So that was when it had happened. Right there and then. And worse, the power of the larimar had contributed to that chaos on the beach. Evie shook with anger while Blackheart Man carried on, calmly enjoying his meal.

"I sensed that you had magic in you, when you came to me. Mi just helped it blossom a little. And once that happened, you were meant to be possessed and fall under my control as another mage of the Heartless, just like the rest o' dem." Evie was shocked by how dispassionately he said this. "That way I could make you give me the larimar willingly, and I could continue to operate in the shadows, as I always have, without revealing my presence to so many witnesses." Blackheart Man held her gaze. She couldn't read the strange expression that appeared momentarily. "For reasons mi didn't understand that night, it didn't quite work that way. But even though you've

given us some trouble, mi knew we'd find you again eventually."
He chuckled.

A cold sweat trickled down Evie's back. She couldn't help but feel responsible for Myal. For unwittingly helping the Heartless. For Nanny Town, for Arthur. Cai. She clutched her temples. How could she have revealed the larimar to Blackheart himself like that? She scolded herself for her costly mistake.

"You've actually been a great help to us, Evie," said Blackheart, his voice steady and sincere. "And now I hope that, despite everything, we can continue to help each other."

Evie glowered at him. There was no disguising her hatred, but he looked back at her serenely. "What do you want, Blackheart?"

Blackheart Man gesticulated as he chewed and then swallowed his mouthful. "Not me, Evie. You. I'm close to achieving everything I set out to – a new spiritual state. A world without any suffering or physical limitations. But what do *you* want?"

A derisive stab of a laugh escaped Evie's chest. "A world without suffering? Don't you think you've caused enough of that already? What about the Maroon towns? The shamans and everyone who stood up to you to protect the gemstones? You're a murderer!"

Blackheart dabbed a napkin at the corners of his mouth, calmly soaking up the attack, simply shaking his head.

"You're missing the bigger picture, Evie. Once the boundaries between worlds are destroyed then there will be no death. The pain we experience in these mortal bodies will cease and only our spirits will exist. No more boundaries. No more fear."

Evie turned her head away. "You're insane. You might have brainwashed Lana and Jujo with your nonsense, but I see through you."

"You don't," Blackheart said, his tone shifting. The slightest hint of offence lent his voice an edge that hadn't been there before. "Not yet. At your young age, you may have experienced loss, but you don't understand this world. You don't even know who you are." Blackheart's chair scraped across the floorboards as he got up then walked towards a wall filled with picture frames. "But you will."

He removed a wooden frame and slid it across the table to Evie. It was a yellowing document, a signed certification for the Xaymaca liberation army.

"I've seen much suffering. Too much death. You see, Evie, I have lived and died before."

"What?" Evie frowned, wondering whether she'd misheard.

"I first discovered I was a spirit waker in another life, when Nanny awakened our magic. They were long years in which we reclaimed the magic of our ancestors and freed ourselves from shackles. But I saw more kin buried, even before that war was waged, than you'll see in your whole lifetime."

Evie was pressed as far back in her chair as possible. Blackheart Man had been reborn? "Mi…mi don't believe it."

Blackheart's small, dark eyes burned into Evie's with a steel that made her doubt herself. "I died then, fighting the British to liberate this island. So when the shamans came for my spirit, to take me to that next place, I wasn't ready to go. Not until I had tasted true freedom." He walked slowly back to his seat and took a sip of sorrel.

"I found that, through death, Obeah took many different shapes. Any longer outside of a body and mi would have become what you would describe as a corrupted spirit – a duppy. But instead I killed one of the two shamans who came for me. And the other, well, I discovered in that encounter that I could project my spirit into other vessels – human or animal. I took the younger shaman's body as a host for my spirit…and I lived another life."

Evie could barely believe what she was hearing – what spirit wakers could be capable of. Blackheart's possession of the jancrows made sense now. He could even send other spirits into unwilling host bodies to become his spies. She realized with a jolt that this is exactly what must have happened to Arthur. Only it was *her* erratic powers that had caused it. She was capable of the same evils…

"I learned much about the shamans in that time. I saw many things change over the years, but human nature stayed the same. And when the time came for that host body to die, I moved onto another." Blackheart Man ate a forkful before dabbing at his mouth again.

"Soon this host body will give out on me too. It's taken several lifetimes to understand how we can truly be free. But that freedom is now within our reach, Evie."

The old stories of Blackheart were of a man who had sold his soul to the devil for demonic powers. Nobody ever suspected that the devil was living among them the whole time. Blackheart Man's spirit may as well have been corrupted for all the evil it bore. It terrified her. She hadn't moved because fear had frozen her. The man may have been calm blue water on the surface, but it was all the more frightening once you understood that a predator lay in the depths beneath.

"I want to see Cai!" Evie had heard enough. Her head swam. She needed Cai's calm and clarity.

Blackheart placed his fork down on his plate softly. "Will you not break your fast? This will be your last meal before the spiritual state comes. Your last chance to enjoy a mortal body."

"I want to see my friend!" Evie yelled.

Blackheart nodded slowly. "You'll see him. But he's... catching up with his brother right now. In the meantime, I'll take you out cliff side. Now that you've had a chance to hear La Diablesse's story, through our talented friend Jujo, she would like to speak with you in the flesh."

Evie's heart thumped at the mere mention of La Diablesse – the woman who had chosen to join the Heartless. Blackheart Man tossed his napkin aside and rose to his feet again. He motioned for her to follow as he headed for the door.

"And really think about it, Evie: what is it you want? Because I think it's the very thing you came to me for when we first met at Myal."

Evie was drawn by the brutal violet glow of Blackheart's eyes. Spirit sight.

"I think you want more than anything to be reunited with your parents. That is within your reach. Right now! Mi can give you this, just like you wanted. But *you* need to help us break through to the spirit world."

As Blackheart gazed at her, several emotions fogged Evie's mind and body at once: fear, longing for her parents... confusion. "How you mean?" she uttered. "You're a spirit waker too. Why yuh need me?"

The beginnings of a smile seemed to form on Blackheart's lips. "Answers soon come."

# Chapter Thirty-Five

## PROPOSITION

### Evie

Blackheart Man led the way across the great house's veranda in silence, leaving Evie unnerved. What was he keeping from her? Whatever surprises awaited, they couldn't be good ones.

From outside, she could see the expanse of the estate and out to the ocean. They left the grand but decrepid building, descending stone steps and making their way through withered fields that once grew sugar cane. Over her shoulder, Evie felt the presence of the two lagahoo brothers. They weren't in their wolf forms, but they wouldn't need much of an invitation to transform. One wrong move, one finger laid against Blackheart Man, and Evie would be in trouble.

Blackheart's steps were firm and fast over the long, dry grass. Despite the old age of his host body, his spirit was strong – full of youthful drive and determination. In the distance, as the fields became a cliff edge, there were three shimmers in the sky. Evie brought a hand to her mouth to stifle a cry as she saw the muscular physique of Quao the Healer, the tall and lean frame of Cudjoe the Diviner, and Sekesu – dear Sekesu the Enchanter – all summoned by Blackheart. Encompassed in green, red and blue light, the three of them appeared to have a singular focus – expanding the dark rift in the sky to help the Heartless break through to the realm of the dead. But there was a spark of hope in the dying embers of Evie's resistance. Nanny's spirit was, thankfully, nowhere to be seen. Blackheart Man must have been unable to reach her.

La Diablesse and Jujo turned at the sound of approaching footsteps, and relief flooded through Evie as she spotted Cai kneeling on the ground behind Jujo.

"Cai!" Evie called, her relief fading when she saw his arms had been shackled and that he looked defeated. Her instinct was to run to him, but Wilfred and Mikey now hovered in her periphery to remind her who was in control. "Why'd you chain him up like that?"

"Hello, Evie," La Diablesse said, uncrossing her legs and rising from the ground. Her hoofed foot trampled the earth as she stepped closer to Evie. All four gemstones were in her grasp. "We understand each other now, don't we?" she said assuredly. "Our run-ins are in the past; all is forgiven and forgotten. This moment is all that matters."

Evie glanced at Cai, who stared back with an intensity she hadn't seen before. He looked more like a boy – afraid, powerless – than ever before.

"It's over for me, Evie. It's all up to you now."

Evie reeled. This wasn't the Cai she knew. What had they done to him? "Don't talk like that!" she begged.

"Arthur was right," Cai said, hanging his head. "We're in over our heads. Mi…mi can't be who the shamans want me to be."

Every feeling of relief at seeing her friend collapsed in an instant.

"But you can stop them, Evie. Don't let them use your power to finish their plan!"

"My… What power?" Evie didn't understand. What could she do that a seasoned spirit waker like Blackheart Man could not?

Jujo grabbed his brother's shirt as a warning for speaking out.

"We need you, Evie." La Diablesse had the amethyst in her grip. "You need to remember everything and awaken your powers so that we can break through to the spirit world." The demon lady glared at her expectantly.

"Mi nah understand," Evie said. She'd tried summoning Nanny, back when she'd confronted Blackheart Man in Nanny Town. She hadn't been able to find her spirit thread. "Mi can't call her."

"No one can," said Blackheart. "Because she's already here. Reborn."

La Diablesse held out the amethyst to Evie. "Reclaim your magic, Evie. Join your sister and brothers in arms. You are the spirit of Queen Nanny."

For the briefest moment, La Diablesse's words were only sound not meaning. The absurdity of the statement made Evie question what she'd heard. How could she possibly be Queen Nanny?

"At Nanny Town mi watched, stunned, as the magic of the amethyst flowed into you – returning to its reborn spirit. It was as though the universe was mocking me, laughing at my plans." Blackheart Man spoke animatedly, his small eyes flickering expectantly. "But mi knew it was the truth when you broke my connection to the four gemstones as easily as snuffing out a candle."

The memory rolled over Evie in waves. Her head swam and she swayed, unable to breathe. It was impossible. Gasping for breath, she looked up to the spirit of Sekesu, who stared forlornly at her. And then she knew. The Heartless were speaking the truth.

"I'm…I'm reborn…" Evie stared at the amethyst. She had only just found answers to who she was – who she believed she was, at least. But now she had to accept she'd had another life entirely?

"You see, Evie, it's fate that brought us together at Myal," Blackheart continued. He nodded warmly, as though he understood how difficult it was for her to fathom. "With my spirit waker abilities, I've lived several lives by taking host vessels. But, o' course, Nanny's magic was even greater than mine. She did it. She found a way to *truly* be reborn, and her magic will be restored when you reclaim the amethyst. And what better use for it than this chance to live for ever?"

"Don't listen to them, Evie!" Cai cried. "Once they have what they want you'll just be—"

"Jujo, silence the boy before I do. Permanently." La Diablesse seethed. Her irises were aglow with a cerulean light.

"Don't make this any harder on yourself," said Jujo angrily, gripping his brother by the scruff of the neck.

The amethyst called to Evie. Magic that had once been hers, as a hero, could now be hers again in the hands of a girl who felt scared and confused. Immense power was within her reach. The power to save a nation. The power to bridge the world of the living to the world of the dead…

La Diablesse turned back to Evie, and her face displayed calm again. "Make the right choice, Evie. You are a courageous girl. Determined. For that you have my respect. Sincerely." Her eyes flickered again, awash with sorrow. "If Rose had grown up to be as strong-willed as you, I would have been proud."

The words startled Evie. She felt La Diablesse's immense loneliness as though it were her own. "I-I respected you too," she admitted. "When mi first met you. You had the kind of grace I wanted. You were smart and beautiful. You moved through the world like I want to."

"Then join us, Evie!" La Diablesse thrust the amethyst towards her. "Your magic is the most powerful Xaymaca has ever seen. Move through the new world as you choose to. Bring your parents back and fill that hole inside yourself."

Evie hesitated, then reached out for the purple gem.

"No!" Cai uttered. From the corner of her eye, Evie saw him thrashing under Jujo's grip. But she couldn't meet his gaze.

"That's it. You knew great suffering too, in your past life," Blackheart Man called. "Your heart and spirit – entrust them to me. Let's make it so no one ever has to suffer again!"

Evie took the amethyst in her hands. A great energy surged through her, just like at Nanny Town. But now she remembered a life already lived – a million memories and feelings rushing like wind through the mountains of her mind. She closed her eyes. It was as though she were recalling each memory, every sensation, as both a child and someone who had lived a long and tumultuous life. There had been so much pain in her past – in this life and the one before. She swam in the ocean of her despair. It threatened to drag her down to perilous depths.

Then she had a vision, as though she were a diviner. She looked up in the sky, at her sister from another life. The love she felt for Sekesu then eclipsed everything. A memory returned, of an older sister combing the hair of the younger. Of Nanny looking at her reflection in the water. Of three Bantu knots. Evie smiled at the memory, mirrored in her second lifetime. Yes, Nanny had seen immense suffering, unspeakable acts of horror among humans. But she had also felt moments of the most profound beauty – when people collided and, somehow, their spirits connected.

There was joy.

There was hope.

There was love so powerful a young woman would cross an ocean to save her sister. Love so vast she would not rest until every enslaved person on this island had their freedom. Love pulled Evie back to the surface. For she was Queen Nanny, and Queen Nanny was her.

Then there was Arthur and Cai, lighting her new life like beacons. There was Ms Bell, and an entire extended family in the shape of Sekesu's Town.

"I wish I had my parents. Wish mi could talk to them just once," she said eventually. "But mi don't want this world to be joined with the spirit world. Mi want to live."

"Evie, there will be no death! Don't you see?" said La Diablesse, her voice tinged with frustration.

"But then there won't be life either!" Evie looked at Cai now. He tried to smile – pride replacing his fear. "You're right. There has been a hole. I've been hurting. But that doesn't mean mi ha'fi destroy the physical world with all its beauty and its imperfections. There are people in my life right here and now. My friends. My mama. Mi want to feel everything with them – in this world. Good or bad."

Blackheart scowled. His eyes flicked towards La Diablesse. The demon woman stared at Evie in confused silence. She took a step backward, and Evie one step forward.

"Lana Walters, mi know you're hurting badly. You were forced to make a choice at your darkest time. But that doesn't ha'fi be the end," Evie pleaded. "I *do* understand you, Lana. Mi know how you feel—"

"You know nothing!" La Diablesse growled. Evie took a step back again. A patchwork of clouds covered the sun and darkness shaded La Diablesse's face. Yet her cruel eyes shone as brightly as ever. "You never really knew the love of the people you lost. You're too young to truly understand what loss is. How could I ever think you would understand?" La Diablesse's head snapped in Cai's direction. A blue flash lit up her eyes. "But I can make you understand."

In a split second, La Diablesse was by Cai's side. She grabbed him by the neck and lifted him from the ground. Cai choked and squirmed, his arms bound in front of him.

"Let him go!" Evie yelled.

"Then join the other heroes and tear through this world!" La Diablesse countered. "Or I'll let him go all right. Let him go slowly and painfully in front of you."

Cai spluttered. It was as though he was trying to shake his head at Evie. His face grew red, and his feather necklace broke under La Diablesse's grip, falling to the ground.

Jujo watched it fall and his eyes widened, as though reliving a half-remembered dream. "La Diablesse!" he yelled. "Stop this."

"Silence, Jujo. Let the girl make her choice," Blackheart ordered.

"Not like this…" Jujo pleaded. Evie stared at him, willing him to move – to do something. La Diablesse gripped Cai's throat tighter.

Evie rushed towards her friend. But like an apparition, Blackheart Man manifested in her path.

"You know what you ha'fi do," he said with quiet menace.

Evie scowled, desperate to charge through the man standing in her way. Then, all at once, a shrill cry sounded in the fraught air.

Blackheart spun in shock towards the sound, and as he did, Evie gasped at the sight. Jujo cradled his brother in one arm, a bloody akrafena in the other. La Diablesse's right arm drooped uselessly, the other arm clutching where Jujo's sword had slashed through her shoulder.

# Chapter Thirty-Six

# BROTHERS

## Cai

Cai gasped for air, clutching at Jujo's shirt with tears welling in his eyes.

"I'm here, brother." Jujo's voice cracked. "Don't worry."

"No!" Blackheart Man roared. "Jujo...what have you done?"

Cai let tears of relief flow freely. He had done his best, yet he'd almost given up hope. But when it came down to it, Jujo had come through. Cai was saved from La Diablesse's clutches only because his brother had defied her. He was right to have kept faith in Jujo after all.

"Even if death is erased," Jujo began, his voice wavering. "I won't watch my brother suffer needlessly in front of me. You have no right."

"You turned your akrafena on *me*!" La Diablesse screeched. "I'll show you what suffering is, you snake."

Before she could pounce, an incensed Blackheart Man appeared at her side. "No. I chose to make him one of the Heartless. If this is the end of our road together, then *I'll* be his dead end. You focus on Evie."

Meeting his mentor's fearsome gaze, Jujo pushed Cai aside and raised his akrafena. With one precise strike, he broke the chains that bound his brother. Cai got to his feet and shook his tender wrists before balling his hands into fists. His magic ignited, fists engulfed in two perfect flames.

There was uncertainty in Blackheart's eyes. Cai could feel the chess match playing out as the spirit waker considered a course of action that Jujo would be least likely to predict.

"Wilfred! Mikey!" Blackheart yelled, pointing at their shaman targets as he backed away. His eyes glowed violet, and he turned to the rift in the sky – magic manifesting in a purple aura.

Cai channelled his magic and steeled himself as the two lagahoo brothers approached, transforming ahead of him. Meanwhile, nightmarish screeches rang out across the sky as Blackheart summoned duppies. They flooded from the rift, hungrily chasing ancestral magic like hounds sniffing prey.

The lagahoos charged at Jujo and Cai, ferocious growls adding to the terrifying din. Jujo unleashed his magic, and in a flash of scarlet his body was shrouded in an aura. Wilfred hesitated. He looked to Mikey and with a swift growl they split apart to make their attack from two sides.

Rather than wait to be rushed, Jujo intercepted Wilfred.

It was only because of the wolf-man's quick reflexes that he was able to avoid Jujo's strike and return the attack with his huge claws. But Jujo had already dodged, leaving the lagahoo swinging at air. He realized too late that Jujo had already seen his movements before they'd happened. He howled in helpless frustration before Jujo's akrafena had even struck – sending the evil wolf spirit within him back to the realm of the dead. Wilfred's wounded, human body fell to the ground.

Cai shot a wall of fire from his palms to block the remaining lagahoo's path, while Jujo prepared for the wave of Blackheart's duppies. Mikey, with his singed head and face, snarled at Cai. He turned and flexed his clawed hands. This would be round three of their battle – and it needed to be the decisive one.

The lagahoo smashed his fists to the ground, causing the dry earth to crumble apart and a veil of dust and debris to rise. Cai darted aside and circled away from the rising cloud of dirt. Mikey had hidden himself well, and he was quick, so Cai knew he had to become a moving target. But what Cai didn't bank on was that he might run directly into his opponent, who struck him down with the ferocity of a wrecking ball. With a victorious howl, the lagahoo dived in for a swift and decisive final strike.

Dazed but finding clarity through pure adrenaline, Cai's body sparked blue, before igniting as a living flame. His opponent backed off, unable to strike again without being burned. Cai climbed to his feet, a human torch. Mikey twitched, his body remembering the searing pain of the fire from their first encounter. Then he howled once more and charged, resolving to make his final strike whatever the cost.

Cai drew his akrafena, glowing in the heat of the flame. The lagahoo leaped with his powerful legs, clawed hands stretched out for Cai's neck. But Cai's sword was swift, and it carved through the wolf-man like a hot knife to butter. The evil spirit inside returned to the spirit world, cursing the young shaman, while Mikey's now human body fell face-first to the ground.

"Two–one," Cai croaked.

## Evie

Amidst the melee, Evie raced to the cliff side where the three spirits of Cudjoe, Quao and Sekesu floated, awaiting further commands from the Heartless who'd summoned them. Sekesu looked at Evie mournfully.

"I'm sorry, Evie," said Sekesu. "There's nothing we can do. Blackheart Man summoned us. His spirit is too strong for us to free ourselves."

"I'm sending you back to the spirit world!" Evie cried above the screech of duppies and the battle being waged. "Mi broke his control before. Mi can do it again."

"Your magic is back from the amethyst. Mi can feel it!" Cudjoe the Diviner spoke, his voice deep and sonorous. "To think Nanny could link with her magic in another life. Mi knew

270

your spirit felt familiar. It's an honour to be in this world again to witness this."

Evie felt as though she were being praised by a legend rather than a brother in arms. It made her all the more determined. "The honour is mine, Cudjoe!"

She focused on finding the spirit threads to the gemstones. But La Diablesse loomed over her in a flash. Her good arm was raised to strike with a sapphire glow. Evie closed her eyes tightly, bracing for the impact. But instead, she felt the earth move beneath her. Opening her eyes again in fright, she watched the ground swell and swallow La Diablesse's hoofed foot as though it were living quicksand.

La Diablesse jumped backwards, alarmed. She broke free of the warped earth only for the same to happen again as she landed. Surprised, Evie looked in the direction of the rippling earth, then upwards to the source.

"Sekesu!"

"Mi…mi can use my magic of my own free will!" said Sekesu in astonishment. "But how—?"

"Evie!" a small, desperate voice cut the earth enchanter short. Evie startled. She knew that voice.

There, darting towards her, was a dishevelled-looking cat in a porkpie hat.

"Arthur!" Evie's heart swelled. He was safe.

"The gems; take them!" Arthur cried as Evie ran towards him. Amidst her confusion, he removed his hat and passed it to her like a church collection plate. There, in all their gleaming glory, were the larimar, coral and emerald to go with her amethyst stone.

Evie stood in shock for a moment, gazing at the gemstones with an ecstatic smile. Somehow, Arthur had managed to pinch them from La Diablesse's pocket. And he'd had to overcome immense fear to do so. "Classic misdirection, right?"

"You make them look to the left while you disappear to the right," Arthur replied. His ears pinned back against his head as La Diablesse roared in anger upon seeing the stolen gems. "You take it from here, sistah. If mi get caught in a shadow mi done for!" And with that, he shot off to hide again.

"Keeheehee! A king of thieves!" Sekesu whooped. "Evie, now you can focus on sending us back to the spirit world while I hold her off!"

"Mi nah have to!" said Evie determinedly, clutching the gemstones. She remembered now what had happened at Nanny Town – that her battle with Blackheart Man on a spiritual plane had resulted in her regaining Nanny's power from the amethyst. It had dispelled all of Blackheart's duppies and freed those who were possessed. "Mi can free you all from Blackheart right here and now by destroying the spirit threads that bind you to him."

Evie channelled the state of calm, of allowing her spirit to see beyond the world in front of her. She let her spirit energy flow into the four gems in her hands, reclaiming the spirit threads of the Four Heroes. But not before La Diablesse struck with an attack of her own.

"The new world is coming, whether you want it to or not!" La Diablesse's shadow stretched rapidly across the ground, taking a hold of Evie's legs, then torso – stretching upwards to her neck. Evie panicked, knowing that in her spirit state, she was like a spectator to the fate of her own body.

It was now or never. Evie's energy cascaded from her body, the gemstones aglow. Sekesu, Quao and Cudjoe's spirit threads rippled, untangling from Blackheart's. Their magic returned in full, flowing from the gems. The colours became a pure white light, exploding from the spiritual plane into the physical world.

Evie opened her eyes, back in her body, and felt weightless. The light of the gems had dispelled the shadows and broken La Diablesse's hold on her. She was suspended in the air, surrounded by the freed spirits of the other three heroes of Xaymaca.

Unable to accept this turn in fortunes, La Diablesse clutched at her head then threw her arm to her side, screaming her frustration at the sky.

Evie proudly turned to her comrades from a past life. Memories of the four of them in younger days, fighting shoulder to shoulder for freedom, rushed through her mind. Cudjoe's masterful strategies, Quao's bravery, Sekesu's fighting spirit. These heroes, who she loved and trusted with her life. "Please fight beside me one last time: Cudjoe, Quao, sistah!"

*   *   *

# Cai

A further swarm of evil spirits flooded out of the growing hole in the sky, yet Blackheart Man was nowhere to be seen. Against a diviner like Jujo, he knew the smartest move was to overwhelm his enemies to mask his movements. Otherwise, the same diviner powers that had served Blackheart so well would now be working against him. It was unfortunate for Cai and Jujo that Blackheart's particular method of distraction was just as deadly as he was.

They stood back to back, their akrafenas drawn and raised to defend themselves against the ghostly onslaught. They slashed through the storm of spirits, moving like mirrored images with the speed and grace of a deadly dance.

*Twenty-eight!* Cai kept his tally.

The intensity of the barrage alarmed him, but he'd faced similar before, and survived, at Myal. He was determined to survive here too. He and Jujo sent the evil spirits back to the realm of the dead as swiftly as they'd come – in a flurry of scythes and slashes.

*Twenty-nine! Ignore the fatigue.*

After everything, after the chasm between them that had seemed insurmountable, they were fighting together. Brothers. Warriors.

More from the left. Twisted, hungry mouths aiming for Cai. He snapped his fingers, calling a burst of blue flames. Two more duppies extinguished.

*Thirty-one!*

This was for Master Mucaro. He sensed, dodged and slashed the duppies clamouring for his spirit.

*Thirty-two!*

This was for himself – to be stronger than he was at Myal.

*Thirty-three!*

Stronger than he was a minute ago!

*Thirty-four!* His master's record was in sight, before a desperate cry broke his concentration.

"Caiiiiii!"

He was bowled over before he could react. Cai landed on his shoulder to break the hard fall, gathering his wits in time to see Jujo standing over him. His brother's akrafena struck the enemy Cai hadn't anticipated – Blackheart Man.

Cai lay in shock, his near miss sinking in. Jujo had predicted the spirit waker's attack, thrusting his sword into Blackheart's side and saving Cai's life in the process. But then, Jujo coughed and blood trickled from his lips.

"Jujo!" Cai had been so focused on Blackheart's wound that he hadn't even noticed Jujo's. A hidden blade jutted from Blackheart's sleeve into his brother's chest. It retracted, and blood trickled down with it. Blackheart grunted, pulling back and clutching at his own wound, the brilliant white of his under-robes now red with blood.

"See you…in the new…world," Blackheart Man panted, eyes flashing purple with his palm out as though to strike. Cai watched Jujo's spirit draining from his body, Blackheart Man snatching it away like a deadly parasite.

"Run, Ca—" was all Jujo could manage before he collapsed, the last of his spirit seeping into Blackheart.

"No!" Cai yelled, recklessly swinging his akrafena at Blackheart, who sidestepped and backed away. Cai held his blade out to defend with one arm, the other covering his brother's body. But Blackheart Man, wounded, watched on from a distance.

Cai knelt beside Jujo. His vision became a blur. His soul felt shattered.

There was no attack that could hurt him as much as this one. Now, for certain, there was no saving his brother.

## Chapter Thirty-Seven

# BATTLE FOR THE BLUE MOUNTAINS

## Evie

Though La Diablesse tried to escape from the reunited heroes of Xaymaca, Sekesu trapped her, enchanting the weeds and bushes of the field to encase her legs and arms. She was a scowling part of the overgrowth, rooted like a nightmarish scarecrow.

It was then that Evie heard the guttural scream that sent shivers through her body like a rip tide.

"Cai!" Evie ran to her friend on instinct, seeing him slumped to the ground. It took a moment to realize it wasn't Cai who was hurt. He was folded over his brother's body, shoulders shaking with the force of his sobs. Blackheart Man was injured, one hand covering a wound in his side. But still, he edged closer to Cai. The hidden blade shot out from the sleeve of the mage's free arm.

"Quao! Cudjoe!" Evie yelled, urging her comrades of past and present to follow her.

Blackheart Man had murdered his own companion, and was about to do the same to Jujo's brother too. But Evie dived for Cai – the force of her body shoving him out of harm's way. They rolled over the harsh ground together before Evie righted herself, ready to defend her grief-stricken friend.

Cudjoe had the grace and speed of a whippet, and he sent Blackheart staggering with a powerful hook kick. Quao was built like a small tank and locked Blackheart's body in his arms like a wrestler, trying to sap the spirit that lay inside his elderly vessel. Cudjoe immediately joined Quao in restraining the injured mage, leaving nothing to chance.

"Damn you!" Blackheart Man looked astonished as the two heroes tried to force him into submission. It must have been infuriating in the first instance that Cudjoe and Quao were no longer under his control. But clearly he hadn't expected that, in their spirit forms, they'd be able to harm him physically. Just like Sekesu, the two heroes were showing a masterful understanding of Obeah to manipulate energy in the physical world.

"I won't let you ruin my plans again!" Blackheart yelled at Evie, straining to get the words out.

Evie shielded Cai, glaring at Blackheart Man defiantly. Cai's relationship with Jujo had been complicated, but they were still family and the strongest bonds made for the hardest breaks. She felt his pain. Evie was shocked at how easily Blackheart had turned on his protégé, but Mucaro had been right. Jujo had been used for his diviner powers – he'd been just as expendable as anyone else.

Blackheart's irises flashed purple. His physical body may have been restrained, but he was still dangerous in his spirit state. Evie stilled her heart and cast her own spirit out of her body to fight him again. But Blackheart's spirit soared towards the rift in the sky – the unfinished tunnel to the realm of the dead.

Something made Evie's spirit stop rather than give chase, as she sensed a small army charging towards the cliff top. She could feel their spirits coming fast. Then came the beautiful hum of an abeng, blowing in the distance. Relief and gratitude sparked in her.

"The Maroons!" she cried, close to tears.

But it wasn't just the Maroons of Nanny Town and Sekesu's Town approaching with a vengeance, it was the Society of Shamans too.

With akrafenas in hand, Chief Marcia and her captain, the revived Omar, led the charge. There must have been a hundred men and women ready to fight for Xaymaca's soul against the Heartless.

"You did this," Cai whispered to Evie's body. She looked down at him from where her spirit floated in the sky; his face was wet with tears. "You set all of the possessed free at Nanny Town. You really are a hero of Xaymaca."

Evie felt a new wave of energy swelling. She turned her attention back to Blackheart's spirit. He was summoning again – duppies even more powerful than before. The sky was darkening around the rift as, one by one, ten enormous bull-like creatures came charging through. With fearsome horns and eyes like hot coals, they bellowed, breathing fire. Their hoofed feet landed with a thump, shaking the earth beneath them. They stood before the army of Maroons and shamans, dragging hoofs and readying to charge.

"Rolling calves!" Cudjoe exclaimed. "Duppies of the wickedest men who lived."

"Maroons! Protect the girl and the boy," Chief Marcia yelled, pointing her akrafena in Evie and Cai's direction. A dozen Maroons sprinted towards them and formed a protective triangle from the fire-breathing rolling calves.

"Shamans! Let's send these duppies back to hell!" one of their leaders ordered. The shamans, in their off-white robes and loose black trousers, charged at the duppies. Blue sparks and fire breath set the air alight like fireworks, as enchantments were activated and the rolling calves unleashed their fury.

Amidst the melee, Evie – in her spirit state – had lost sight of Blackheart Man. She suddenly felt his spirit travelling at pace back down from the rift, hurtling towards his vacant body. But when his spirit passed the vessel by entirely, Evie stared open-mouthed in horror.

Blackheart Man wasn't returning to his own body, held fast by the spirits of Quao and Cudjoe.

"It's time for one last change of host, Evelyn Bell!" he yelled triumphantly. "What a fine vessel you'll make. Then control of the heroes will be mine again!"

Blackheart was heading straight for her vacant body. Not even the guarding squadron of Maroons could protect Evie from spirit possession.

# Chapter Thirty-Eight

# SPIRIT WAKER
# VS SPIRIT WAKER

## Evie

Evie sent her spirit back to her body. Her eyes opened but she wasn't in control.

*No!* Blackheart's spirit lingered there at the front of her mind. She felt the struggle like a tug of war. He was fighting to break her spirit; she rallied to expel his.

*Get out, you thieving jancrow!*

*Give yourself to me, Evie. Don't fight me! It will all be over soon when the new world comes.*

"Evie!" Cai's voice sounded so distant. "Something's wrong!"

"It's Blackheart! He cast his spirit into Evie's body," answered Cudjoe. "She's fighting for her life now!"

Though Cai begged the Maroons for assistance, there was nothing they could do but watch in horror as the fight took place beyond their physical reach. None of them were spirit wakers – the rarest of mages. And even if they were, how could they contend with Blackheart Man to help the reborn spirit of the Mother of Magic?

Evie and Blackheart Man were locked in battle – their spirits repelling each other like two mirroring magnetic poles. With one misstep, Evie could be relegated to the fringes of her own mind. She felt her grip on her body weakening. Blackheart's spirit, his resolve, was it that much stronger?

"Evie!" another voice called to her… A friend. A brother.

Through her body's eyes she could see him – Arthur pressed his furry face right up close to hers.

"Are you the spirit of Queen Nanny or what?! Fight him, man! You've always been a fighter!"

But it felt futile. Blackheart Man was worming his way into her memories. Recalling her loneliness, her fears…showing her all of her weaknesses to sap her fighting spirit.

"You're my best friend, and the only family mi have. I'll never abandon you, Evie! You hear me? So let's put an end to the Heartless – together, like we've always been!"

*Feline fool!*

Evie could feel Blackheart trying to reach out with her hands to strangle him.

No! She couldn't let him hurt another friend. She couldn't let him win. Not after all the awful things he'd done. She pushed every ounce of spirit energy she had left against Blackheart's, forcing the good memories to block out the bad.

**283**

Blackheart faltered, while Evie's spirit energy swelled – a purple storm erupting beneath them.

Blackheart Man roared. *This is our one chance to reset this wretched world, Evie! Why do you fight me?*

*I'm fighting you because mi can't accept the living world is the forsaken place you see. Mi can't give up. I'll fight for a better world – one that's not ruled by a murderous, heartless beast like you!* Evie felt a new surge of strength. She felt the power of her Maroon ancestors – the spirit of resistance. It was as though they stood alongside her, smeared in mud, dressed for battle. She could see warriors from ancient African kingdoms, in fearsome armour and beautiful paints, akrafenas and spears in their grip, reaching out as though to lend her their magic. Their blue, red, green, purple auras combining with hers in a flood of white. *It's in my blood!*

Blackheart's spirit was desperate. He resisted, but Evie could feel him weakening. With spirit sight now Evie could see it was he who was full of doubt – that he could ever match the power of Queen Nanny. He was used to having his way, to spirits succumbing to him. Well not any more.

Blackheart's spirit form began to crack like broken glass from the strain of trying to hold fast while being ejected from Evie's body – the spirit magic of generations proving insurmountable. Evie seized her chance. She followed the threads of the ancestors in the spirit world, and made her connection. She wouldn't just force Blackheart Man out of her body, she'd send him where he should have been all along – the realm of the dead.

Her spirit burst from her body once more, finally thrusting Blackheart's weakened soul out with it. Upwards they soared, Blackheart cursing as they ascended towards the rift in the sky, until Evie had got as close as she dared. Blackheart stared back at her with abject fear as she gave one final push.

"Dispel!" she roared into the dark void above, using every sinew of spirit strength left to sever Blackheart's remaining threads.

A radiant, violet blast sent the monster to his end, the shock waves rippling through their world into the next. Blackheart cried out in defeat, his fractured form shattering in the rift. The darkness dispersed.

# Chapter Thirty-Nine

# DARKEST LIGHT

## Evie

Evie sat up with a lurch. Cai was calling to her, but she was lost in the sheer elation of feeling and controlling every precious part of her body. She looked around to see Arthur and the Maroons watching her closely.

"Evie?"

"It's me," she said as Cai eyed her concernedly. "Bowlhead," she added.

Cai visibly relaxed and placed a comforting arm round her shoulders. Arthur pounced onto Evie with a laugh and licked her face. She hugged him right back.

Across the field, the remaining six rolling calves were dispelled – returning to the spirit world with their vanquished summoner. The shamans and Marcia's Maroons sheathed their akrafenas amidst colossal trails of fire where the rolling calves had attacked. These warriors were strong in numbers, and those who'd been injured were being tended to by the healers among them.

"What happened to Blackheart Man?" Quao asked when the spirit waker's body didn't move.

Gasps of surprise sprang from the dozen Maroon guardians, as Blackheart's body withered like a raisin. Quao and Cudjoe released the decaying body in alarm. It hit the ground and turned to dust.

"It's over," said Evie.

"No." Cai shook his head. He was staring at the cliff side, where Sekesu and the restrained La Diablesse waited. "Not yet."

Evie swallowed back the relief that had seeped through her weary body. Every pair of eyes beside her saw La Diablesse.

But she saw Lana Walters.

Cai and Arthur tried to hold Evie back as she got to her feet. Before she knew it, her aching legs were sprinting towards the shadow enchanter; she ignored the calls of the Maroons and Sekesu's look of surprise.

"Lana!" Evie called. "You're free now. You don't ha'fi keep fighting!"

"Evie, stay away!" Sekesu warned. "The shadows!"

But Evie stood firm. Lana peered back at her, eyes probing, face sallow. Her hat had been lost to the sea during their earlier battle, and where two devilish horns had protruded from her head before, now there was skin as smooth as the face beneath it. Blackheart's hold on her was no more.

"Blackheart Man is gone, you hear me?" Evie said. "Mi know what he turned you into. But it doesn't ha'fi be that way."

Lana's shoulders shook within the grip of Sekesu's earthen magic. Then the tremor turned to a quake as an uncontainable sob escaped her. Evie watched the tortured woman, who must have felt lonelier than ever. Tears streaked down her own face, but she could only watch, along with the crowd of Maroons that had gathered behind her.

"Sekesu, please. Let her loose," Evie pleaded. She deserved at least a little dignity.

Sekesu begrudgingly did as Evie asked. As the weeds and roots receded, Evie noticed that Lana's hoofed foot had gone, and a human leg had been restored. She walked slowly towards Lana, who was curled on the ground. Placing one hand first round Lana's back, she drew her closer with the other and let her cry into her body as she held her. There they stayed for a while, as the crowd watched on, speechless.

"Mi know you were forced into this, Lana. Mi know you felt you didn't have a choice. But you do now."

The blazing sun hid away for a moment, dropping behind a patch of cloud – dimming the light and cooling their skin. Evie held Lana until her cries died down, and as she pulled away, Lana uttered, "It's too late, Evie."

Dread clutched at Evie's spirit. She felt as though she was sinking under Lana's impenetrable gaze. "H-how you mea—?"

"It's too late for me to turn back."

In that moment, Evie realized the pair of eyes staring back

at her didn't belong to Lana Walters. They belonged to La Diablesse.

Evie was entrapped in her shadow, unable to move a millimetre while La Diablesse snatched the four gemstones away from her. "I can still get my family back. If you won't break through to the realm of the dead from this world, then I'll just have to take *your* spirit there by force. Then the choice will be yours: death or to break through to the living world instead…if you ever want to see your friends again."

With the four gems glowing, La Diablesse's body slumped to the side and her spirit emerged – the deadly result of Jujo's treachery in teaching her the secrets of the shamans.

"Evie!" Sekesu yelled, admist cries of panic from all around.

Too stunned to think and powerless to react, Evie found her spirit in La Diablesse's clutches once again, fighting against the urge to swim for the light in the spirit ocean – the space between worlds.

# Chapter Forty

# A RECKONING

## Cai

Cai watched helplessly as La Diablesse and Evie's soulless bodies folded over each other on the ground. He gripped his akrafena and gritted his teeth. La Diablesse's last act was desperate. She'd given up her body and taken Evie's spirit with her. If La Diablesse succeeded in reaching the realm of the dead, Evie's only way back to the living world would be to destroy the barrier between worlds – the very thing they'd been fighting against. What could he do to stop this?

"It happened again!" Arthur cried. "They're in *that* place again. What do we do?"

"You go after them," called a voice that surprised boy and cat alike.

"Mi laaaawd!" Arthur exclaimed, darting away from the speaker.

Cai felt the blood drain from his face, because he was staring at a ghost. Jujo's spirit loomed over him, prompting nearby Maroons to draw their akrafenas.

Jujo simply stared at his brother, unfazed. "It has to be you, Cai. Take me to the spirit world." A wistful smile played on his lips.

Cai rubbed away tears, struggling to find his voice. "Jujo…" he managed to utter.

"You can still fulfil Mucaro's wishes by taking me to the other side. And you can bring Evie's spirit back too," said Jujo, drifting closer to his brother. "Mi was misguided. Mi see that now. Misguided by Blackheart Man, but by the shamans too."

Cai frowned. "W-what are you saying?"

"When Blackheart Man gave me the coral stone mi saw back through time. Saw all the monstrous things mankind has done to each other on this island. Because of that, what he said made sense to me. He wanted to reset all o' this – to change this cruel world." He paused, looking ashamed. It was a moment more before he was able to look at Cai again. "But it's taken your capture for me to realize what we've become in order to achieve our goal. We are monsters too. It shouldn't have taken your suffering for me to see it. But it did."

The Maroons surrounding them were wary, unsure of how to react.

"Mi still believe the shamans need to change their ways," said Jujo. "If not to help the dead, then to break the cycle of torment for generations of young shamans to come. Cai, you can do better than I did. Better than any of them. You can be that leader to bring about change in the Society of Shamans."

Cai's head lowered as he thought about Mucaro – how hard he'd tried, but how he'd ultimately failed to live up to his master's expectations.

"Raise your head, brother!" said Jujo. "I'm ready to go, and you're ready to become the true shaman this world needs."

Cai looked his brother in the eyes. The same deep brown, unyielding eyes gazed back at him. Jujo nodded assuredly as Cai drew his akrafena. They moved in perfect symmetry, sitting back on their heels. Then, his heart racing, Cai steadied his hands, exhaled and projected from his body. His blade cut through his brother's spirit and the very fabric of their world.

The sea of spirits came rushing to them, submerging them. Cai peered around frantically. The spirits of the dead drifted towards the light – the water break at the surface. Among them was Evie, kicking out as La Diablesse dragged her towards it.

Jujo placed a steadfast hand on Cai's shoulder. He was with him all the way.

Cai swam as hard as he could towards his friend, fighting against the fatal pull of the realm of the dead, which called to his spirit. No, it wasn't his time. He wasn't here to die. He was here to make sure that Evie lived.

As the brothers approached, La Diablesse locked eyes with them and dragged harder. Evie seemed to be losing the will to fight now that she was so close to the spirit world. Cai grabbed hold and wrestled for her.

Jujo grappled La Diablesse to help him break Evie free. All the while they struggled against La Diablesse, they drifted closer and closer to the light at the surface. Cai pushed and kicked with all his remaining might. His life force was being sapped, metre by metre.

As they drifted ever nearer to the break, bubbles rose from the deep. Cai gaped as another spirit joined Jujo and took hold of La Diablesse.

*Master Mucaro!*

La Diablesse mouthed a panicked scream, and Cai saw a clash of shock and regret in Jujo's gaze. But Mucaro was calm, resolute. He cast a glance at his former pupil that exuded peace. He had reckoned with his own death. Mucaro then turned to Cai. He nodded proudly, tight jawed as he held onto La Diablesse. Together, they wrested Evie free from her clutches. Cai kicked away, holding Evie close with one arm. The three spirits – Mucaro, Jujo, La Diablesse – drifted to the surface, succumbing to the pull of the spirit world, the light swallowing them up.

Before the same fate could befall Evie and himself, Cai slashed with his akrafena. The flow of water became a split tide, water gushing past until daylight embraced them again. They were back in the living world.

Cai sputtered, lurching into his body once again. Arthur peered at him with his bright cat eyes. "You're back! Is Evie...?"

Cai turned over, gazing anxiously to where Evie's body had fallen. He scrambled to his feet, calling her name. Arthur bounded alongside him. He knelt by Evie's side as she shot up – coughing, adjusting to the shock of having her spirit back inside her body.

"Arthur...Cai!" she said breathily.

"We're here," Arthur called. He scrambled towards her in blessed relief, and nestled into her body. Cai leaned into her as well, and the friends held onto each other as though their spirits were about to be stripped away again.

Evie whispered into Cai's shoulder. "Thank you, Cai. Thank you for coming for me."

"It's me that should be thanking you," said Cai. "If it weren't for you, Blackheart Man would have...would have—"

Evie flinched suddenly. "Cai...your arms!"

Alarmed, Cai looked down at his arms to find them glowing blue. A heavenly light was emitting from spirit markings covering his arms.

"It's happened," Cai said quietly. He stood tall, gazing at the iridescent symbols in awe, before looking at his friends proudly. "I'm a true shaman."

# RETURN OF THE HEROES

## Evie

Seeing that the three friends were all physically safe, the dozen guardian Maroons tended to them quickly to make sure all was well spiritually, and to find out what had happened to La Diablesse in the space between worlds. Cai took it upon himself to do the explaining, while Evie was checked over. Before long, the Maroons excused themselves to see to their comrades, leaving Evie, Arthur and Cai to take stock of their unlikely survival.

Evie stroked Arthur's head. "When mi needed you most you were there. If mi never heard your voice…who knows if mi woulda had the strength to beat Blackheart Man."

"Mi know," Arthur said with a sad smile. "Mi saw it."

"How you mean 'saw it'?" asked Cai, his brows meeting in an inquisitive frown.

Arthur flashed his teeth. "Let's just say Evie wasn't the only one who had an awakening."

Evie watched Cai's mouth fall open. As her thoughts raced to make sense of it all, she soon came to the same realization.

"Arthur! You're…"

"A divinerrrr," he purred with a satisfied smile. "Back in Nanny Town, when mi was about to climb the clock tower. That's when it happened."

Evie chewed her bottom lip, struggling to pinpoint how and when exactly he'd found out. "Then…Blackheart Man found magic in you too?"

"Nuh Blackheart Man. *You.*" Arthur's eyes shone brightly. "Whatever you did to dispel the duppies and free the mages, that blast of energy woke up the ancestral magic in me too. Mi saw the clock tower collapse *before* it collapsed!"

"So that's how you survived." Cai sounded impressed.

Evie shook her head disbelievingly. "Lawd have mercy, Arthur!"

"Mmhm! All mi could do when the Heartless took you both was lay low. Mi was still trying to understand what had happened to me. But at least mi was able to explain everything to the Nanny Town Maroons and the shamans. And mi knew there was no time to waste. Mi had to come after you both like you woulda come after me."

Evie smiled at her friend with admiration. Gratitude was an understatement. "When mi fought Blackheart for my body, mi saw a vision of the ancestors. It was so real, like their energy flowed through me. It was your doing, wasn't it?"

Arthur beamed at this like he'd just had a fish supper. "Yeah man. I'm pretty great, nuh?" Evie laughed and playfully pushed him aside.

"Master Mucaro was right about you, Arthur." Cai grinned. "You are more heroic than you ever thought."

The friends were approached by the spirits of Sekesu, Quao and Cudjoe; the heroes hung back, wary of spoiling their shared moment. But Evie reached out to embrace them all.

"When La Diablesse took you, mi thought it was the end," said Sekesu sombrely. "It was my fault for releasing her."

"Mi know you only did so because mi asked. It's not your fault at all," Evie replied. She turned to Lana's vacant body. Immense sadness rushed through her, and she thought that she might cry again. "Could I have saved her?" she asked. "Could I have done something differently?"

"It's not on you to save her soul, Evie," Sekesu said firmly. "You tried your best, that's all you coulda done. But grief consumed her long ago. As sad as it is, sometimes people get lost in it and never come back. Just think yourself lucky that you do have love in your life to anchor you."

Evie glanced at Cai and Arthur appreciatively before turning to Sekesu again.

"Don't be afraid to keep reaching out to others because o' this. It's a wonderful quality to have, sistah. And one day you just might save somebody's life."

Evie walked towards Lana's body and placed a hand on her

shoulder. Evie hoped that she would find peace in the spirit world – find her family.

"Could we bury her, Sekesu?" Evie asked the enchantress. "We can't leave her like this." ·

"Wait! The gemstones," said Cudjoe. "We ha'fi retrieve them first."

"Uhh…about that."

Everyone turned to Arthur as he coyly lifted his porkpie hat, revealing the coral, emerald, amethyst and larimar.

"When did…? How…?" Cai uttered incredulously.

Evie grinned despite herself. At least that took care of that.

Sekesu nodded in agreement at Evie's request. Evie stepped away and allowed Sekesu to enchant the earth, letting the churning soil swallow Lana's body and sink her slowly, deep below.

With the Heartless and the summoned duppies defeated, the shaman and Maroon warriors were able to take stock of their injuries and losses. Quao joined the healers, working doggedly to tend to as many of the wounded as possible. Those who hadn't survived the battle with the rolling calves were buried and their souls taken to the sea of spirits by the shamans.

Marcia left her fighters to speak with Evie and her friends. The Maroon chief looked over them proudly. "If I'd known that you were Queen Nanny's reborn spirit, mi woulda accompanied you to Nanny Town myself."

"That was the past," said Cai, surprising the group with his interjection. "Here and now, the name Evie Bell deserves to be spoken in the same breath as the heroes."

Evie was speechless. A feeling of warmth flushed through her. Praise from Cai of all people didn't come easily.

"She's saved our world, not just our island."

"You're quite right, Cai." Marcia nodded. "And that goes for you as well – bringing her back from the brink of death. What you've done here today is remarkable."

"Mi saved her life as well, yuh know…" Arthur licked a paw and brushed it over his head, doing an awful job of pretending not to care that hadn't received praise.

"Yes, you too, puss."

"Puss?! My name's Arthur Nansi, and may the history books remember that!"

Marcia spread her arms as if to give an embrace. "And now, with everything set right again, the gems of the Four Heroes must come back into the care of the Maroons."

From the corner of her eye, Evie caught Cai glancing at her. Arthur also turned questioningly. They both wanted to be sure that she was all right to be giving up her link to the past. But Evie was only concerned with Sekesu, who hovered beside her.

"It's okay," said Evie. "My mami and papa left the larimar with me so that Sekesu could protect me. She already did that. And besides, the gemstones may have helped with my journey to magic, but mi need to master it by myself."

Sekesu pointed at the rift in the sky. "We're not done yet," she said. "We ha'fi close the rift. And that should be the last act of our magic. The gems should be destroyed."

"That's right," Cudjoe agreed. "We can't risk our magic falling into the wrong hands again. This time, it should disappear from this world with us."

The Maroons and shamans murmured among themselves. Although some were indignant at first, in the end no one could deny that the heroes were right. And, after all, it was *their* magic. Their choice. For as long as the gems remained in the living world, there would always be a danger that the power could be abused.

"We're agreed," said Marcia eventually. "Use your magic to end this horror for good."

Evie swallowed nervously, staring at the rift and taking in the scale of the task. "Mi nah sure mi have the strength left," she admitted.

"Let me help with that," said Quao cheerily. "We'll have you good as new again."

Quao placed his hands over Evie's head and a green glow emitted. In a magic minute, Evie felt her spirit replenished. Healers truly were incredible.

Sekesu grinned. "All right then – let's get to work."

Evie knelt on the ground and projected her spirit once again. One by one, she and the three heroes rose into the air. They were shadows in a sky of pinks and papaya. Halos of light surrounded them like a celestial vision: red, green, blue, purple collided. The light surrounded the rift in the sky and the hole slowly closed as though being sewn up by an invisible hand. The last of the darkness slipped away into the light, and the streams of their ancestral magic scattered. Now, it was over.

Their duty done, Evie and the three spirits floated in the air above the cliff, regarding one another affectionately.

"Mi can't believe mi having to say goodbye to you again." Evie sighed.

"For now at least. No one lives for ever. Your time soon come," said Quao drily.

"But wait, Quao. Why you ha'fi rain on her parade?" Sekesu chastised. "She has her whole life ahead of her yet."

Evie grinned at the squabbling spirits. "Mi couldn't have done none o' this without you," she said to Sekesu. "Thank you for showing me the way."

"You already knew the way, deep down." Sekesu smiled. "Mi just nudged you back on the path."

"Ay, last chance to tell me the secret to a second life, yuh know," Quao called.

"Hush now!" Sekesu and Cudjoe cried in unison. But Evie laughed.

"Mi wish we all coulda been reborn. Together, like this," said Evie. "I'll ha'fi wait to be with you again."

"Don't look too far ahead," said Sekesu. "You'll have many rebirths in your lifetime, Evie. Everyone does, in a way."

Evie's brow crumpled in confusion. "But how you mean?"

Sekesu's melodious chuckle escaped her. "You'll change the way you think about the world, sistah. Even the way you think about yourself. You'll be challenged. You'll forge new friendships, perhaps lose some along the way. You'll give your heart, maybe have it broken, but you'll heal and rise again like the phoenix you are. *Sankofa*. You'll learn from the past and build your future."

These words overwhelmed Evie. It felt scary and exciting at the same time to think about how she might change, how she might develop her magic, where her abilities might take her.

Evie looked down below at her body, kneeling tranquilly on the ground. The gems were in her palms – now dulled like dishwater, the magic returned to their owners. "Take it easy now, you hear?" she told the heroes tearfully.

"We can't exactly put ourselves in danger now, can we? We dead!" Quao quipped, prompting Sekesu and Cudjoe to tell him off again.

As Evie let go of the spirit threads that bound the heroes, Quao faded first, followed by a smiling Cudjoe. "Blessings upon you, Evie Bell," he said as he slipped away.

Then there was Sekesu. She held out her hand and Evie mirrored her – their spectral fingers lacing together – until she too faded away.

"Until we meet again, sistah."

# Chapter Forty-Two

# MEMENTO

## Evie

"Evie...Arthur Nansi, yuh ready?"

The two friends turned away from the cliff side where they'd been speaking with Cai to see Marcia waiting while the Maroons piled into a convoy of trucks in the distance.

"We'll be there in a minute," Evie replied. It wasn't that she particularly wanted to stay at this dilapidated old great house. Her stay had been *far* from pleasant. But she wanted this last memory to be the one that would stay with her.

Marcia nodded patiently, and as she was turning to walk away, she hesitated. She pulled the four no-longer-magic gemstones from her waist pouch. "As the magic is gone, why don't you take the larimar back? To remember them by."

Evie smiled as Marcia held out her hand, and walked forward to take it. Sekesu, her mother and father – they'd remain with her after all.

"Thank you, Marcia."

"Do you mind if I take the amethyst?" Cai's request appeared to take Marcia by surprise just as much as it did Evie.

"Mi suppose," said Marcia, looking inquiringly at the boy. "Call it a graduation gift."

"Well now, mi don't suppose you want to bless *me* with the emerald and coral, nuh?" Arthur pried, sitting back on his hind legs expectantly.

Marcia cleared her throat awkwardly and quickly pocketed the two remaining gemstones, eyes firmly on the cat. "I'll be in the truck."

"Cho!"

And then the trio were alone again – the sun beginning its descent over the ocean in peach and pink.

"I don't know if a more incredible thing will happen in my whole life," said Cai, looking out to the sea.

Evie laughed at that. Not cruelly, just considering how much more there was out there over the horizon. "It'd be a shame to think the best isn't still to come."

Cai glanced at her, then back to the sea. He nodded to himself, acknowledging that his friend was right.

"Will you...do you think you'll maybe stay with the Maroons?" asked Cai. "You can honour your parents by following in their footsteps. And the shamans, we pass by the towns often too." Cai's face was redder than usual. Evie supposed that they had been under the glare of the sun for a while, after all.

"I'm proud to have the blood of the Maroons. I'm so proud of my parents," said Evie. "But that's not my path. Now that I have some answers about the past, mi want to go and build for the future." She knelt down and landed a playful pat on Arthur's hat. "For a start, we need to head home, find Ms Bell, and get Arthur back into his real body."

The pair exchanged heartful smiles. Arthur's tail batted quickly. "Yeah man."

Cai nodded sombrely. "Of course."

"We'll meet again, promise," Evie assured him. "You ha'fi come back to Ochi. Or maybe we could meet again every year – at Myal night! All three of us."

Cai smiled. "I'd like that very much."

"Cai!" one of the shamans called out. The three friends turned once more, and it appeared the shamans were ready to move on too.

"You're all right, Cai," Arthur said, holding out his paw.

Cai grinned, knelt and shook it with two fingers and a thumb. "You too, Arthur Nansi. Look after this one."

"So long, Cai." Evie threw her arms around her friend.

"I'm glad I'll have the amethyst close to me," said Cai softly. "That way you'll always feel close too."

They pulled apart and Cai, red-faced, turned and joined his shaman comrades. He was metres away before he came to a sudden stop. There he knelt down, picked something up and held it for a moment. Evie squinted to see.

"The necklace Jujo gave him," said Arthur quietly.

Evie could have cried. She hoped that he'd be okay – that he wouldn't feel he had to mourn alone. Cai turned back to them with the necklace in his hand.

"Jujo and Master Mucaro never saw me become a true shaman," he said. "But they both helped me in their own way. They had their own convictions and points of view. Now mi think mi should find my own too."

Evie offered an encouraging nod.

Cai pocketed the necklace and smiled. "Until the next Myal, then. I'm going home to pay my respects to my brother and my master."

Evie and Arthur watched the shamans disappear. A handful of Maroon trucks remained, idling by the great house, and the two friends started walking towards the vehicles. Evie wasn't sure that what they had accomplished together had fully sunk in.

"You think we can get a ride all the way back to Ochi?" Arthur asked.

"Mi wouldn't say no to a compartment on the Xaymaca Express again!"

"With what money?"

"A-true." Evie admitted defeat, daydreaming about train meals past.

"But don't worry," said Arthur with a mischievous lilt to his voice. "You know how easy it's gonna be for me to become a master thief with diviner powers?!"

"Arthur!"

"Me-a joke! Me-a joke! Lawd have mercy…"

But Evie wasn't too sure that he was joking. And if she was honest, as quickly as the world around them had changed, she would be quite content if just a few things stayed exactly the same.

# EPILOGUE

## Montego Bay, 1963

On a November evening when the moon was full and the tide high, the carnival of magic returned. Nerves. Evie was full of them as she stepped off the bus – even though it wasn't her first Myal *and* she was meeting with friends. She supposed that, given the circumstances of the last carnival, it was understandable to feel a bit apprehensive. But it wasn't that memory alone that agitated her. It was anticipation.

She pulled at the hem of her white dress and adjusted the bandana on her head for the millionth time, letting her two braids hang loose at the front while looking around for the familiar face. There were shamans everywhere this year as added security. But none of them were the one shaman she was looking out for.

In fact, it was Cai who spotted her first. He was already

grinning when her eyes met his. He was taller, his hair falling longer, and he stood proud in the off-white garments of the shamans. Had she changed in a year as much as he had? Nervous energy replaced with joy, she brushed through the crowds to meet him, and he mirrored her.

When they arrived together, they stood apart for a beat of a hummingbird's wings before diving into a warm embrace.

"You're okay?" Cai bumbled.

"Better than okay," Evie answered. "Look at you! The long hair suits you."

"And you look...older too," said Cai. "I mean...in a good way. You look better. I mean—"

Evie laughed. "Take it easy."

"Where's Arthur?" Cai asked, eyes darting left to right.

Evie's lips curled upwards. She nodded nonchalantly to Cai's left. He turned, looking down to see the familiar Burmese cat.

"Oh, Arthur," said Cai, looking deflated. "It's...it's good to see you."

The cat blinked then walked disinterestedly away.

Evie threw her head back and laughed. "That's Clinton."

Cai's eyes flicked upwards in confusion, landing on a young man leaning against a crafts stall with arms folded and a porkpie hat cocked back. Arthur grinned at him – all perfect umber skin and pearly whites.

"Arthur?!" Cai asked, but his smile suggested that he knew as much to be true. The boys ran at each other with giddy laughter and hugged, clapping each other on the back overenthusiastically. A loud, mellifluous laugh tumbled out of Evie at the sight.

The friends danced to the drums, laughed to the moon and caught up on every detail of their lives in the year that had passed. Cai was especially keen to know how Evie had managed to return Arthur's spirit to his body, a tale Evie was only too happy to tell.

"It took three of us just to pin Clinton down. You shoulda seen him scampering around in Arthur's body – trying to leap to the top of cabinets and failing badly."

"Him bruk up Ms Bell's crockery. She was vexed, you know! Left me to inherit a few bumps and bruises too!" Arthur added.

"But once we had them beside each other, mi was able to force out their spirits, just like with Blackheart. Only, switching them back to the right bodies."

"Sounds like you have plenty of new abilities to show me," Cai sang excitedly.

"Well…" Evie cast a contented smile at Arthur, "we've been travelling from parish to parish, like the strays we are. Mi searching for the other four per cent of spirit wakers to learn from, and to share with."

"But we always have a base to go back to in Ochi," said Arthur. "You remember the Soulless Sailor?"

Cai nodded, a bemused look on his face. "You're living at that dutty saloon?"

Evie and Arthur grinned at each other. "It's…under new ownership," said Evie.

"Ms Bell had more than enough insurance money from the hotel to buy out the place," Arthur explained. "Ol' Mr Bennett is *very* happily retired."

"Ever since Ms Bell found out she's got a magical adopted daughter, she's been seriously keen on providing a sanctuary for mages, and learning about Obeah. She cleaned up the place proper." Evie smiled. "But mi have dreams of bringing magic back in a big way, so the whole of Xaymaca is a sanctuary. There's so many others like me who don't know the magic they have inside o' them. Mi want to help people wake it. Understand it. Embrace it."

Cai nodded proudly. "That's a wonderful dream, Evie," he said. "Well, mi haven't been no slouch neither. I'm a shaman captain now. I'd love to show you how my enchantments have come on."

"Plenty time for that later – mi ready to nyam!" Arthur exclaimed, licking his lips at the grills and food stands lined up on the beach. "Let's eat before it's all gone."

Evie stared out at the still water, glistening like diamonds in the light of the full moon. "You go on ahead," she said. "I'll catch up to unuh shortly."

The boys got up without needing to be told twice and walked along the shoreline – arms around each other's shoulders and deep in animated conversation.

Evie turned to the languid sea and waded ankle deep,

kneeling down so that the gentle tide was at her waist. From a sewn pocket in her dress, she drew out the photograph of her and her parents. She held it in both hands, took a long, deep breath of the warm air and her eyes fluttered to a close.

Light cascaded as her spirit left her body. The threads to the realm of the dead became clearer second by second. She felt buoyant.

Then came the welcome presence of two other spirits. She opened her eyes to the two spectral forms in front of her and smiled to the very depths of her soul.

# Author's Note

This is a work of fantasy grounded in real history. Although the real-life Maroons of Jamaica didn't have a magic system to fight off the colonial British, they had something much more important. They had an inextinguishable spirit to fight for their freedom, their history and customs. To me, that is true magic.

The Maroons used their knowledge of the mountains and island landscape to defeat a military that was more technologically advanced. The British would eventually cease their wars and sign treaties (agreements) with the Maroons, allowing them to keep their own separate settlements on the island. Real-life Maroon settlements still exist to this day, such as Accompong, Charles Town, Moore Town and Scott's Hall (where my maternal great-grandfather was from).

Despite being set in an alternate reality, *Spirit Warriors* symbolically takes place in a momentous year for Jamaica: 1962. This was when Jamaica gained independence from Great Britain.

When the British seized control of the island from the Spanish for the slave trade in 1655, they didn't let enslaved Africans practise their own religions and customs. They were fearful of what they didn't understand and perceived it as supernatural dark magic. So *Spirit Warriors* began with a central, fantastical idea – what if Africans on the island really had used magic to drive off the British and liberate themselves?

This led me to research so many fascinating points in the history of the island, and to learn about incredible figures, from Queen Nanny and the other leaders of the Maroon Wars, to the historic indigenous South Americans who settled in the Caribbean over hundreds of years and eventually became known as Taíno people. They named the island "Xaymaca", meaning land of wood and water. Taíno *bohiques* were the inspiration for the shamans.

As with the majority of former colonies, the dominant religion in Jamaica today is the one the British brought with them: Christianity. Real-life Obeah, which is derived from West African spiritual traditions, mixing in some Christian practices, was first made illegal in 1760 and still tends to carry incredibly negative connotations among the island's populace to this day. Anti-Obeah laws have never been repealed, making it clear how colonial perspectives can endure, and providing one small insight into how the legacy of empire is still strong.

# Acknowledgements

To Em. Thank you for your endless patience, love and support. You are wonderful.

Thank you to my agent, Alice, as you secured me the chance to tell not just one but now two stories of my soul.

To the Usborne team: Sarah, Charlotte, Ayesha, Anika, Fritha, Jess, Jacob, Will, and the whole engine behind this book, thank you from the bottom of my heart.

Thank you to the Society of Authors for crucial funding that allowed me to take a research trip to Jamaica to build on my draft zero. This book wouldn't be as rich without your help.

Major thanks to the Charles Town Maroon community for accommodating me, showing me another way of life, and helping me discover another piece of myself. Rest with the ancestors, Colonel Marcia Douglas, who sadly passed away a year after my visit.

Thanks to the University of the West Indies Mona Campus for allowing me access to their special collections, to the helpful folks at the National Library, Institute of Jamaica, and the Greenwood Great House. And to Davida and Joan, my awesome drivers who got me from A to B!

Thanks to Professor Diana Patton for providing a second pair of eyes to ensure some historical accuracy within the fantasy!

To my Manchester writing pals – Kai, Danielle, Diana, Maria and Kim – who were so supportive as I worked on this book, and prepared myself for debut year with my first. I appreciate you.

Rest in power, Alex Wheatle, and thank you endlessly for your warmth and support. What a legacy you built.

To my grandparents, those still striving – Justin – and no longer with us – Noel, Cisyln, Ivy – you inspire me every day. This book would not exist without you. I don't need a spirit waker to know you'd be proud.

# Also by Ashley Thorpe

Kayode dreams of eating the forbidden fruit of the Orishas, so he can gain the power of the gods and stop them terrorizing his people. So when a fruit mysteriously appears in his path after the Orishas snatch his sister, he leaps on it.

Surging with new and difficult-to-control powers, he joins forces with a shapeshifting trickster god and a vengeful princess to save his sister and put an end to the mighty Orishas. But each has more fearful powers than the last – and Kayode's stolen half-god strength won't last for ever...

"A fast-paced, first-class debut with action scenes that will leave you breathless and characters who will have you cheering. I loved it!"
A.F. Steadman, author of the *Skandar* series

Ashley Thorpe is an author and editor,
who helps other writers to create epic stories
through his work at Storymix. His greatest wish is to
bring diverse characters to life that he would have
loved to have seen, but sorely missed, as a young
reader. When he isn't writing or reading, Ashley
enjoys making music, outdoor pursuits, indulging in
anime and gaming. He lives in Manchester.

@ashley__thorpe